IN JUPITER'S SHADOW

Henry Walker

ISBN: 978-1-0689578-1-9

CHAPTER ONE
Journey's End

Seventeen hours.

Seventeen hours stuck in a damned elevator with eight sweaty crewmen.

At least the view was good. The broad ribbon of the climber cable plunged straight down, guiding Jacob's gaze to Europa's glinting expanse. Blues, silvers, and whites swirled amidst the inky blackness, of a celestial canvas. The jagged, frozen terrain spread out beneath him, with the surface base barely visible as a minuscule fleck at the bottom of the cable. Other than this one mar, the landscape was endless fractal spires of ice and rock, scarred by the red-brown streaks of salt from the subsurface oceans. It stretched out in all directions, blurring with the distance as it reached the perfect ring of the horizon.

To the left of the approaching disc, Europa's smooth surface glimmered faintly. The sun, seeming cold and weak this far out into the solar system, was disappearing around that side of the moon, only a thin sliver like a fingernail remained. On the right, the distant crimson crescent of Ganymede hung in the void like a blooded sickle.

This was the sight he had travelled over six hundred million kilometres to see and he couldn't help but feel a surge of excitement. He took a deep breath, reining in his enthusiasm with the practiced calm he had developed over the years. He knew all too well how easily his own enthusiasm could get the best of him and now more than ever, he needed to maintain his delicate internal balance. Besides, it would do no good to his reputation to act like an over-eager schoolboy around the crewmen.

Not that they were any different. They were twelve hours into their long descent and had barely ceased bouncing from viewport to viewport. Jacob took another steadying breath, directing his thoughts away from the overwhelming surroundings. His mind worked backwards through the long, tedious journey that had brought him here, through the arduous training and further back to the countless hours spent writing business cases, the tense negotiations over contracts and the meticulous management of construction schedules.

Each step had been a key part of this monumental project, all the way from that first initial planning session. Thinking back through this rhythm of hard work and success reminded him of his own competence and resilience and of all that he had already overcome. His breathing steadied as the weight of his past accomplishments did their work to ground him.

Even with his newfound composure, the knowledge that fewer than six hours remained in this year-long journey from Earth kept prickling beneath the surface, threatening to sweep the calm away.

Jacob pushed off the deck plate beneath him and drifted up to his cot. After more than a year in space, his movements were practiced, a delicate ballet in the microgravity that had become second nature during the long trip. The cot was little more than a hammock but it stopped him from meandering out of control over the climber with each little judder. At this point in their descent, there was in fact some small sensation of gravity tugging at them, but it was still very low due to their near orbital velocity. It was all too easy to send yourself spinning into the roof with a carelessly exuberant kick or push.

As he lay, Jacob's eyes inevitably drifted upwards, drawn by the commanding presence looming overhead. Jupiter, massive and awe-inspiring, dominated the view with its immense size. Named for the king of the gods, the planet's vastness filled the sky with swirling bands of cream, tan, and rusty orange. It more than lived up to its name.

The planet's famous red spot, a roiling, tumultuous storm larger than Earth itself, stared back at him like a baleful eye, with an intensity that seemed almost sentient. It was a staggering sight, beautiful and terrible, a mesmerising display of nature's magnificence on a scale that dwarfed everything he had ever known or imagined.

As he gazed at the seething orb of gas, Jacob felt his sense of awe begin to be tinged with unease. The sheer scale of Jupiter was overwhelming and despite his efforts to maintain his hard-won self-control, a creeping anxiety began to surface. The planet's turbulent display, its massive storms, so grand

and powerful, made him feel insignificant and vulnerable.

He tried to anchor himself in the calm he had painstakingly achieved moments ago, but the gaze of that baleful eye pressed heavily against his mind. It was like standing on the edge of an abyss, feeling the pull of something dark and terrifying and the unsettling urge to surrender to it, to fall, even to jump.

The balance he strove to maintain threatened to slip to the other end of the spectrum with this black reaction and he struggled to find that fragile middle ground.

He realised he was holding his breath, too focused on the internal struggle, against giving in to his anxieties. The extremes of his emotions, always so hard for him to control, were heightened by his situation, by the weight of his responsibility, by the looming presence above and the adventure awaiting him below.

Finally, he exhaled sharply, deciding he needed a distraction.

"Evans," he called out, his voice carrying easily in the confined space of the climber's cabin.

"Yes, Mr Callaghan?" Evans's reply, soft and steady, filtered back through the cabin. Despite the decades the two had worked together and the undeniable fact that they were firm friends, Evans's tone, as always, carried the quiet respect of a junior.

"How long now?"

There was a brief pause as Evans consulted the control console.

"Coming up on four hours, sir." Despite his usual

deference, Jacob could hear the eager anticipation in the man's response.

"Just about time for a game then?" The intellectual exercise was a reliable way to steady his mind.

"Always," Evans replied with a hint of a smile.

He pushed himself gracefully towards a locker, returning with the familiar board and pieces. Without comment, he also brought Jacob's wash bag and a pouch of water. Evans always knew.

Jacob discreetly removed a pill from the bag as Evans carefully steadied the board in mid-air between them. Jacob, with a last contemplative look towards the viewport, took the black pieces, arranging them in their usual ranks.

They had played many times before and Jacob's racing mind finally quieted as he fell into the well-worn patterns of the Benko Gambit. Evans, with his usual methodical precision, accepted the gambit and quickly overcame the resultant positional disadvantage. The game unfolded the pace of each move slowing as they left the familiar opening patterns and a complex mid-game developed. All the while, Evans quietly murmured advice in his usual, unassuming way.

Soon, the space around each player began to fill with the captured pieces, each one drifting like a small moon in its own personal orbit. The cloud of black pieces surrounding Evans was noticeably larger than the white ones around Jacob, who had managed to blunder a cluster of pawns.

As they moved into the endgame, Jacob found himself in a frustrating position. His remaining pieces were limited—his options narrowed by Evans's relentless pressure. Despite this, he defended with determination, his brows furrowed in concentration, grimly refusing to concede. Each move was a carefully calculated bid to delay the inevitable, but Evans, by far the stronger player, continued his methodical advance, pushing Jacob inexorably into submission.

Finally, the end came and, after a long moment of studying the board, Jacob extended his hand in defeat. "Good game, Evans."

"Thank you, sir. You must be careful to guard against my passed pawns in the future." Evans began collecting up the pieces and Jacob took off after an errant rook which had wandered away towards the ceiling. As he reached out to grasp the wayward piece, his momentum carried him towards the viewport.

There it was again—Jupiter in all its immense glory. The sight of the giant planet, with its turbulent storms, was still awe-inspiring, but now he could shake off the intrusive thoughts. The game, and the prescribed help, had done their work.

He caught the rook and, for a moment, let himself float there, the chess piece clutched in his hand, his gaze briefly fixing on the hypnotic swirling patterns. He braced himself against the wall with one hand to avoid drifting away from the viewport. The cool, slightly textured surface of the climber's walls was reassuring under his fingertips. The steady, rhythmic rumble of their descent down the cable transmitted through the contact and he unconsciously matched his breathing to it, filling his lungs with the recycled air. Satisfied with his regained control, he smiled quietly to himself, finally able to simply enjoy the view that so few humans had ever been privileged enough to witness.

As he floated there, drinking in the scene, Jacob still could hardly believe his luck. Here he was, commanding a mission to Europa, venturing as far into the solar system as humanity had ever dared to go. It was beyond anything he had ever imagined for himself.

When he had begun his career with TAURS, he had never dreamed it would actually take him off-world. His highest ambition had been to climb the corporate ladder, but now here he was, boldly going where no man had gone before! Not many men anyway.

The path to this moment had been filled with challenges, hard work and a fair share of luck. More than his fair share if he was honest. The thought was humbling and exhilarating at the same time.

Jacob knew he was hardly the type who would have been considered an astronaut in the Apollo days of the previous century. He was no top gun test pilot, no steely-eyed missile man; he was a wiry man in his forties, whose joints ached more often than not. His frame was lean, built for endurance rather than strength, and his years squinting at spreadsheets had recently put him in eyeglasses. He was definitely more nerd than jock. Buzz Aldrin probably would have stolen his lunch money if they'd been at school together.

Focusing as he was on his physical shortcomings, he became acutely aware of the strange, unanchored feeling of the joints in his spine, floating free without the usual pressure of his weight to bear down on them.

Stretching, Jacob cursed softly. "I'd pay a lot of money for just ten minutes of Earth gravity," he muttered, more to himself than anyone else. The weightlessness had been a fun novelty at first, but it wore on you after so long in space.

"What was that, sir?" the ever-attentive Evans inquired.

Jacob considered ignoring the question but then thought better of it. Keeping the crew's morale high was part of his job and it wouldn't do for them to think he was brooding. Turning away from the viewport, he pushed himself the twelve or so feet to the deck, his knees barely bending as they took the gentle impact.

"Oh, nothing, Evans. Just being old and crotchety." Jacob said with a chuckle, trying to keep the mood light. "Now, how about a bite of breakfast? I think we could all use it."

Evans smiled at his boss, who was a good fifteen years younger than himself. Turning, he drifted over to the galley station and started pulling dehydrated coffee pouches out of the ration bins along with sausages for himself and Jacob's favourite apricot porridge. After adding hot water from the reclamator and handing a pouch to Jacob, he distributed the rest to the other crew members before taking his own seat on the edge of his cot. The crew gathered around to eat, their bodies bobbing gently in the low gravity of the confined space.

Evans, with his closely cropped, thinning hair, stood out as by far the oldest there. Without Jacob's intervention, he would have likely been deemed too old for the mission, but Jacob had insisted. The others were all physically fit, intelligent and irritatingly young in Jacob's eyes. Three were payload specialists for the new mass spectrometry filter; three more were additional mining crew for the extraction operations; and the last was an additional operations crew member, a skilled engineer who could maintain, fix, and fettle the base and its core equipment.

They had spent fourteen months together since launch from Olapa Space Port and in just a few more hours, they would join with the team who had been on the ground since mission day one.

Cadmus Outpost, the base below them, with its promise of more earthly comforts, loomed large in their imaginations. The thought of real showers, where water didn't float away in frustrating droplets, was almost a fantasy. Then there were the aeroponically grown vegetables—a luxury unimaginable compared to their diet of rehydrated and packaged food. The idea of fresh, crisp greens was tantalising, a small but significant reminder of the Earth they had left behind, even if it would still only be an extremely rare treat.

Jacob was unusually quiet as he ate, acknowledging the crew's conversation with nods and a few absent minded words. His thoughts were preoccupied with the prospect of seeing Mark, who was already on the surface, serving as the Mining Director of Cadmus. He felt an undercurrent of excitement at the thought of their reunion, tinged with the complex emotions that always seemed to accompany thoughts of his little brother.

Despite the hubbub around him, Jacob found himself lost in reflection. He and Mark had taken different paths in life, yet their careers had both led them to this distant moon of Jupiter. Jacob, the elder and more outgoing of the two, had always pursued success with a certain flair, climbing the corporate ladder with a mix of charm and determination. Mark, on the other hand, had turned his talents to engineering.

Theirs was a relationship built on a foundation of mutual respect, peppered with the inevitable rivalry that siblings often share. Jacob had always felt a sense of responsibility for Mark, a protective instinct that had driven him to call in favours to secure Mark's position on the mining team. He knew Mark was more than qualified for the role – his expertise and dedication were beyond question. But in the competitive arena of space exploration, where opportunities were as scarce as they were coveted, Jacob had wanted to ensure his brother had every advantage. He doubted there could be many on the surface below who did not, in part, owe their presence to nepotism of one sort or another.

Finishing his breakfast, he tossed the packets into the recycling bin and dropped down to the deck again. He slumped onto a thinly padded bench, feeling the faint judder of the climber's movements. Evans proffered him a laptop and he cracked his neck before opening it and tapping in his password. He wouldn't get another data dump until they arrived at the base and so he began to kill the time, finalising the time sheets for the next few mission days and familiarising himself even more with the maps of the base.

The detailed planning and logistical considerations of the mission provided a welcome way to kill a few hours. He immersed himself in spreadsheets, Gantt charts, and risk logs, knowing the work was mostly redundant; he was already well-prepared for every conceivable scenario. But the familiar routine helped pass the time. The focus required for these tasks kept his mind occupied and helped to stave off the boredom of the long descent.

An hour passed in what felt like mere moments, his engrossment in the details of the past quarter's osmium yields uninterrupted until Evans called out with an urgency that couldn't be ignored. "Commander, come quickly!"

Startled, Jacob leapt from his seat and rushed to the viewing port at Evans's beckoning. He didn't need the guiding hand to see what had got everyone so excited. The plume's crest, a spectacular fountain of ice and vapour, was prominently visible against Europa's bleak landscape. At their current altitude, it seemed to be erupting from right beneath them, reaching up with questing fingers to snatch at their fragile little craft.

As he observed the glittering plume, Jacob was struck by the stark contrast it presented against the moon's lifeless surface. The harsh, cold landscape of Europa, with its rugged ice formations and deep crevasses, was suddenly animated by this geyser-like eruption. The top of the plume, shimmering in the weak sunlight, scattered prisms of light that danced across the rough terrain. It was a breath-taking sight.

It was also a vivid reminder of the unpredictable and potentially dangerous environment they were about to step into. Europa, with its hidden oceans and geological activity, was a world of unknowns. He and his crew would be protected from that harsh environment by no more than a few thin layers of canvas and aluminium.

Leading the crew on this mission was a tremendous responsibility, one that Jacob had willingly embraced, yet occasionally found himself questioning. He wondered if he was truly prepared for the challenges that awaited them. The unknown depths of Europa's oceans, the unpredictable nature of the mission, and the weight of the lives under his command weighed heavily on his shoulders.

Leaning against the bulkhead, Jacob let out a deep sigh. The camaraderie and banter among the crew behind him helped to ease his anxieties, if only a little. They had been through months of training together, bonding over shared goals, shared drinks and the excitement of the adventure. But Jacob knew that the true test lay ahead and that they could succeed or fail, live or die and the accountability would be his. The mixture of excitement and fear stirred yet again within Jacob, emotions that, as always, he struggled to reconcile.

Reaching for positivity, he consciously reframed his own self-perspective. He had worked hard to earn the respect and trust of his crew and he was determined to lead them through this mission with confidence. The nervous anticipation that bubbled within him at the thought of the upcoming arrival at the surface base was not just a prelude to anxiety but a rallying call to adventure. It would mark a crucial turning point, where tensions and challenges would undoubtedly arise, not least when he relieved Commander Okoreye.

The Commander was one of Earth's finest, his career a testament to skill, discipline, and unwavering dedication. Starting as a decorated officer in the Kenyan navy, he had transitioned seamlessly into the role of a nyotanaut under the banner of the United African Space Association, bringing with him the rigour and precision of his military background. His command of the outpost since its inception had been marked by a string of successes, with the base being brought online a full three weeks ahead of schedule. In the eleven months that followed, not only had the mining platform surpassed its projected output, but the research team had made notable strides in their experiments. Jacob certainly had a lot to live up to.

As he imagined the moment of transition, Jacob couldn't help but smirk. He visualised Commander Okoreye's composed expression, an attempted mask of professionalism, barely concealing his disdain as he handed over the reins to someone he probably saw as a corporate puppet. Jacob knew the stereotypes all too well—the profit-driven executive, out of his depth in the real world of exploration and danger. Stereotypes which, to be fair, might have some truth to them, but deep inside he knew he was more than that.

As the climber steadily crept ever closer to the surface, Jacob's thoughts drifted to the base itself—Cadmus Outpost. A remarkable feat of human engineering and exploration, named in the old NASA style after a Greek mythological figure. Cadmus was more than just a research base, it was a symbol of humanity's unyielding desire to venture into the unknown and extract the untapped resources of the cosmos. The original Cadmus had founded a great city and while this small outpost was no Thebes, who knew what the future might bring? It was more than just a temporary research station; it was a first small step to achieving giant leaps in mankind's exploration of space. It was a symbol of the potential for humanity to not just inhabit but to thrive in the far reaches of our solar system.

The base's establishment was a joint effort between the planet's major space agencies and TAURS, a collection of privately owned multi-nationals known as the Terraforming and Asteroid Utilisation Research Syndicate. Their collaboration in and of itself represented a milestone in cooperative space exploration, the enablement of scientific curiosity fuelled by commercial aspirations.

Cadmus was primarily focused on osmium extraction, a rare and valuable element abundant in Europa's frigid ocean as osmium chlorohydrate. If enough of the precious resource could be extracted to offset the monumental costs of the base, the success could pave the way for even more ambitious projects.

As the domes of Cadmus loomed into view, their rounded contours were stark against the icy landscape. Each dome, a bubble of life in the desolation of Europa, was strategically placed and interconnected through a series of tunnel-like corridors. These passageways snaked across the surface, creating a lifeline between the domes.

The domes themselves were marvels of engineering, constructed from a combination of durable alloys and a multi-layered, high-tech canvas. This material was not only resilient to the harsh temperatures but also to the radiation and micrometeorite impacts that were common on the moon's surface. The reflective outer layer of the domes served to insulate the interiors and deflect harmful solar radiation, providing a safe haven for the crew and their research.

Deep beneath these structures, the mining platform was the core of Cadmus's operations. The elevator shaft that connected it to the surface was a vertical lifeline, descending more than eight hundred metres, through layers of ice and rock, to reach the subglacial ocean below. Much like an iceberg, the true expanse of Cadmus remained unseen, with only a small portion visible above the surface. The majority of its complex and intricate workings were ensconced deep below, shrouded in the icy embrace of the alien world.

Inside the base, researchers and engineers from many nations worked side by side, pursuing ground-breaking discoveries and laying the foundation for a new era of space exploration. Jacob envisioned the atmosphere as one of collaboration and shared purpose, with scientists and miners cooperating to ensure the success of the mission.

Beyond the confines of Cadmus, the landscape of Europa unfolded in a spectacle of stark, alien beauty. The ice sheet, a vast expanse of brilliant white, stretched endlessly to the horizon, its surface marred only by the occasional rise of a rugged ridge, the shadow of a vent hole or great rusty streaks of magnesium sulphate. The ice gleamed under the weak sunlight and jovelight, refracting it into a spectrum of subtle blues and whites, shot through with dusky orange.

As the remaining journey time ticked by, the excitement onboard the climber grew palpable. The sensation of gravity gradually became noticeable and increased as their orbital altitude reduced. The crew members took turns at the cramped windows, scanning the landscape below, eagerly awaiting their arrival, their banter filling the confined space.

As they neared the base, the mood shifted subtly. The joviality quieted, replaced by a sense of eager anticipation, building to its peak after the years of training and more than a year of travel.

Jacob's own journey had begun in San Diego with a business class flight to Dubai, then a notably less comfortable seat to Mombasa before a modified troop carrier in the UASA colours brought him at last to Marsabit and the Olapa spaceport. The downgrades in luxury had continued as he was blasted off the planet to meet the Fulgur in orbit and settle himself into the tiny sleeping pod onboard the ship that would be his home for the next thirteen months. The climber was the ultimate end of that sorry decline into cramped, smelly and spartan accommodations and he could not decide if he was longing more for his small ration of aeroponic veg or the thought of a bed he could actually lie flat on.

"Five minutes to docking," Evans announced, breaking the contemplative silence that had settled over the climber. Jacob nodded, acknowledging the update, and stood up from the hard bench. He walked over to the windows once more, gazing down at the wide sweep of Europa's icy surface below.

Far closer to the surface than before, he could see the plume vent, now a quiet pool of gently lapping water, quickly being reclaimed by ice skimming across its surface. The water was perfectly black, save for slight ruddy reflections on the wave tops from the great orb of Jupiter hanging above them. It was easy for his mind to throw up visions of grasping talons, leering eyes and all sorts of monstrous appendages emerging from the infinite depths. Jacob shuddered before forcing his anxiety to one side and pulling away from the window to walk across the cabin and find a different view.

Now he could see the domes of Cadmus Base seeming to cover much of the alien landscape with their maze of interconnecting tunnels, pipes and bundles of cabling. The closest dome loomed large and was soon blocking any other view from sight as a loud rattling filled the small space.

The climber came to rest in its cradle, the airlock connected to its counterpart on the base with a hiss of pressure and at last, they had arrived.

CHAPTER TWO

Diamond Rain

Diamonds fell about Abuya as she lay sprawled on the ground. The usual rhythmic hiss and exhalations of her suit's life-support system were drowned out by a discordant tinkling, the sound sending an autonomous tingle down her spine.

She blinked rapidly, her vision swimming as she tried to focus. The ground beneath her hands felt distant, almost unreal and her breath came in short, sharp gasps. Each inhale tasted like metal, the suit's recycled air mixing with the metallic tang of blood. She'd bitten her lip as she fell.

Her hands trembled slightly as they pressed into the icy surface, the cold seeping through her gloves. She forced herself to count her breaths, attempting to bring some measure of calm and slow her frantic heart.

Abuya slowly began to rise, her movements cautious and measured. The impact of being hurled to the ground had left her slightly stunned. Her mouth was still bitter with adrenaline and she had to make a conscious effort to calm herself down and take stock of her situation.

She swept her gaze across the barren, icy landscape, searching for the sampling drill that had slipped from her grasp during her dive. Her shoulder clicked painfully and her mouth formed a curse, inaudible through her visor.

The plume had surprised her. They weren't due to begin for several more days and she had thought herself quite safe working around the jagged crack of the vent. The diamonds that were not diamonds continued to fall and she smiled wryly to herself at her own luck, peering towards the edge of the vent from where the plume still gushed. This one had only been a few kilometres high, quite weedy really in comparison to other plumes she had seen, but still no less beautiful or terrifying.

The frozen moon of Europa is a cracked shell of ice, concealing a vast ocean beneath, kept liquid by the immense gravitational pull of Jupiter. This cosmic tug-of-war generates colossal tidal forces that can heave thousands of kilos of its ocean per second into the sparse atmosphere, where it freezes kilometres in the air, raining down as a tumbling barrage of tiny crystals. For Abuya it was hard to appreciate the awe-inspiring beauty of something that had nearly killed her.

To an exobiologist such as herself, the vents were treasure troves. Each plume offered a rare glimpse, kilometres beneath the moon's surface, potentially carrying organic compounds and minerals essential for understanding if life could, or ever did, exist in the dark ocean below. An excellent resource for any scientist, as long as you didn't get too close to one and almost get blasted into space.

Muttering a stream of half-hearted curses under her breath,

Abuya methodically began to collect her scattered tools and the few precious samples she had managed to gather. The ritual of running through her equipment checklist as she did so helped to calm the last of her anxious tremors.

As she turned to make her way back towards the rover, the voices that had been crackling through her radio gradually began to filter into her consciousness. The combination of the rattling on her helmet and the shock of the eruption had allowed her mind to not even acknowledge the voices' presence. Now though, the concern and urgency in her team's calls to each other began to pierce through the haze, pulling her back to the present reality.

"Her com system must be down—She's moving, she looks ok—Still. I am worried—Henning are you close?—Ja, Scott, I am almost there."

Abuya's surface suit limited her peripheral vision so she had to turn her whole body to see Henning skipping towards her. They had been doing surface operations for over two hundred mission days by now and yet she still found the sight of her fellow researchers skipping about the place very comical, especially the giant form of Henning.

She waved to him as she interrupted the continuing comms chatter. "Ok, ok, I can hear you. I'm fine guys, sorry just a bit shaken."

"Yeah, we saw you taking a little lie down, you had us scared for a moment." Scott's voice came through the radio, settling back to a relaxed drawl that belied the urgency it had held a moment before.

Henning had reached her by this point and was fussing over

her, trying to visually inspect the suit for tears or weaknesses. The attention embarrassed Abuya, making her think of her mother's ministrations before the first day at school. It felt like a spotlight on her mistake, on her vulnerability and she shied away from the attention.

"I'm not leaking Henning!" Abuya cried, exasperated, making to slap his hands away.

"Ruhig Kleine," Henning muttered, bodily turning her to and fro as if she weighed nothing, scrutinising the gauges on the back of her suit.

Scott's voice over the comm cut into his checks, throwing her a lifeline, "Just bring her back Henning, you're only a few hundred metres away, I'm sure she can survive to the airlock."

Henning didn't answer but nodded to Abuya who turned toward the rover. They took off together at a jaunty skip—the strange gait far more efficient than walking or running in the bulky suits and low gravity. Each bound carried them forward, covering significant ground with a minimum effort. The terrain of frozen ridges and shallow craters passed beneath them in a blur, their movements synchronised like some bizarre dance.

The rover loomed into view, its bulky frame a reassuring sight against Europa's desolate backdrop. Normally, visibility on the moon's surface was clear, but today, flurries of hail, stirred up by the recent plume activity, swirled around them in the sparse atmosphere, shrouding their surroundings in a ghostly veil. The vehicle was already in motion, trundling over the icy terrain towards them and soon they were bundling themselves into its airlock, Henning's broad shoulders barely making it through the hatchway. Abuya squeezed herself into what little space was left and they both stood brushing melting ice crystals from their suits as the airlock cycled and came up to pressure, sealing them away from the harsh world outside.

Henning's expression was tight with concern as he assisted Abuya in removing her helmet, his big hands surprisingly gentle as they unfastened the clasps. Initially it irked her. Yet, seeing the genuine worry in his bright blue eyes, her annoyance gradually gave way.

As the helmet came off, her braids, slightly damp from perspiration, tumbled free. The fall had set them loose from the tight bun she typically used to squeeze them into her helmet.

"I'm okay, Henning, really. It was close, but I'm alright," Abuya reassured him. She placed a hand on his cheek, her rich brown skin contrasting sharply with his pale complexion and light brown stubble.

"I know this, but still, you were almost hurt."

"Not your fault."

"Still." He looked so forlorn that Abuya couldn't help but grin. She punched him playfully on the shoulder and realised her smile was all he had been after.

"Stop it you! We are back inside safely and that's what counts. Did you get any of your samples?"

"Some yes, but not all."

As the rover began its homeward journey, its movement caused a gentle lurch beneath them, signalling their departure from the perilous site. Henning and Abuya stepped into the main cabin, a compact space lit by the dull glow of an array of monitors and equipment, each screen flickering with data or maps of Europa's surface. The air was filled with the subtle hum of machinery and the stale aroma of humans performing manual labour in airtight suits.

In the front seat, Scott, the research team lead, was hunched over a digital log, his brows furrowed in concentration as he meticulously recorded the day's incident. His salt & pepper beard and the laugh lines etched around his eyes spoke of his years of experience and a warmth that had earned him the respect and trust of his team.

Even in the midst of documenting their brush with danger, there was a calm assurance about him.

Beside him, Delun was manoeuvring the rover with practiced ease. His thin hands flitted deftly over the controls, guiding the vehicle around a jagged spur of ice with precision. Delun's focus was unwavering, his boyish face a picture of concentration. The occasional furrow of his brow or quick adjustment of the joystick was all that betrayed the challenges of navigating Europa's treacherous terrain.

As the rover rumbled its way back to the Cadmus outpost, Abuya leaned forward around Scott's shoulder, peering out of the front window. Her eyes scanned up and down for the distinct silhouette of the climber on the cable which stretched umbilically up into the vastness of space above. She could just make it out—a small speck, like a high-flying aeroplane, but rapidly descending towards the base below.

Abuya wondered what the new arrivals would be like. The prospect of fresh faces and personalities joining their little community at Cadmus was a welcome change. They were, after all, the loneliest humans to ever exist, the furthest their species had ever been from home, from the other eleven billion people, from Starbucks.

Currently, Cadmus was home to thirty-two individuals, each playing a vital role in the smooth functioning of the outpost. In overall command and directly responsible for the surface operations was Commander Okoreye. The surface maintenance crew, comprising just two individuals, was responsible for keeping the upper elements of the base in full working order in the harsh conditions and the base's doctor performed the same service for the crew. Finally, the four researchers in the rover, along with their colleague Alistair back at the base, completed the small surface contingent.

The majority of Cadmus' population lived and worked on the mining platform below. The mining director oversaw nineteen miners, with seven more arriving today.

Abuya had always thought 'miners' to be a rather unglamorous term for such accomplished engineers, but when she had raised this to the others over a meal, they had come up with the term 'sievers' instead and so she had quickly dropped the issue before she made things worse.

While she knew her colleagues looked down somewhat on the miners, Abuya could at least appreciate that their work was the lifeblood of the base, crucial to the economic viability of their mission.

The arrival of the new miners and the company officials was set to increase their total numbers to forty-one, edging closer to the full complement of fifty. For Abuya and the rest of the crew, it meant adjusting to new dynamics, new collaborations, and the continuous evolution of their small, extra-terrestrial society. For her friend Okoreye, however, it marked the end of his tenure as commander and the beginning of his journey back to Earth and a well-earned retirement.

She smiled at the thought of Mark, the mining director, and his barely contained excitement. His brother was among the new arrivals and Mark had been a whirlwind of activity, buzzing around the base with an energy that was almost palpable. In his eagerness, he had done more commanding than the commander himself, orchestrating preparations in all sections with an enthusiasm that was both endearing and immensely aggravating.

Despite the subtle divide that sometimes existed between them and her fellow researchers, she found herself fond of some of the miners. The researchers themselves were astronauts, taikanauts, cosmonauts and nyotanauts, each a testament to rigorous training regimes and incredibly strict selection processes. They were the crème de la crème, chosen for not just their scientific prowess but also their adaptability and resilience – qualities deemed essential for space exploration.

In comparison, the miners, while exceptionally intelligent and proficient in their specialised fields, didn't always receive the same level of admiration. All of them held PhDs and had considerable experience on Earth, yet they didn't necessarily fit the mould of what the old NASA would have termed 'the right stuff.' At least, that's what Scott and some of the others seemed to believe.

A jolt from the rover broke her train of thought and she blinked as the back of her head hit the wall behind her. Wincing, she rubbed the sore spot as she once again peered between Delun and Scott's shoulders and through the front window. They were approaching the base now and Delun was heading for the hangar airlock as the great domes grew before them.

Cadmus, was an exo-architectural marvel, a testament to human ambition and engineering. It was comprised of three primary domes, each flanked by one or two smaller secondary domes. Aluminium struts formed the ribs of the domes, gleaming faintly in the weak sunlight, their strength evident in every joint and joist. Between these sturdy ribs stretched layers of industrial hab-canvas, a multi-layered shield designed to protect the inhabitants from the harsh cold and relentless solar radiation and to maintain a life-sustaining atmosphere within.

Alongside the corridors that interconnected the domes was a network of conduits, like the veins of a living organism, snaking across the frozen ground and carrying not just the lifeblood of power and data, but also the essential systems for life support. The three main domes all met at the squat climber station, with their smaller subsidiaries branching off them in an erratic fractal pattern. Looking up from the station, one could see the climber cable stretching upwards, a broad ribbon that disappeared into the sky, reaching for a geostationary orbit far beyond sight.

Each of the three main domes sported a separate logo

emblazoned on its flanks. The dome they were approaching bore the symbol of TAURS, a ring of the solar system's eight planetary bodies surrounding a stylised pickaxe. The same logo adorned her surface suit below the scarlet mission patch and above the black, white, red and green of the Kenyan flag. It was also splashed across the rover, all her clothing and pretty much any piece of research equipment within their dome. TAURS were certainly loud and proud and seemed to like advertising themselves to the inhabitants of Europa for reasons Abuya couldn't begin to fathom.

As impressive as it was, the base itself paled into insignificance in its magnificent setting. The surrounding icy terrain, a landscape of frozen waves and ridges, contrasted sharply with the technological marvel that was Cadmus. Above it all, the immense orb of Jupiter hung in the sky, a constant, looming presence that dwarfed the base with its colossal size and swirling storms. The juxtaposition of the human-made structure against the backdrop of this alien world and the giant planet above created a scene of surreal beauty and awe, a harsh reminder of humanity's small place in a vast universe.

The rover shuddered to a halt and the four researchers donned their helmets. It was irritating to have to suit up just to move from the rover to the base but it was far simpler than the rover docking directly. The four of them trudged the few metres from the rover to the airlock with Delun pausing to connect the power feeds to ports on the rover's nose.

As Abuya waited for the airlock to cycle and admit them, she looked down at the ridged ice beneath her feet, imagining that she could see through it to the under-decks of Cadmus. They plunged down into Europa's frigid ocean with the lowest dangling sensor array almost a kilometre below her.

Scott swung the lever and the airlock door clanked open, the sound weirdly muted, transferred mainly through her feet in the thin, almost non-existent atmosphere. The four of them stepped inside and sealed off the door, relaxing subtly as air rushed in to pressurise the confined space.

It was a few moments before the strip lights on the ceiling flicked from red to green and Scott could crank the heavy inner door open. A grinning face appeared at the other side, framed by a mop of tousled hair. The corresponding arm grasping Scott's and pulling him through into the dome.

"Welcome home, welcome home. Thought we'd lost you there Abs," chattered Alistair amiably. "Who'd have thought a plume like that this early. Ah well, all's well that ends well, eh?" He was busily tugging at her gloves at this point, helping her get the suit off, nattering on all the while. Abuya wasn't fooled, she knew it was just his way of showing concern.

Henning was walking towards the equipment racks with three of the crew's helmets tucked under his huge arms when they were almost knocked flying by a blur of white-blonde hair that came streaking past him.

Abuya woofed out a lungful of air as Annika collided with her. Delun chuckled and placed a steadying hand on the small of her back to stop the pair from careering back into the airlock.

"I'm ok dear, really. Don't worry, I'm fine." Abuya gasped out as she tried to refill her lungs.

Annika's hands were worriedly patting her down and her light blue eyes were filled with concern. Her normally pale face was flushed and the snarls of her hair showed where she'd been pulling at it in her worry. She had clearly been scared by what had happened.

"Du er trygg, du er trygg!" the usually unflappable woman was almost whimpering.

"Yes darling I'm safe." Abuya smiled, gently lifting Annika's small, pointed chin to ensure their eyes met. She could see the fear and worry etched in Annika's flushed face. Abuya leaned in to plant a quick kiss on her nose before resting their foreheads together, taking a moment to feel each other's presence. Annika placed a hand on Abuya's cheek, her touch tender and familiar. Annika's expression softened with relief, the flush gradually fading from her pale skin as the tension melted away.

"I also am safe," declared Henning looking a little put out.

Annika turned her head and the two exchanged a brief flurry of German, too fast for Abuya to catch the meaning, but when Annika turned back, she was smiling.

"Sorry."

"That's Ok."

"It's just, when I heard on the comms…"

"I know, but I'm fine, really."

Abuya kissed her on the forehead and gave her a final squeeze before shrugging off the remnants of her surface suit and peeling off the thermal vest beneath it.

Delun, now in a fresh jumpsuit, came over, accompanied by the aroma of the steaming mug of tea in his hands. "They will be arriving in just over three hours," he announced, his tone carrying a note of subdued excitement.

Scott came up behind him with tea and coffee for them all according to taste, his lined brow furrowed in concentration as he struggled not to spill.

Abuya gratefully accepted her coffee from Scott, wrapping her hands around the mug and feeling the warmth seep into her palms. The freeze-dried swill was a far cry from what she'd enjoyed back home, but, in the confines of the station, it was a small, cherished luxury. She brought the mug to her lips, taking a cautious sip, the hot liquid a welcome contrast to the lingering chill of the surface that had seeped into her bones.

She took another mouthful and heaved a heavy sigh, part relief and part fatigue. "Well, I'm going to go wash up before we greet our guests."

Turning, she made her way towards the researcher's quarters, her steps slow, each one shedding a little more of the weight of her recent ordeal. The promise of a hot shower beckoned, a brief respite to cleanse and rejuvenate her before facing the new arrivals.

"Doctor Pedersen, please report to the mining level, we've had a small incident," Mark's voice emanated from the intercom panel by the entryway.

Annika hesitated in the act of following Abuya before hurriedly turning on her heel and striding out of the room towards the centre of the complex and the elevator terminus.

• · · · ·

Abuya did not see Annika again until a couple of hours later. Standing in the climber station, clad in a fresh uniform, she felt somewhat rejuvenated. The fabric crisp and clean against her skin, was a welcome relief to her earlier dishevelment. She kept her back straight, shoulders squared, projecting an air of calm and control. Inside, however, the memory of the plume's unexpected eruption still lingered, causing her heart to skip a beat whenever she thought about it. Her hands, though steady now, had been shaking as she fastened her uniform. She was determined not to reveal how the incident had rattled her, not to her colleagues and most certainly not to Annika. She always worked to maintain her facade of strength and resilience, even to herself half the time, although she was sure Annika would see through her quickly enough. She always did.

She looked around at the familiar faces. It had been months since the entire complement had been together in one area like this and it made the base suddenly seem relatively crowded. She noticed Mark standing to one side, concern and excitement fighting for dominance on his eager face. She assumed he was merely nervous to see his big brother until Annika slipped beside her and squeezed her hand in greeting.

"Everything ok down below?"

"Yes, I think so. Some of the miners were fighting, I just had to disinfect a few scratches and tend to a bruise or two."

"Fighting? Really?"

"Well, I don't know. They said it was just an accident but it didn't look like that. I think Mark knows more about it but we had to hurry up here for the new crew's arrival."

"They can't have bee—" A sudden, resounding clang cut through the air, slicing Abuya's sentence in half and abruptly redirecting her attention. The sound, metallic and jarring, echoed through the compartment, suspending all conversation. It was quickly followed by the loud, rushing hiss of atmospheres being equalised, a familiar and yet still startling sound.

In front of them, the double hatchway began to open. It moved slowly, almost ponderously, its heavy panels swinging outward with a deliberate, grinding motion that spoke of robust construction, designed to withstand the rigours of the environment. The gap widened, revealing the silhouette of a tall man framed in the doorway.

The man had to duck slightly to clear the coaming, his movements awkward and exaggerated in the unaccustomed gravity of the station. He was a striking figure, his height accentuated by a slim build. His hair was an unruly mass of dark curls and his skin somehow still bore the tan of someone used to sunnier climes. His eyes, bright and alert, he scanned the room of faces before him.

He was grinning, his smile broad and somewhat toothy, an expression likely intended to be friendly and disarming. However, to Abuya, it came off as slightly predatory, more hungry than hospitable.

Abuya couldn't help but compare him to his brother, Mark. They shared a similar build and facial features, though Mark was a little shorter and broader. Despite Jacob being the elder, he wore his age well and it would be hard to tell on sight who was the older of the two. Where Mark was more demure and shy, Jacob's eyes were bright and eager, actively seeking eye contact with everyone in the room.

The man was clearly bursting with barely repressed excitement as he straightened up and stepped towards Commander Okoreye.

Abuya watched the two men look each other up and down as they shook hands. The new commander was handsome if a little too carefully put together. He wore the standard blue-grey uniform jumpsuit, but too well, as if he'd taken it to some fancy tailor before leaving Earth. The TAURS logo was emblazoned across his shoulder above the Stars and Stripes and beneath the epaulettes that showed his rank. Gathii would be gritting his teeth at the pips on the epaulettes, knowing that this new Commander had not earned the rank as he had. She was looking forward to reacquainting with her friend in the few weeks before his departure. Now he was no longer her commanding officer, she hoped she might get him to relax some of his strict formality.

"—and I'm sure we will all build a great working relationship and exceed all the expectations put on us."

She snapped her attention back to the moment. Commander Callaghan had finished reading himself in and was now addressing the crew.

"I look forward to getting to know all of you more over the coming weeks. In the meantime, please feel free to come to Evans here with any problems and he will pass them along to me."

Abuya's focus shifted to the man the new commander had

indicated. He stood a little behind Jacob, observing the scene with an air of quiet composure. He was old to be on this mission, probably in his late fifties, but he looked wiry and strong and his eyes flicked about with a keen intelligence, drinking everything in. His movements were measured and deliberate, each gesture precise and controlled with none of the clumsiness the other new arrivals were showing in the unaccustomed gravity.

The introductions over, the miners started drifting away towards the elevator terminus while Mark hurried over to his brother, clearly madly excited at the reunion and utterly failing in his efforts to hide it.

The pair were joined by Annika, Scott and Okoreye. Along with Mark, they were the four department heads of the base; medical, research, command and mining respectively. Jacob greeted them all warmly, shaking hands and seeming genuinely thrilled to meet them. Abuya, observing from across the room, couldn't help but feeling a pang of sympathy for Okoreye, as he stood with the group, but somehow apart. A fifth wheel.

He was tall and proud, his military background evident in his posture and his closely cropped hair. Abuya couldn't help but compare him to the new commander. Though a little shorter than Jacob, his shoulders were significantly broader, lending him a commanding presence. His sharp, neat fade presented a striking contrast to Jacob's more wayward curls. Gathii's skin, a rich, deep hue even darker than Abuya's own, made Jacob's Californian tan seem pale and somewhat unhealthy in comparison.

The group, with Jacob still holding court, began to move away, presumably towards the commander's office and a more formal meeting. Annika would be stuck in conference for at least an hour.

She was woken abruptly from her contemplations as Henning's huge hand clapped her on the shoulder, bucking her knees a trifle. "Come then, we should eat."

She smiled up at him, turning to follow his lead.

"Might I join you?" The softly spoken voice behind her belonged to Evans. He was not following the little knot of officers, currently drifting towards the Commander's office and had instead come to shake hands with Alistair, Delun and the two surface maintenance engineers, Lena and Tomas.

"Of course," smiled Henning, enveloping the man's thin hand in his own huge one and pumping it enthusiastically. "Always good to meet a new face, when I have been stuck with these ugly ones for so long."

Abuya gave Henning a playful shove and headed towards the mess, calling back over her shoulder. "Come on, we might even be able to get you some food before Henning eats it all."

. . • . .

Henning took charge of rehydrating ration packs while Evans took his seat with the others. Abuya was struck by the man's eyes – sharp and alert as they darted around the room. They were the eyes of someone who missed nothing, taking in every detail and filing it away for future reference. There was a certain intensity in his gaze, a focused curiosity that seemed to dissect the room and its occupants, understanding far more at a glance than others might with prolonged scrutiny.

Above them, the curved canvas of the dome stretched overhead like a protective canopy, its surface a pale, neutral colour that helped to reflect the light and give a sense of spaciousness to the otherwise compact room. An intricate lattice of support struts crisscrossed the ceiling, their sleek metal surfaces glinting faintly in the artificial light. These struts converged gracefully towards the dividing wall at the back of the mess, creating pleasingly symmetric patterns.

Lighting in the mess was provided by a series of cold, sterile strips that ran along the top of the walls, casting an even, unobtrusive light across the room. The light was efficient and functional, lacking the warmth of natural sunlight but sufficient for the needs of the crew. It bathed the room in a consistent glow, eliminating shadows and giving the space a clean, almost clinical ambience. The utilitarian tables and benches were arranged in a neat, orderly fashion, the furniture sturdy and minimalist, designed to be as light as possible while still surviving the rigours of life on a space station.

Alistair was chattering away, telling the story of that morning's misadventure with the plume. Abuya chimed in with her own details, building up a fancifully exaggerated version of the story and laughing off Scott's insistence that she be more careful next time.

As the conversation shifted away from Abuya she took a moment to watch Evans. He was quietly observing the scene, listening far more than he was speaking. She felt sure he was carefully cataloguing his observations of her fellow researchers so as to brief Jacob later on. Well, he was welcome to. They were a weird bunch one way or another and she didn't envy Jacob the task of trying to manage them.

Abuya's train of thought was broken as the entry hatch rumbled open and Annika stepped through, accompanied by Okoreye.

"Sorry to interrupt." Annika flashed a smile at Abuya and continued, "I need to steal Evans for a moment."

"You need the new crew's medical intake Doctor?"

Abuya grinned. The top of Annika's jumpsuit was turned down and tied about her waist and the t-shirt underneath did not bear her medical insignia. Evans must have memorised everyone's photo before he arrived. He seemed the type.

"Yes, Commander Callaghan tells me you have them."

"I do indeed, after you," said Evans and so saying, rose to follow her, nodding to the table's occupants before stepping through the hatchway.

With Annika gone, Abuya's attention returned to Okoreye, who had taken a seat at the table and was glumly contemplating his cup. He had been extremely proud of his role as base commander and now Jacob, in his eyes some trumped-up businessman, was taking over. Abuya reached over and clasped his arm. "I guess I can call you Gathii again."

He snorted and rolled his eyes. "I think you called me commander once on this whole mission Abs and that was probably an accident."

"At least three or four times!" Abuya feigned indignance

and pouted at him until he couldn't resist a small smile.

"So, tell us about the new boss Gathii. Uh, Commander." Henning asked, correcting himself with a sheepish grin in response to the former commander's sharp glance.

"He certainly seems driven," Okoreye mused, gazing down into his cup as he considered his response. "I can't fault his qualifications. I just hope he understands the challenges of leadership out here."

"He's got big shoes to fill that's for sure." Scott clapped Okoreye on the back. "Besides, we've got a few more weeks before you ship out, I'm sure you can give him some pointers."

"Of course," Okoreye said with a nod, seeming to relax and finally taking a sip of the drink he'd been staring at. "It's just that I've always believed a space agency member should be leading such an important outpost. But times change and decisions are made." His tone was measured, but Abuya detected the bitterness in it.

"It'll be interesting to see how things go with Jacob," she said, hoping to change the topic slightly. "I heard he was involved in some major ventures back on Earth before this."

"Yes, he has quite the reputation," Okoreye acknowledged, only a little grudgingly. "I suppose it can be an advantage to have someone with a different perspective running things. It's just a matter of getting used to it, I suppose."

Scott spoke up, his tone matter-of-fact. "TAURS's money is why we're here. Their methods may not align with ours, but their funding is essential. It's just how space exploration works these days."

Abuya, not really in the mood for another lecture about the economics of space exploration, turned to Delun and Henning to join their discussion of the samples they had collected that morning.

Before long, Delun excused himself to tend to routine maintenance on the rover while Henning and Alistair headed off to finish cataloguing the samples.

Abuya, left Scott and Okoreye, now debating the finer points of baseball, and headed down the connecting tunnel towards the medical bay. Entering the pristine room, she found Annika dabbing at a wincing Mark's forehead with disinfectant. The sharp scent of the antiseptic filled the air, mingling with the usual sterile coldness of the room.

"Skjera kosepus, just one moment." Annika greeted her with a smile, turning to toss the cotton ball into the recycler.

Abuya hopped up onto the opposite examination table and winked at Mark. "What was it this time then?"

Mark looked sheepishly at her "I was talking to Jacob and wasn't looking where I was going."

Abuya chuckled "I can imagine you were very excited to see him and I'm sure he will be reassured that a few months off world hasn't cured his brother's clumsiness!"

Marked scowled briefly before hissing in pain and reaching gingerly up to the now rumpled bandage that Annika had just finished applying. She rolled her eyes before fixing it smoothly over the cut once again.

"So, you're pleased to see him again then?"

"Obviously, he's great, I really missed him."

"And you don't mind being his subordinate?" Abuya

teased, nudging his foot with her toe.

Mark chuckled. "I've been that since I was born!"

Annika stepped back from his forehead, pocketing the roll of dressing tape. "There, all done," she told him.

"Thanks, Doc. I'd better be getting back down below." Mark dropped down off the examination table and headed for the elevator terminus.

Annika wiped down the table and started tidying the refuse from her first aid, giving Abuya a perfunctory peck on the cheek as she bustled past. "I swear that man's used half my supplies already."

Abuya sniggered at that.

"Evans says he's always been like that though, we'd only just finished transferring the new medical records when Mark arrived."

She turned away to pick up an errant bandage wrapper. Abuya leaned back on her perch, her legs swinging rhythmically as she watched Annika flit about the medical bay, her eyes following every move as her mind wandered. She thought back to their conversation earlier before Jacob had arrived. Something about a fight down in the mining section. "So, you never finished telling me about your house call to the miners?"

"Oh, that. Mark was just giving me the details before you came in. There was a scuffle between two of the miners, Cole and Wei-Yun. He reckons it was just an isolated incident, nothing to be too worried about."

Curious, Abuya leaned in, urging Annika to continue. "Tell me more. no one was actually hurt, were they?" She liked

Wei-Yun and was amazed the mousy little engineer had been fighting.

Annika shook her head. "Not at all. I treated some minor scratches and bruises, nothing major."

"Still weird though, never had anything like that happen before."

"To be honest it's almost strange it didn't happen sooner. We're all so cooped up here, it was bound to happen eventually. Not like we can step outside to take a breath of fresh air and let off steam."

Abuya nodded thoughtfully, still surprised. Shrugging, she chalked it up to the stress of preparing for the new commander's arrival. She hopped down from the examination table, looping her arm around Annika's waist and pulling her close for a kiss. "You're probably right, you normally are anyway."

"Always," grinned Annika. "Now, I'd better get on, go play with your rocks and I'll see you tonight."

Abuya smirked and gave her a quick hug before heading back through the hatchway towards the research dome and her awaiting samples, hearing Annika's clattering keyboard behind her.

CHAPTER THREE

Lost On Mars

Two weeks passed on Cadmus Outpost, each day blending into the next as routines settled into place. The arrival of the new crew members had brought a sense of renewed energy to the base and the novelty of having fresh faces around added a welcome touch of variety to the daily activities.

Abuya's days followed their usual steady rhythm. Her mornings began with the soft artificial dawn of the research dome's lighting strips. She shared the researchers' dormitory with her colleagues Scott, Delun, Henning, and Alistair, at least when she didn't spend the night in Annika's quarters.

Showering on Europa was a unique experience, requiring an active drain to suck down the water. The droplets clung to her skin much more than on Earth, the low gravity almost matched by the surface tension. This made rinsing off much harder, as the water clung to her in large globules that needed careful coaxing to flow towards the drain.

Afterwards, she would take a moment to apply her carefully hoarded supply of dehydrated shea butter. The dry air of the base could be harsh on her skin and she was determined not to let herself get ashy. The familiar scent and the ritual of moisturising were small comforts that reminded her of home.

She would then catch up with her colleagues, already eating their breakfasts, and exchange sleepy greetings with them while she rehydrated her pouches of eggs and coffee.

Their mornings were normally dedicated to research, either maintaining equipment or obtaining and analysing samples. If this work didn't take them out onto the surface, then they could generally be found amidst an assortment of sophisticated instruments or huddled around computers, faces lit by the glowing displays.

On one memorable day, Abuya found herself accompanying Alistair out onto the surface to aid in his observation of the Aurora Joviana, Europa's answer to the northern lights. Abnormally high magnetic field activity from the gas giant hanging above them had caused the dancing lights to appear far further from the distant pole than was normal and to Alistair, an exo-aerologist, this was a godsent opportunity. They had stood together, gazing up at the flickering lights while Alistair's equipment collected data. It was the quietest she'd ever known the man. She even suspected he had been weeping behind the visor of his surface suit. She could hardly blame him; the sight had moved her deeply too, making her feel so small, so insignificant, so lucky to be on this incredible adventure.

But such events were exceedingly rare and most of her mornings involved cataloguing and studying sample after sample of ice or, if she was lucky, titrating something very slowly.

At lunchtimes, with the morning's research carefully packed away, Abuya would generally make her way to the medical bay to eat her ration packs with Annika. If it was just the two of them, they'd cosy up together to share their meal or, if Annika had patients, they would chatter together while she attended to the inevitable cuts, bruises and minor injuries collected by the crew. Abuya loved watching Annika's calm and competent movements as she swabbed, tended and mended. She had a remarkable knack for putting even the most anxious crew member at their ease and more than one of them seemed to come more for a friendly chat than for any real medical need.

Abuya also liked to take the chance to talk with the miners Annika treated. The researchers didn't get much opportunity to mix with them on a day-to-day basis with their work and living quarters separated by the long slow elevator ride below the surface. It was always fun to swap stories and gossip and, because of these interactions, she would sometimes be invited down to the mining platform to join in after-hours game nights. The miners were generally too nerdy for poker, it was usually Scrabble.

After lunch, she would move on to the carefully choreographed dance of tasks and responsibilities that all the crew shared to maintain the base. One of Abuya's main responsibilities was maintaining the small aeroponics bay but there were always endless diagnostics, restocking and just plain old cleaning to keep her busy. She enjoyed supporting Tomas if he had to fix something and whenever she could, she joined him in rover maintenance, hoping to increase her own competency and eventually qualify as a rover driver.

At first, the new commander had tried to overhaul these schedules and patterns of work but to his credit, he had quickly seen that the team were already working well and so he had left them to it. He had been proving himself to be a perfectly capable leader, in Abuya's opinion, as she observed Jacob's interactions with the crew. He took the time to understand their individual strengths and supported innovative approaches to problem-solving in the research dome. He had brought a fresh perspective to some aspects of their work and Abuya appreciated that he respected the established routines in other areas, earning Okoreye's grudging approval, even despite his insistence that everyone call him Jacob. She could sense that he genuinely cared, not just about the team's success but their well-being as well and his friendly demeanour fostered a positive atmosphere among the crew.

As the days went by, Abuya found herself spending more time with Evans. He was eager to learn and assist in any way possible and was always keen to shadow one of the crew. He quickly integrated into the routines of the base and showed genuine interest in the research being conducted. It was hard to say if this was just personal interest or on Jacob's orders but he was quiet and helpful and the researchers were happy to have him around.

The surface crew's evenings were typically spent together unwinding in the communal area, sharing rehydrated rations and relaxing after a day's work. Conversations generally started as serious scientific discussions. The researchers, still in the thrall of their work, would exchange ideas and insights, debating theories and findings. But as the evening progressed, the conversation would invariably be derailed and topics would wander to old sci-fi movies that everyone had seen a dozen times, personal anecdotes from Earth, or the latest base gossip.

Soon after the new arrivals came, however, there was a welcome addition to their evening routines.

Abuya had casually mentioned to Evans during one of their afternoon chats that the surface crew, engrossed in their own world of experiments and data analysis, seldom interacted with the miners. There was a subtle divide between their two worlds, enforced by the literal and far less subtle divide of four hundred fathoms of frigid ocean.

She felt sure that this observation had been passed along to Jacob for it wasn't long before the commander suggested a movie night for the whole crew. Okoreye with his more traditional command style had never considered such a thing in his eighteen months of leadership but Abuya was delighted by the idea of mingling more often with more of the crew.

Evans bustled around the base frantically for the whole day, clearing out the conference room and pinching all the benches from the surface-level mess, leaving the researchers to sit grumpily on the floor for their lunch. Even with his efforts some of the crew had to sprawl on piles of spare uniforms and blankets and Lena had to modify the dome's atmospheric regulator to handle that many people's life support.

As the request for film suggestions had gone around, Scott

had been found to have an endless supply of classic space movies on his personal drive and had provided 'Robinson Crusoe on Mars' for the evening. The movie was over a century old but it seemed to fit the theme of the base.

The elevator started the long process of bringing up the mining crew from the lower levels. A round trip took about fourteen minutes, and the elevator was a tight squeeze with even six of the miners, but eventually, everyone was up and crowded into the makeshift theatre, jostling for elbow room.

Annika had found a cosy spot for herself, nestled on a wadded-up section of spare dome canvas as a surprisingly comfortable makeshift pillow. As the lights dimmed and the theme tune started playing, Abuya squeezed herself in between her and the dome wall. She snaked her arm about Annika's waist and felt the weight on her shoulder as Annika rested her head on it affectionately.

The movie went down well with lots of chortles at the kitschy sci-fi and booming laughs from Henning who seemed to be particularly fond of Mona the monkey. Abuya, snuggled next to Annika and helped her with a few of the references and puns. Like many a Norwegian, Annika's English was technically much better even than many native speakers but some of the nuances escaped her.

Finally, as the weird, early CGI ships came roaring down towards the survivors, the crew cheered and the lights came back on. Sore limbs were stretched and the chattering crowd made to head towards the chair-free mess where a stash of snack-based ration packs had been prepared ready for them. As she began to clamber to her feet, Abuya realised that the knees she had been leaning back on belonged to Wei-Yun, one of her friends among the miners. He grinned at her struggles to stand and reached down to help pull her up.

"Heya Abs, enjoy the movie?"

"It was weird, but I liked it. I like weird."

"That was Batman, right?" Annika chimed in making Wei-Yun laugh.

"Adam West? Yeah, he was the proper Batman in the silk suit."

They chattered about the movie, waiting their turn to squeeze out of the conference room and into the connecting tunnel.

After a while, Abuya leaned towards Wei-Yun, her voice hushed. "Hey, Wei-Yun. Can I ask you something?"

"Sure, what's up?"

"I wanted to talk about what happened between you and Cole," Abuya said gently. "You know, the fight you had."

Wei-Yun sighed and looked away for a moment before meeting Abuya's gaze. "It was ridiculous, really. We were just having a normal conversation over a tea break and then Cole started telling this bizarre story. It was like something kids would tell at a campfire to scare each other."

Abuya's curiosity was piqued. "What sort of story."

"It was about some terrifying creature that supposedly lives in the ocean here," Wei-Yun explained. "According to Cole, this creature emerges from the depths and devours miners, one by one. He said it was some ancient, mythical being that had been awakened by our filtration plants… or something like that."

Abuya furrowed her brow. "That sounds... odd. Did he seem serious about it?"

Wei-Yun nodded. "That's the weird part. He seemed dead serious, as if he genuinely believed what he was saying. So did some of the others actually, they looked frightened! I just laughed, thinking he must be joking, but that just made him suddenly all furious and he lunged at me!"

"That's really weird. I've talked to Cole before, he doesn't seem like the type to get offended by anything, let alone someone not liking his story. Has he done anything else weird?"

Wei-Yun considered the question for a moment. "Now that you mention it, yeah, I guess. He's been more on edge than usual for the past couple of weeks. I just chalked it up to stress but maybe there's something else going on. Maybe bad news from back home or something."

Annika had been listening in. "Maybe I'll have a chat with him. He didn't mention anything when I treated him for that beautiful black eye you gave him Wei." she said this with a disapproving raise of one eyebrow, "but I'll try again tonight."

Wei-Yun looked thoughtful. "Not a bad idea Doc, thanks."

They'd made it into the corridor by now. They were the last to arrive at the mess where Jacob was standing on a table, holding court. He was taking advantage of the gathering to make a few announcements and further ingratiate himself with the crew. Annika sidled away to find Cole in the crowd while Abuya perched on one of the tables to listen.

"I want to thank all of you for these two incredible weeks we've had together," Jacob began, his voice projecting easily across the room. "You've welcomed me with open arms and I couldn't have asked for a better team to lead. The work we're doing here is ground-breaking and your dedication and passion for science are truly commendable."

Abuya's gaze wandered around the room, noticing how the newcomers, including Evans, were already fitting in seamlessly with the rest of the crew. Jacob had done a good job integrating them it seemed.

"As we continue our research and exploration on Europa, I have no doubt that we'll face challenges and obstacles," Jacob said, his tone becoming more serious. "But I firmly believe that together, as a united team, there's nothing we can't overcome. We're pioneers here, exploring new frontiers and that requires the kind of courage and adaptability that I can see in all of us here tonight."

He paused, scanning the faces before him, meeting each crew member's eyes.

"I want to create an environment where all of you feel heard and valued. If you ever have concerns, ideas, or suggestions, my door is always open. Your insights and feedback are crucial to our success and I look forward to hearing from each of you."

The crew responded with nods and murmurs of appreciation. Jacob carried himself well—confident yet approachable, although Abuya still rebelled slightly at the corporateness of it all.

"Now, on a lighter note," Jacob said, switching back to the lighter tone, "I've been hearing whispers about some more movie night requests. Well, with thanks to the efforts of Evans here, I'm proud to announce Movie Night will officially be a regular thing!"

The crew cheered at that and Evans looked down bashfully as Jacob hopped to the ground and clapped him on the shoulder.

Before long the small room was filled with a hubbub of laughter, stories, and an overall sense of camaraderie. Meanwhile, Jacob moved through the crowd, engaging in conversations with different crew members, showing an honest interest in their work and lives. He seemed eager to learn from them and to build meaningful connections. Almost too eager to Abuya's eyes, like he'd learned how to be that way at a seminar. He caught Abuya watching him and made his way over to her.

"Ah Abuya, how are you enjoying the movie night?" Jacob asked, his eyes sparkling, seeming genuinely keen for her opinion.

"The crew seems to be having a great time. I can't thank you enough for organising this. It's wonderful to see everyone coming together."

"I'm glad to hear that," Jacob said, his gaze drifting across the room at the mingling crew members. "Building strong connections between us is essential for our mission's success. And speaking of connections, how did you and our dear doctor become such good um… friends?"

Abuya's cheeks flushed. Okoreye had done a remarkably good job of failing to notice her relationship with Annika, even when it was right under his nose. She had been a little worried about the new commander's reaction, fraternising was quite definitely against regulations after all, but she saw him grinning at her worried face and realised he was just trying to tell her he knew and reassure her that it was fine.

She softened to him then and shrugged as she told the story. "We hit it off on the journey from Earth. Actually, we bonded over a noise. There was this annoying high-pitched squeaking in the mess room from one of the vent fans. No one else seemed to be able to hear it but it bugged the hell out of us. We started eating our meals in one of the cabins to avoid it and one thing led to another."

"Well, here's to you two bonding over more than being irritated!" Jacob raised his aluminium mug and took a swig of his reconstituted orange juice.

"We are. I never had much luck dating anyone in Seattle at Uni, then I was in the Danakil desert for nearly six years doing my PhD, not loads of options there either."

"Well, I'm glad you found someone. Officially I disapprove of course but between you and me I completely get it. It's lonely out in space." Despite how flat he was, Abuya recognised the tune he sang these last words to and grinned

"On such a timeless flight." she replied.

"It is timeless! That's why it's been stuck in my head this whole time. We are making history here together. Who knows what you researchers will discover, to say nothing of the miners proving the financial viability of this sort of exploration. The idea of being part of discovering something brand new is… intoxicating!" He took another swig from his mug and winked at her. Abuya wondered if there might be more than orange juice in the mug.

"But then look who I'm talking to, the great discoverer of Dunaliela Eritretes."

Abuya blinked in mild astonishment. "You've read my papers?"

"Of course. It was a very long journey here after all, I read up on pretty much everyone. I found your dissertation particularly fascinating."

"It's over a hundred thousand words! I'm not sure the doctoral panel even read the whole thing." Abuya laughed at him, secretly quite pleased. Discovering a new type of foul-smelling, eukaryotic algae smeared across the salt pans of a barren desert was very exciting to someone studying extremophiles but not really to anyone else. Even Annika glazed a little when discussing the topic.

Jacob was about to discuss her discovery with her further when Abuya caught sight of Annika pushing her way back through the crowd, looking slightly puzzled but clearly enjoying the atmosphere.

"How was Cole?" she asked as the doctor joined their little group, nodding to Jacob and accepting the proffered mug he had somehow conjured from nowhere.

"Couldn't find him in the crowd actually, no one saw him at the movie either."

A look of concern furrowed Jacob's brow. "Hmm, I don't think I saw him now I come to think of it, I hope he's alright. I'll ask Mark to go down to the lower levels and check he's ok."

"He's way ahead of you, he went down a few minutes ago. He reckons Cole just wanted some quiet time to himself but he said he'd make sure he was alright anyway."

Jacob brightened. "Excellent, well I won't keep you two, I must go and speak with Scott about the next movie night, see what else he has in his dusty archives."

As Jacob slipped away, Henning loomed into view, moving like an icebreaker through the crowd with the far slighter Alistair bobbing along in his wake. He leaned in close to Abuya as if to whisper in her ear.

"Tag, you are it," he muttered, before engaging Annika in a flood of voluble German. Abuya gave a tiny internal sigh and settled herself into Alistair's stream of consciousness about the movie. He was always happy to expound at length on pretty much any topic and to be fair she had rarely found one in which he was not well-stocked with interesting tidbits. He was just in the middle of explaining how one of the stars, Victor Lundin, went on to play the first ever Star Trek Klingon when he was interrupted. With a sudden bleat of static, the room's intercom panel burst into life with a message that made the room fall silent.

"There's been an incident on mining level three, section D. Commander Callaghan and the Doctor please report here immediately." It was clearly Mark, but he was panting and sounded distressed. Jacob rushed over to the intercom, causing chaos as those he bumped past struggled to keep to their feet in the low gravity.

"Jacob here, Mark what's happened?" he demanded.

"Just get down here Jake."

Cursing, Jacob hurried towards to exit. Annika had already vanished in a flash of blonde hair, most likely running for her medical kit.

"Would you need a hand Commander?"

"Thank you, Henning, it couldn't hurt." Jacob called back over his shoulder.

Henning moved away after him and Abuya tagged along behind, worried about Cole and wanting to make sure Annika stayed safe. Mark had not seemed himself. He had sounded shaken, even scared and Abuya was sure she wasn't alone in feeling a pit in her stomach at the idea of some terrible accident having taken place down in the depths while they were all above having fun.

She had to scurry, almost running to keep up with Henning's long strides, and they got to the elevator terminus just as a panting Annika arrived from the opposite corridor, clutching her emergency bag. She was breathing hard, either from running or perhaps her heart, like Abuya's was pounding in her chest with sick anticipation of what they might find. The urgency of the situation sent little jolts of anxiety down her spine and her mind raced with worry. She glanced at Jacob, who didn't waste a moment. Without a word, he strode purposefully into the elevator, the others quickly falling into step behind him.

As Henning swung the grating closed and the dim lighting of the elevator shaft enveloped them, Abuya took a deep, steadying breath, bracing herself for whatever awaited them below.

CHAPTER FOUR

She Will Feed

Abuya's heart thrummed in sync with the descending elevator's rumble, each unpredictable thud making it flutter and skip a beat. Cold sweat prickled at the back of her neck and she fought to control her sharp, shallow breathing. She did not want to seem this fearful in front of the others and she glanced to either side almost guiltily.

She could see the tension in their expressions as well, hidden to various degrees. Henning tapped his fingers against his thigh in a steady, restless tattoo while Jacob alongside him was gnawing at his thumbnail.

Only Annika seemed genuinely unaffected, digging through her medical bag and checking she had everything she might need. Despite her tiny stature and general light-heartedness, Annika was tough. She'd spent her residency working in the Haukeland Hospital emergency room before taking two separate rotations with the United Nations peacekeeping force as a front-line medic. She'd dealt with some pretty awful situations in her time and this would be nothing new to her.

Abuya strove to follow her example, forcing her hands to unclench and her mind to think clearly. It wasn't easy, but Annika caught her eye and flashed her a small, reassuring smile which helped to settle her somewhat.

The elevator shaft's walls were made of sturdy metal gratings, past which the dimly lit walls of the shaft slid. She forced herself to study the intricate network of cables and support beams, tracing their paths with her eyes as they passed in an attempt to ground herself. The dull red glow of indicator lights dotted along the shaft provided intermittent illumination, casting ruddy shadows that danced eerily on the walls. With a jarring whoosh, a looming dark shape appeared to her left and flashed by the gratings, making Abuya jump. The counterweight. The massive cage of ballast had passed by unexpectedly, disrupting her fleeting sense of calm. She clenched her fists, frustrated at her own reaction, inhaling and exhaling slowly, trying to regain her calm. The cold, mechanical smell of the elevator, the faint scent of metal and lubricant, filled her nostrils. It was oddly comforting.

With a final rattle and a dull clang, the elevator at last arrived in the main body of the mining platform. The usual smells of machine oil, closely packed humans and traces of ozone left over from the electrolysis process, washed over them as they stepped out into the brightly lit central hub of the first level.

Abuya, who had visited most often of all, was used to the mining platform being loud and crowded with the crew that worked and lived there. Now, emptied of its inhabitants, it was like nothing she had ever experienced before—a vast expanse of bare metal walls, creaking and groaning in the currents of Europa's subsurface ocean. The constant awareness of the immense weight of water above them added to the eerie atmosphere and Abuya couldn't help but imagine the utter darkness beyond this brightly lit environment, hiding secrets and unknown dangers. Cole's story about some horrifying creature outside swam back into her memories and suddenly it was not so hard to imagine the noises she could hear as the tapping of claws on the hull or the hungry moans of something desperate to get in.

Annika stood close to Abuya, her medical bag clutched tightly in her hand, her knuckles white with the pressure. She reached out to squeeze Abuya's arm, but it did little to ease her nerves. Jacob's demeanour was one of intense concentration, his gaze flickering across the metal walls with an almost obsessive attention to detail. There was an air of strained control about him as if he were wrestling with thoughts that darted too quickly to grasp. His hands, though steady, occasionally flexed or clenched in a rhythmic pattern, betraying a hidden tension. Every so often, his head would shake slightly, as if trying to pin down a fleeting thought or ward off an unwelcome one.

Jacob led the way forward, moving quickly towards the outer ring. The mining platform was a stack of five doughnut-shaped rings. Each with a central room housing life support, mining machinery or, in the case of this upper section, the elevator station.

The walls of this central room were lined with control panels, gauges and monitors, each flickering with data and status updates. The hum of machinery and the occasional hiss of pneumatic systems filled the space with a constant background noise, a testament to the ceaseless activity of the platform's filtration operations.

The sections were connected along the outer ring by laddered hatchways, each offset by one hundred and twenty degrees. Jacob was heading for the nearest ladderway. Passing an intercom panel on the wall, Jacob hit the talk button. "We're down Mark, just heading to the level one ladderway now."

"Ok, Cole's awake again. Please hurry!" Mark's reply came back after just long enough for them to worry.

"Is he hurt Mark?" Annika had pushed Jacob aside to speak into the intercom.

"I don't know Doc. I think he's sick, or crazy or something. I had to tie him up."

"Ok Mark, you hold tight we'll be there as soon as we can."

Abuya heard Henning mutter some curse in German before he and Jacob took off at a run. Abuya and Annika followed closely behind and watched anxiously as Jacob hurled himself down the first ladderway, barely avoiding falling down the last few rungs in his haste.

Reaching the second level they ran together along the curved outer walkway that ran along that level's hull, nearly sprinting the hundred or so metres to the next hatch and the next ladderway.

Henning managed to interpose himself, climbing into the shaft first before the frantic commander had a chance to take the ladder too fast again.

Now on the third ring, they cut across the centre of the circle, winding their way through the maze of crew quarters, maintenance workshops and other rooms before finally reaching section D.

"In here." Mark's call drew them into the egress chamber, a large room containing pressure suits, maintenance equipment and the huge reinforced hatch that led to the external pressure lock. At the moment it also contained Mark, sprawled ungainly against the cold metal wall, a grimace of pain warping his features.

He was trying to cradle his leg, the ankle of which was twisted at a nauseating angle. At the opposite end, thrown against the hatchway, was the huddled figure of Cole. His legs were hobbled with what looked like a torn jumpsuit and a length of gauge wire had been used to lash his wrists to the railing of the steps beside him. He was curled into a tight ball, rocking silently with his bound hands scrabbling at the top of his head.

"Mark, what the hell happened?" Jacob exclaimed, his voice drawn and panicked as he dropped to his knees beside his brother.

Mark turned to them, his face ashen and his hands trembling slightly.

"I'm not sure," he began, his voice unsteady. "I was on my way down to Cole's quarters to check on him; he wasn't at the movie night, so I wanted to see if he was ok. I was passing through this level and I heard a loud noise, clattering like something heavy had been dropped. I called out with no answer so I came along here to investigate." He paused, pushing past the pain to collect his thoughts before continuing. "When I arrived, I found Cole, muttering to himself and apparently oblivious to me. He was lugging a load of supplies and equipment, looks like he'd been loading them into the pressure lock. I couldn't understand it." He sucked in a hiss of air through his teeth as Annika gently probed at his injured ankle. "When I confronted him, he started babbling about it being a gift and then when I tried to stop him, he leapt on me."

Henning looked about, seeing the disarray of the egress chamber. There was equipment tossed about and broken glass from some of the instruments scattered on the floor.

"You fought?" he asked.

"Yes. He was completely out of control, like he wasn't even seeing me." Mark's voice was strained. "He just kept lashing out blindly. In the struggle, he shoved me off those stairs over there." He gestured vaguely towards the steps Cole was currently tied to, his face contorting with pain as the gesture caused a slight movement in his injured leg. "I grabbed onto him as I fell and we both went down together hard. My ankle got caught and it wrenched around real bad. I... I think it's broken." His voice faltered as the nauseating crunching sound came back to him. "On the ground, I managed to get my arm around his neck and I just held on. When he finally went limp, I was scared I'd killed him, but I found a pulse. I didn't know if he'd be out long so I tied him up before I crawled over here to the intercom."

Jacob was clearly at a loss for words at Mark's story, his mouth working silently. Annika stepped in before he had a chance to recover himself. "Henning, can you handle Mark while I check on Cole?"

Henning, who had been in the military himself in his youth and had experience in first aid of this sort, nodded brusquely.

Annika called out to him as she turned to make her way towards Cole. "Don't move him and don't try to treat the ankle, just check there's nothing else wrong and I'll take over when I'm done over here."

Abuya followed Annika across the chamber to stand at a safe distance from Cole. He was still rocking back and forth, his hands pulling at hanks of his hair. His legs writhed over each other as if trying to pull free of the rags that bound him.

"Cole?" Annika's query elicited no response.

"Cole, can you hear me? Nathaniel?" At Abuya's use of his first name, a low moan started to emanate from the pitiful form but the writhing and rocking continued.

Annika looked to Abuya. "I may have to sedate him. Keep trying to speak gently to him while I prepare an auto-injector."

So saying, she turned to rummage in her medical bag.

Abuya could hear loud clanging footsteps echoing closer as she crept towards to Cole. The sight of the man lying before her filled her with sickening dread, she couldn't imagine what could have caused him so much pain, so much distress. The air felt thick and oppressive, the recycled atmosphere thick with the sour tang of human sweat.

"Cole? Can you hear me, it's Abuya. Cole?"

Okoreye came bursting into the room, Evans and a handful of miners hot on his heels. They must have barely all fit into the elevator to make it down. They took in the sight, slack jawed before Okoreye hurried over to help Henning with Mark. Evans took Jacob by the arm and drew him to one side for a muttered conversation.

"Cole?" Abuya tried the wretched man's name one more time. There was still no response and she leaned forward, reaching out to gently clasp his shoulder.

With a convulsive gasp, like a drowning man breaking water, Cole stiffened. His arms and legs shot out straight and his back hyper-extended until she thought his spine must surely snap. He held the position for one heart-stopping second and then, drawing breath into his lungs in a shuttering wheeze, he screamed. It was a wordless, mindless, throat-tearing howl that echoed around the aluminium walls until the entire lungful was spent. His body thrashed violently from side to side, knocking Abuya flying. He thrashed mindlessly, ripping his hands free of their bonds and screaming again and again at the absolute top of his lungs. Abuya scrambled out of his reach, hearing his screams crack out behind her, mindless sounds interspersing themselves with desperate curses and cries.

"SHE WILL FEED! LET ME SAVE US!"

"Henning," Annika shouted above the noise, "hold him!" Her voice was remarkably calm, issuing clipped, curt orders.

Henning strode across, enveloped the man's hands in his own huge fist and lay heavily across his thrashing legs. Okoreye rushed to grab the man's other hand which was clawing at Henning's face and with the man finally secured Annika darted in, found the man's neck and pressed her auto-injector pen to it.

After a few seconds, the screaming faded to be replaced with rattling breaths and finally stillness. Henning clambered to his feet, dabbing gingerly at the scratches on his cheek with the cuff of his sleeve.

The room fell into a heavy silence, the aftermath of Cole's frenzied screams hanging in the air. Abuya's hands quivered uncontrollably, the rush of adrenaline leaving a tingling sensation in her fingertips and a bitter taste in her mouth. She felt her heart pounding in her chest, each beat echoing the intensity of the moment. Her eyes met Annika's, finding a reflection of her own shock in the other woman's wide, disbelieving gaze. The man who had been their colleague now lay before them, broken and unconscious. He had torn at the flesh of his hands and Abuya suspected some of the fingers must be broken after thrashing so hard against his bonds. Blood seeped gently from lacerations where he had wrenched against the wire binding him and his light brown hair was matted and red.

They all stood in stunned silence, staring in disbelief at the scene before them. Evans, his complexion ghostly, turned towards Jacob, looking to him for some sort of explanation. His voice, when he finally spoke, was barely above a whisper, yet it cut through the silence sharply. "What the hell happened here?"

The question seemed to echo around the room, hanging unanswered in the air. No one could muster a response. There was a palpable sense of bewilderment and fear that damped their minds and stopped their voices.

Jacob shook his head slowly, trying to process the events. "I… I don't know," he stammered, his voice faltering as he struggled to maintain his composure amidst the overwhelming circumstances.

Evans, observing Jacob's evident difficulty in grappling with his emotions, stepped forward decisively. With a steady, assertive tone, he cut through their collective reverie. "We need to get them back to the surface right now. We're not equipped to handle this situation down here."

Henning nodded in agreement. "I will help with Mark. Imobilise his leg and we can carry him on a stretcher. But Cole...He will need something stronger to hold him. He may still be… unpredictable."

"He will be out for hours Henning, I've seen to that," put in Annika. "There's only one carrying brace down here and we'll need that for Mark. Do you think you can manage Cole on your own?"

"Of course," shrugged Henning, as if it was nothing. To be fair they were in only about a fifth of normal gravity, they could all perform feats that would have been superhuman on Earth.

Abuya looked down at Cole's prone form, lying motionless on the floor, his eyes closed. He seemed almost peaceful compared to the thrashing monster that had knocked her sprawling only a few moments ago. She couldn't shake the image of his violent thrashing from her mind any more than she could forget the wild, terrified look in his eyes or that unearthly screaming.

Annika sent one of the miners to bring the stretcher from

storage and set about doing her best to immobilise Mark's leg for the journey. There was only so much she could do with what she had available and, despite the morphine she gave him, there were several winces and hisses from the wounded man. She declared that he was fortunate only to have dislocated the joint and not to have broken anything. At this pronouncement, Jacob seemed to come back to himself with a jerk. Once more in control of himself, he thanked the doctor and took charge again, arranging a team of bearers from the ever-growing crowd of miners that were arriving one elevator load at a time.

Abuya couldn't comprehend the varied reactions of the miners upon seeing Mark injured. Shock and concern were evident on many faces, as she expected, but there were others who seemed to glance at Mark with something that looked disturbingly like anger. She caught fleeting glances exchanged between a few of them, their expressions unreadable but tense. This mix of emotions puzzled her deeply, leaving her unsettled and confused. but before she could dwell any further on it, she felt a tap on her arm from Henning.

"Can you watch his head for me as I go?"

He was standing, quite casually with Cole slung over his shoulder. Even in the low gravity, it wouldn't be trivial to manoeuvre the ungainly weight through the maze of passages and up two narrow ladderways. Abuya nodded and set off behind Henning, laying a hand carefully on Cole's head as it bounced on the man's broad shoulders.

As they approached the first ladderway, they encountered Wei-Yun. He looked as pale as a ghost, the shock still clearly affecting him greatly. Despite his state, he remained focused on his duty, rigging a block and tackle at the top of the ladder to aid in bringing up Mark's stretcher. Abuya wanted to say something to comfort him, but her mind drew a blank. She settled for placing a reassuring hand on his arm, eliciting a grateful yet worried look that quickly shifted away when Wei-Yun's gaze landed on Cole's motionless form.

Abuya couldn't help but glance back nervously into the mouths of the corridors they passed, her mind filled with unsettling thoughts. What could have driven Cole to such a state? What was down here in the depths that could cause such terror? She felt the unnerving sensation that something was watching her, a prickling between her shoulder-blades.

"She will feed." She whispered the words Cole had screamed to herself under her breath. Henning heard her and stopped; she walked straight into his back with a muffled umph.

"You heard this too then?" He asked the words softly, half turning to look at her over his shoulder.

"Yes… I did.. what do you think it mea...."

"It meant nothing at all, the ravings of a mad man," he cut her off abruptly. He clearly wasn't as calm as the appearance he was trying to project.

"But what made him that crazy? What if he saw something that scared him so much it drove him mad?" Abuya wasn't sure what she thought at this moment. Panic was overruling her reason, spurring her imagination.

Henning placed a heavy hand on her shoulder and looked steadily into her eyes. "Come on Abs, you are a scientist. You are an exobiologist verdamnt! You should know better than anyone how impossible this thing would be."

He was right of course. Abuya closed her eyes, trying to put herself out of this paranoid frame of mind. She pictured herself back on the surface in her bunk, trying to let images of normality block out the dark fantasies her brain was busily concocting. Henning was quite right. Her research here was looking for single-celled organisms and the chances of them existing were already minute. The possibility that some giant monster, to say nothing of a whole supporting ecosystem, could have evolved out here and not left any trace to be discovered was ludicrous.

"Thanks," she said in a small voice. "I'm just a bit shocked. I don't know how to deal with a problem like this."

"I sat on him." Cole's frame bobbed as Henning shrugged. "I find most problems can be solved by sitting on them."

It was a terrible joke, but Abuya let out a snort of laughter despite herself. Suddenly the mining platform didn't seem so scary. She looked at Henning's face, carefully set with a serious expression. "I'll try that next time you're snoring in the back of the rover!"

Henning turned away with mock indignation and continued towards the terminus. As he did so, Cole's face was turned back into her field of view. She laid a protective hand again, this time on his cheek, feeling a rush of tenderness and pity for this poor, fragile man. He was only in his early twenties, probably one of the youngest on board.

As they reached the elevator, they carefully brought Cole inside. Just as Abuya was sliding the grating closed, she heard running feet and Annika hurried out of the corridor behind them.

"Hold that!"

She clattered inside and Abuya shut the grating behind her. "The others will take a while getting Mark up to me, I'm most worried about Cole in any case."

She stooped over the man's prone form where Henning had set him down, checking for his pulse and opening up his jumpsuit to feel the rise and fall of his chest. "He is burning up," she said to no one in particular. "Pulse is rapid and weak."

Abuya and Henning squeezed themselves against the wall, trying to give Annika as much space as possible in the confined elevator. Annika worked swiftly and methodically, her hands moving with practiced precision. She palpated Cole's abdomen, checking for any signs of internal injury, and gently probed his limbs for fractures or other damage. The man's skin was slick with sweat and Annika's fingers left faint trails on his feverish body as she examined him.

"Breathing is shallow," Annika noted, more to herself than anyone else as she leaned in close to listen to his laboured breaths. She gently opened one of his eyelids, shining a small pen light to check his pupillary response. "Pupils are dilated but reactive."

The elevator shuddered as it continued its slow ascent, the mechanical clanking echoing through the confined space. Annika's brow furrowed in concentration as she ran her hands over Cole's limbs, checking for any signs of neurological response.

"He's responsive to pain stimuli, which is good," she murmured, rubbing hard on the man's sternum with her knuckles. Her hands moved to check his pulse again, frowning at the irregular rhythm beneath her fingers. "We need to get him to the medical bay as soon as possible."

Abuya kept her eyes on Cole's face, trying to read any sign of consciousness or recognition. The elevator felt like it was moving at a snail's pace, each second stretching into an eternity. The confined space amplified every sound, from Cole's ragged breathing to the rhythmic clank of the elevator's ascent.

Finally, the elevator reached the surface and they were greeted by the bright lights and open space of the main elevator terminus. Delun and Scott were there having rightly assumed that help would be needed and they unburdened Henning, hurrying Cole down the corridor towards the medical bay with Annika scampering at their heels.

Henning declared that he would stay to help with Mark when his elevator arrived and Abuya found herself suddenly at a loose end. The adrenaline flowed out of her in a rush, leaving her swaying on her feet. Henning took her by the shoulder and gave her a gentle push towards the researchers' dormitory. She let her stumbling feet carry her there and collapsed onto the nearest cot, too tired even to climb up to her own. As sleep quickly overtook her, echoes of Cole's anguished cry drifted through her mind.

"She will feed."

CHAPTER FIVE

Invisible Wounds

The dim red glow from the strip lights in the researchers' dormitory brightened through orange and yellow to their daytime white, rousing Abuya from her slumber. As she slowly opened her eyes, blinking away the remnants of sleep, there was a fleeting moment of normality, a brief interlude of peace before the events of the previous day rushed back into her consciousness with vivid clarity.

With a deep, steadying breath, she sought in vain to wrest some semblance of sense from amidst the chaos of her memories of the night before. As she did so, a wave of guilt washed over her as she thought of Annika. She would have spent the night dealing with the aftermath, the luxury of rest denied to her. She needed to check on her right away.

Swinging her legs off what she now realised was Delun's bunk, she gave perfunctory replies to the morning greetings from the other stirring researchers and strode away down the connecting passages towards the medical bay.

The familiar waft of bleach and antiseptics stung her

nostrils as the bay's hatchway swung open before her, revealing Annika's dishevelled appearance. Her eyes were puffy and red, evidence of a sleepless night filled with anxious work. She was sitting on one of the examination beds, head bowed over a steaming tin mug. Abuya stood hesitantly in the hatchway and it seemed to take a moment before Annika even noticed her presence.

"Hey Abs," Annika said with a weak smile, her voice thick with exhaustion. "Nice of you to visit."

Without a word, Abuya enveloped her in a warm embrace, holding her head to her chest and breathing in the warm mix of coffee, disinfectant and unwashed human. They stayed there for a moment, finding solace in each other's presence before Abuya released her and turned to gaze at the other examination bed.

There lay Cole, his skin drawn and pallid, a stark contrast to the dark, discoloured bruises marring his flesh. His body was motionless, save for the faint, uneven rise and fall of his chest. His face, usually animated and expressive, now lay eerily still, accentuating the hollows beneath his closed eyes and the sharp angle of his cheekbones. His light brown hair, usually neat, was now a dishevelled mop, giving him a forlorn and abandoned appearance. The unconscious figure looked so fragile and vulnerable, lying there at the mercy of machines and medicine.

"How is he? Did anything happen after I fell asleep?"

Annika sighed heavily, gesturing helplessly towards the unconscious man. "Not much. I've been keeping him sedated. He has a mild fever and his blood work shows some weird neurochemistry, but until I let him wake, there's not much I can do to understand what's going on."

"How about Mark?"

"He's back below." She held up her hand to quell Abuya's worried exclamation. "He insisted. I relocated and splinted his ankle; not much else I can do for him. He's going to have a tough time getting around, but he'll manage, especially with the low gravity here."

"That's a small mercy I guess." Abuya's brow furrowed in concern. She had taken a step closer to Cole as Annika spoke, wanting to look down into his sleeping face, and had seen a network of angry red abrasions at the base of his neck. Annika anticipated her question.

"He's covered in those scratches; I think he has been clawing at himself. It's odd though, there aren't any in spots where they wouldn't be hidden by his uniform."

"You think he was trying to hide them?!" Abuya asked incredulously.

The implications of this sent a shiver down Abuya's spine. He had been distressed enough to gouge his skin, but conscious enough of the wrongness of his actions to hide them.

Before Abuya could respond there was the sound of approaching footsteps down the connecting tunnel followed by a sharp rap on the hatchway.

Both of them turned to see Okoreye framed in the entrance, his gaze inexorably drawn to the unconscious man. "Good morning, Doctor, Abuya." He nodded to them both. "Doctor, the commander has called a senior meeting to discuss last night's events. He has asked that you give your initial report."

"Can't it wait a little, she's exhau…" Annika cut Abuya off mid-sentence, placing a restraining hand on her shoulder.

"It's fine Abs, I'll be ok." She smiled at the look of worried concern on Abuya's face. "Why don't you come keep an eye on me if you're worried? Reckon that's ok?" This last she addressed to Okoreye who nodded and turned on his heel, disappearing back through the hatchway.

With a sigh, Annika picked herself up and stepped beside Cole, checking the controls of the intravenous feed tube to ensure he wouldn't wake while she was gone.

Abuya placed a hand on her shoulder and together they followed Okoreye towards the main conference room.

· ·• · ·

It took Abuya a moment to remember why the conference room was in such disarray. The main table had been hurriedly set up once more, but around the edges of the room was a litter of chairs and benches that had yet to be returned to their rightful homes. The movie felt like it must have been weeks ago, but she realised it could be barely more than twelve hours.

Annika took a seat at the main table and Abuya went to pull an extra chair from a nearby pile. The room was already full of the base's upper ranks, all with tightly drawn expressions of worry. Jacob, Scott and Okoreye were there along with Evans, Wei-Yun and Henning. Mark's face was on the main screen, presumably to save him an unnecessary journey on his wounded leg. Abuya grinned internally, knowing just how severe the usually sweet Annika could be about the need for bed rest.

Mayumi, one of Mark's two sub-directors, occupied his usual seat at the table. Abuya didn't know her very well, only having observed her in meetings and passing interactions. From what she had seen, Mayumi was typically composed and assertive, often veering into micro-management.

Today however, her anxiety stood out, even among the anxious crew. Her fingers tapped an irregular rhythm on the tabletop as her eyes, wide and alert, darted around the room. It was as if she expected something to jump out at her.

Every so often, her gaze would lock onto Abuya and the intensity of her stare was unsettling. There was a suspicion in those eyes, almost an accusation, that made Abuya shift uncomfortably. The once confident woman now seemed frayed at the edges, her paranoia palpable. It was as if the news of recent events had shattered her composed exterior, leaving behind someone unrecognisably defensive and wary.

She tried to offer a reassuring smile, but Mayumi's intense stare only narrowed slightly in response.

Before she could dwell on this odd interaction further, Jacob spoke, cutting over the hubbub of individual muttered conversations that had pervaded the room. "Welcome, thank you all for coming. As I'm sure you are all aware, we are facing an unprecedented situation," Jacob swept his gaze around the room, making eye contact with each of them in turn before continuing. "Cole's condition remains stable, but he is still unconscious and under close observation." So saying, he gestured to the screen where, next to Mark's image, there was a camera view of the medical bay and Cole's prone form.

"For those of you not yet fully apprised of last night's events, Cole attacked Mark without any apparent provocation. The incident escalated quickly into a significant physical struggle. Mark suffered a severe injury to his leg, and Cole was restrained only after sustaining multiple abrasions and lacerations."

"Do you have any idea what might have triggered this, Mark?" Scott directed his comment to the screen. Mark's only response was to shrug helplessly.

Jacob sighed, "That's unclear. Cole was found in a highly agitated state, muttering incoherently about...feeding something. It's possible he's experiencing some kind of psychotic break." He let the words hang in the air, allowing the team to digest the unsettling news. "Since the event occurred, Mark and Evans have uncovered more details which we urgently need to discuss. Moreover, we have witnessed some surprising behaviour among several of the mining crew." Here his eyes flicked to Mayumi and hastily away, as if he didn't trust himself to meet her gaze.

"Evans's, I think we should hear your report first."

Evans cleared his throat and looked about the room before beginning. "After Cole and Mark were removed from the mining platform early this morning, I, along with Mayumi and a small team, began trying to piece together what happened. We began with an examination of the lower egress chamber where the altercation took place. Upon checking the chamber's pressure lock, we found it to contain a large pile of supplies, primarily food rations but also emergency medical supplies, laboratory equipment and even some personal items, presumably belonging to Cole."

This was news to Abuya and clearly to several of the others at the table judging by the murmuring that arose at Evans's words.

"I had inventory checks carried out on all supply stores. This revealed that, on three of the five mining rings, supplies are missing. The shortages were of a significant quantity, indeed clearly more than were found in the pressure lock. Searches have been conducted and so far, none of the unaccounted for supplies have been found."

Abuya was baffled by this. There was no benefit to anyone stealing supplies. Food was rationed yes, but the rations were generous.

"I'm afraid that's not all. In attempting to discover from security footage what had happened to these supplies, we discovered that several of the cameras in the mining platform have at some point been tampered with."

"They don't like people watching them all the time!" This was Mayumi butting into the conversation, her voice an angry, staccato hiss. The room fell still at her outburst.

"Mayumi, no one even looks at those unless there's an emergency. We weren't even aware that they had been disconnected until we checked today," Jacob explained placatingly.

"People are watching." Mayumi's reply was a sullen

murmur as she sat back with a scowl.

Evans cleared his throat quietly, bringing attention back to himself. He met Mayumi's dour gaze and held it unwaveringly as he spoke. "I asked Mayumi to join us this morning as her concerns are typical of those I have found in a subset of the mining crew. I thought it would be useful for their opinions to be heard."

Now under the gaze of the whole room, Mayumi looked about petulantly as if she would refuse to answer, then her feelings burst forth in an angry torrent. "Who gave you the right to barge into our domain, disrupt our work and accuse us of theft?" Mayumi hissed, her voice scornful and bitter. "We know how to survive down there, better than any of you! You have no idea what it's like down below. We're constantly at the mercy of the deeps, struggling to extract what we need without waking whatever lurks in the shadows. It's a delicate dance and we know how to do it without putting the entire base at risk. You should just leave us alone. You're not wanted down there."

As Mayumi's tirade lapsed into silence, the room sat stunned, gazing at her incredulously. Abuya's eyes flicked to Wei-Yun and was relieved to see he was as shocked and baffled at these words as everyone else. Mark's voice came through the speaker at the centre of the table. "I have heard similar sentiments from seven of my crew this morning, including the three that shared Cole's dormitory. I have called an all-staff meeting for the mining base at noon today for us to discuss everyone's concerns."

"What has got you so upset Mayumi?" Jacob turned to the

scowling woman, his tone attempting to be reconciliatory.

Mayumi however would only glare back at him and with a sigh, Jacob turned back to the rest of the room.

"I want to try and get to the bottom of this. Annika, please continue to tend to Cole, let me know when he wakes and I'll come and speak to him. Mark, I shall join your meeting later today and try to come to an understanding with your crew. I hope Mayumi that we can allay some of your concerns." The woman still scowled back at him. Abuya couldn't begin to understand her hostility.

"Evans, I'd like you to accompany Mayumi and Wei-Yun back down to the mining platform. I'm sure Mark could use your support and I'd like to hear your opinion as a relative outsider as to what is going on down there."

Evans nodded and stood with the two miners to leave. As the hatch closed behind them Scott sighed and pinched the bridge of his nose. "Just what the hell is going on?"

The tension in the room was palpable and Abuya could feel the weight of uncertainty settling over them all. "We can't just ignore what's happening," she said, breaking the silence that followed Scott's outburst. "I thought maybe Cole might have cracked under stress or something, but there's more to this. We need to investigate."

Okoreye nodded in agreement. "You're right, Abuya. We can't afford to dismiss this as a simple breakdown.

Annika, who had been quietly listening, spoke up. "I want to analyse Cole's behaviour, see if there are any patterns or triggers that might shed light on what's happening to him." She paused and turned to Jacob, "I'll need to wake him up for that though."

Jacob considered her words and then sighed. "Very well. Annika, go ahead and wake him. Henning, you and Okoreye keep an eye on the doctor, make sure Cole isn't a threat to her."

"No Henning, I'll go, I want to ask the man some questions," Scott interjected.

"No!" Annika's voice was firm. "No interrogating my patient, we don't want to illicit another fit like last night."

Jacob nodded slowly, his expression contemplative as he considered the doctor's advice. "You are quite right, Doctor," he agreed, though his voice was tinged with a hint of reluctance. "We must give Cole the time he needs to recover before we start pressing him for answers."

He paused, looking thoughtfully at the screen displaying Cole's condition. He seemed to zone out for a moment, anxiety and the weight of responsibility clear on his face, before coming back to himself with a small shudder. "When the time is right and only then, we'll seek insights from him." He turned away from the screen, addressing the room in a more decisive tone. "For now though, let's focus on maintaining the stability of the base and its crew."

He gave a final, affirming nod, signalling the end of the meeting.

With their tasks assigned, they dispersed, each consumed by their own thoughts and responsibilities. Abuya tried to immerse herself in the familiar rhythm of her daily tasks, seeking refuge in the methodical nature of her work. She had planned to dedicate her morning to a meticulous enzyme kinetics experiment, a task that would normally require her complete attention and precision. The experiment involved monitoring the rate of enzyme-catalysed reactions, a process that necessitated careful preparation of samples, precise timing, and accurate measurement of reaction rates.

She methodically set up her workstation, laying out the array of pipettes, test tubes and reagents needed for the assay. The process of preparing the enzyme and substrate solutions, usually a task she performed with practiced ease, now felt unusually burdensome. Her hands moved almost mechanically; mixing, measuring, and pouring, but her thoughts were scattered. Her mind, instead of focusing on the delicate balance of the reaction conditions, kept drifting back to the medical bay. Images of Cole lying unconscious hooked up to monitors, invaded her thoughts. Each beep of the timer, signalling the end of a reaction interval, jolted her back to the present, but only briefly. Despite her best efforts, the gravity of the situation elsewhere in the base pulled at her, dividing her attention and making the normally absorbing tasks feel distant and disconnected, unable to anchor her restless mind.

By midday, Abuya realised she was fighting a losing battle with her concentration. Her work, on any other day a source of satisfaction, now felt trivial. Giving in to her overwhelming concern and curiosity, she decided to visit the medical bay, hoping for some reassurance or at least more information.

Even as she entered the tunnel leading down towards the bay, she heard sobbing. She wanted to turn back, but her feet kept her moving forward, drawn irresistibly onwards until she stood before the open hatchway. Annika was standing by the examination bed. Cole was sitting up, head in hands gently rocking. But this wasn't the mad paroxysms that had possessed him the night before. These were the cries of a hurt child, one who is lost and scared. Abuya's heart went out to the man, wishing she knew anything that could relieve the pain she could hear in those sobs.

"Hi Cole." She spoke the words timidly, barely even aware she was doing it.

Both Cole and Annika spun around, neither having heard her approach. Annika's face was worried, Cole's was a twisted mask of fear.

"She is coming! Please, please. She's coming. She will FEED!" The voice rose in pitch until with the last word the sobs became a strangled scream. Abuya's heart skipped a beat as she recognised the phrase from the night before.

"Who Cole, who is coming?" She could barely push her voice above a whisper.

"She is old, so old. She is dark, she is darkness, she is coming! She will feed! I have seen her and she has seen me. She has looked into me and seen my all. SHE WILL FEED!"

Annika gave Abuya the tiniest shake of her head before she could speak again and beckoned her into the far corner of the small room where Henning sat, previously unnoticed. Cole went back to sobbing, plucking feebly at the restraints that bound him to the examination bed.

She sighed, shaking her head sorrowfully. "He has been talking like this since he woke."

"Verrückt," muttered Henning beneath his breath.

"Maybe," said Annika reproachfully, turning to him, "but if

he is crazy, it is not his fault."

"Sorry Doctor, I know." Henning looked a little abashed. "He is setting me on edge, that is all."

"What do you think he is talking about?" Abuya asked the pair. "Has he made any sense at all."

Annika and Henning exchanged glances.

"It's mainly been the sort of thing you've seen. He seems to think there's some sort of creature outside, down in the ocean."

Abuya nodded. "That's the sort of thing he was saying to Wei-Yun too."

"He says he has seen it and he thinks it is coming to eat him." Henning put in.

"ALL OF US!" The anguished wail at their backs told them Cole could hear their conversation.

Abuya winced and tried to ignore the cry. "Does he know himself at all?"

"I think so, he knows his name at least. I've tried talking to him about other things but he won't be swayed."

"Perhaps I could go and bring some of his personal effects up, maybe he has some photos or something that could bring him around."

"That's an excellent idea Abuya, he might just respond to that." They all turned to see Jacob standing in the doorway.

"Hey there, Cole." He addressed the man, stepping over the coaming. "How are you feeling?"

"Let me go!" The imploring moan was pitiful.

"I will Cole, as soon as we can get you calmed down." Jacob was speaking softly, soothingly, almost as if to a spooked horse.

Cole's eyes flickered with confusion and fear. He tried to focus on Jacob, his breaths coming in short, erratic gasps. "It's important—you need to understand," he hissed out harshly, his voice barely above a whisper, edged with urgency.

"I'm trying to understand Cole, I'm trying to help, okay?"

Cole didn't answer. Jacob's voice, despite its calm tone, seemed to unnerve him. "Can you tell me Cole, why did you put the supplies in the pressure lock?"

There was a long pause as Cole rocked back and forth, clearly unsure what to say. "For her." It was a hoarse whisper that came out, they could barely hear it.

"You were planning to jettison the supplies, weren't you?" Jacob persisted, trying to get some sort of straight answer.

"If we feed her, then she will stay away." The voice was small, like a young child explaining why he had been bad.

"You were trying to feed the creature?"

Abuya started at this, Jacob hadn't heard their discussion about a creature, where had he heard it from? "Some of your friends on the mining platform, they told me they saw a creature, it seems to have really frightened them. Is that right? Did it scare you too Cole?"

Cole's eyes were wide with a sort of terrible hope. He nodded vigorously, gulping back sobs.

Jacob sighed. "Ok Cole, you rest now, I promise I'll deal with the creature."

"Give her what she needs." Cole implored, but he slumped backwards onto the bed as he said it.

Annika stepped closer to Jacob to murmur in his ear. "I

think I should put him back under sedation. He only seems to be distressing himself while he's awake. I'd like to run a few more tests, see if I can't work out some sort of treatment before I bring him to again."

Jacob nodded to her. "Do as you think best, Doctor. I'll bow to your judgement." He stepped away from the examination bed to stand next to Abuya. Annika took up a prepared syringe and carefully applied it to the tubing of Cole's intravenous drip. They all watched as the man's eyes slowly drifted closed and his fluttering chest settled into a calmer, slower rhythm.

Seeming satisfied, Jacob gestured for the two women to follow him.

"Keep an eye on him please, Henning."

"Ja, sir,"

In silence, they followed Jacob out of the medical bay and along the corridor to the conference room where he slumped down at the table wearily. Scott and the other researchers were already there, along with Okoreye. Mark was back up on the screen, his concerned look mirroring Jacob's.

Jacob's dull gaze methodically swept across the faces around the table. His voice, usually so buoyant and assertive, was now laden with sombre gravity. "Has anyone seen or heard anything about a creature in the water?"

There was silence for a long moment, the words hanging heavily in the air and then Abuya spoke up. "Wei-Yun said Cole was talking about it a couple of weeks ago. That's all I've heard."

Jacob nodded slowly, digesting this. "I went down to the

mining platform for a spare torsion wrench last week," Delun chimed in. "Some of the miners were staring out through one of the viewing ports. I asked what they were doing and they said looking for the monsters. I thought they were joking."

There was a long pause as Jacob arranged his thoughts. Several people shifted uncomfortably in their seats while others fidgeted or tapped their fingers on the table.

Finally, Jacob spoke. "At our meeting with the mining staff today, Mark and I spent some time trying to understand the concerns of some of the more… reticent of our colleagues. Eventually, they started to tell us they were aware of some sort of creature outside the base." Jacob paused at this point, glancing at Mark on the screen who took over.

"I did hear a few rumours of such a thing a couple of weeks ago. I laughed it off at first, thinking it was some weird joke I didn't get. That does happen quite a bit. Then a few days ago, we did some exterior maintenance. Cole had to go out to replace an outer filter assembly that had ruptured. I came down to the egress chamber and found some of the crew trying to scare him into not going out. I thought it was some sort of weird bullying and I upbraided them for it. I told them I wouldn't tolerate any more talk of this creature. Cole went out for his egress and I hadn't heard anything more about it, until last night. Perhaps I should have taken them more seriously, maybe there is something out there after all."

The atmosphere of the room felt oppressive and heavy as the group once more lapsed into silence. Rational minds were grappling with inexplicable ideas, failing to find a handhold.

"Abuya," said Jacob, breaking the silence, "for the sake of

my own sanity, please give me your expert opinion. Is it possible for there to be some sort of creature living in the ocean here?"

Abuya hesitated, wanting to give a sweeping affirmative. "My work here is looking for extremophiles, single-celled microscopic organisms. We're talking about something potentially akin to algae or archaea, extremely simple life forms. Something that is so small and so simple that it can survive the high chemical contents of the water, the low oxygen, the frigid temperatures."

Jacob nodded "So you're saying nothing any larger is possible?"

She bit her lip. "Literally impossible? No, I can't say that. We don't understand enough for me to be able to say that. But based on what we do know, a large, complex organism is unlikely. Extremely unlikely. Ten big foots and a Loch Ness monster kind of unlikely."

"Plus, if something big lived in these waters, we'd have had to find smaller things that it ate." Scott chimed in. "A big creature would have to imply a food chain."

"True," replied Abuya nodding, "although there could be regions deeper below us, more amenable to life. We've only ventured about a kilometre down, the ocean is at least a hundred times that deep, maybe more. I don't think there really can be anything, but I can't give you a certain no Jacob, I'm sorry."

"Not wanting to alarm anyone, but didn't Mayumi mention 'the deeps' or something like that?" Alistair, who had been uncharacteristically quiet, interjected this point, reminding

Abuya of the strange phrase. It was not one she'd heard any of the miners use before."

Mark was shaking his head before Alistair could finish his comment. "Even if there was a creature, Mayumi couldn't know anything about it or where it came from." Mark pointed out. "There's a lot of paranoia down here, clearly. They felt afraid of me, of us. They seemed to think we were the enemy; they clearly aren't thinking straight. These are good people. I simply don't believe that just being scared by some creepy mermaid would make them behave this way."

"Well, it's clear that Cole isn't himself," Annika piped up. "His monoamine oxidase level is extremely low and that could certainly make him more irrational and paranoid." She paused for a moment, considering. "Then again, a severe enough traumatic event could make him act that way and the chemical imbalances could be just a resultant symptom, not a cause."

"If I might suggest, Commander." Okoreye alone had refused to drop Jacob's rank and still used it religiously. "Speculating won't help us at this point. We need to re-establish some order and some trust with those who have been disaffected. In the meantime, we need to do our best to help Cole and to understand what has caused his condition."

Nodding in agreement with the suggestion, Jacob leaned forward, his demeanour shifting subtly as he took charge of the room once more. "Delun, go and relieve Henning in the medical bay. Scott, you can brief him when he's free."

Delun nodded and rose to leave, his chair scraping loudly against the bare aluminium floor.

"Abuya, I liked your idea. Go down below and fetch up any of Cole's personal effects that might help bring him back to us." Abuya nodded, glad to have something useful to do at last. "Doctor, go and get some sleep, then get back to work studying Cole."

"Commander I'm fine to conti…"

"No Doctor, that's an order." Jacob cut Annika off. "Abuya, put her to bed before you go down."

Abuya winked at Annika. "I may have to use force sir, but I'll manage it."

Jacob gave a wan smile, rising stiffly. "I'm going to send a report back to TAURS control, see if they have any suggestions of what to do. Let's meet back here in twelve hours."

The room slowly emptied, with the team members breaking up into smaller groups, their conversations sober and subdued.

Abuya led Annika towards her quarters. For all her protests, the slight woman was drooping more with every step having barely slept two hours out of the past thirty.

"You need some sleep love. Just think how much better that brain will be working after a good rest." Abuya teased her.

She hooked an arm around the woman's waist and steered her towards the cot. Kneeling, she began to unpick the laces of her boots.

"I know, kosepus." Annika laid a hand on her shoulder and bent to kiss her forehead. "Be careful down there ok."

"I will love, don't worry about me."

"Don't go getting eaten by any creatures!"

It was a half-hearted joke and Abuya hoped that her answering grin could inspire her partner with a little confidence. She wished she could inspire confidence in herself too, but she couldn't think of any words to serve that need. Her chest felt tight and cold as if she was already sinking down into the icy clutches of Europa's ocean.

As Annika finally lay down on her cot, Abuya lingered for a moment. She stood watching her drift towards sleep, before quietly leaving the room and heading towards the elevator terminus.

CHAPTER SIX
Dark Currents

The close confines of the elevator's stark metal walls had never bothered Abuya before today. This time though, with her mind filled with anxieties and confusion, she felt a sudden, overwhelming sense of being trapped the moment she slid the metal grating shut. The walls seemed to close in on her and the elevator shaft felt like it was swallowing her whole. She had to fight down a rising wave of panic, forcing deep, steady breaths into her lungs in an attempt to quell this unexpected sensation.

She dug her fingernails into her palm as she tried to pull herself together. She'd never felt claustrophobic before. No one who lived on a space station could afford to be claustrophobic.

She took deep, slow breaths, trying to steady her nerves as the familiar sensation of the descent began, her stomach lurching as the elevator began making its slow way down. With each passing metre, her anxiety seemed to grow. She felt more than ever like she was being swallowed by the ocean itself.

Closing her eyes, she wrenched at this unsettling train of thought, willing herself to focus. She called up before her mind's eye a picture of Annika's calm, reassuring smile. She pictured Annika's pale blue eyes, her thick, golden hair drifting chaotically about her face. She remembered the comforting feel of Annika's arms around her waist and the soft touch of her lips that always seemed to melt her worries away. She let herself sink into the memory and allowed the warmth of it to wash away her anxiety. Releasing a slow, steady breath, she opened her eyes once more and was finally able to turn her mind back to the situation at hand.

She would be arriving at the mining platform in just a few moments and she tried to prepare herself for what might come. She thought about the many times she had visited the platform, shared drinks, games and laughs with its inhabitants. But now, uncertainty gnawed at her, making her unsure of the reception she would receive. Mayumi's tirade earlier had shown a level of paranoia that was unsettling and Abuya didn't know how widespread that sentiment would be.

Considering how on edge the miners might be, she knew she needed to tread carefully. The last thing she wanted was to exacerbate the situation further. She would get in and out as quickly as possible, focusing on her goal of investigating Cole's quarters. If she could bring back something personal, something that might help him in his current state, it would be worth the trip. Satisfying her curiosity about the miners' state of mind could wait for another time.

The elevator's gentle jolt as it reached its destination

brought her back to the present. Abuya slid back the grating and stepped out into the terminus chamber of the mining platform, her eyes scanning the familiar surroundings.

The platform, typically alive with the buzz of machinery and lively chatter, now felt like a besieged town. Miners moved about with a grim determination, their steps heavy and interactions minimal. Faces that once greeted her with warmth were now sullen and guarded. Conversations were hushed, reduced to terse exchanges and quick glances, as if an unseen threat loomed over them all. The usual hum of activity was muted, replaced by a tense silence that made the air feel heavy. No one acknowledged her arrival beyond wary stares. There was a pervading air of fear and stoicism, like defenders resigned to a final stand.

Abuya's polite nods were met with brief, wary glances. Some miners forced a smile, but most avoided eye contact, their gazes fixed on the ground or lost in the distance. As she passed, she felt their eyes on her back, suspicion and unease burning into the back of her neck.

She hurried through the chamber, her boots clattering over the perforated metal deck plates. The air was thick with the smell of machine oil and ozone, a pervasive, metallic tang resulting from the osmium extraction process. The walls were lined with an ordered chaos of pipes and conduits, broken up by a glowing strip light every few metres.

Navigating the maze of the platform, she climbed down several ladderways, each rung icy and unyielding beneath her fingers. The air seemed to grow more stale with each level, the confined spaces pressing in around her.

Finally, she reached the fourth ring, where she knew Cole's dorm to be. She moved quickly, her fingers trailing along the cool, slightly damp surface of the walls as she followed the outer ring around its circumference. Reaching one of that level's four vestibules, she saw Mark near one of the viewing ports, leaning heavily on his crutch. His silhouette was starkly contrasted against the dim glow from outside, his posture weary and contemplative.

"Mark," she called out softly, not wanting to startle him. He turned sharply to look at her, his expression weary but alert.

"Abuya, what brings you down here?"

"Jacob wanted me to pick up Cole's effects, remember?"

Mark nodded distractedly, "oh right, of course." He turned back to peer out of the viewing port once more. Abuya considered carefully and then took her chance.

"I wanted to talk to you about Cole," she said tentatively. "He said some pretty strange things and I was hoping someone down here might be able to shed some light on them."

Mark sighed, rubbing his forehead. "I spoke to him after the incident last night and he was adamant about what he saw, when he made sense anyway. I've heard similar stories from some of the other miners too. It's unnerving, to say the least."

Abuya nodded, her mind racing with possibilities. "What do you think, Mark? Is it possible that there's something out there?"

He looked at her for a moment, weighing his words before answering. "I want to believe it's just fear and paranoia playing tricks on their minds, but...I can't ignore the mounting evidence. Cole seemed genuinely terrified…" he tailed off, turning back to the viewing port and staring glassily into the void of dark water.

"So, you think there's a chance the creature is real?" Abuya probed.

Mark's eyes flickered with uncertainty. "I can't say for sure, but I think we owe it to ourselves to investigate further. Just imagine what a discovery like that would mean!"

"I can't see how anything could possibly live out there, but if we're wrong, then sure. Nobel prizes all round!" Abuya's weak attempt at breaking the tension fell flat. Mark nodded vaguely, still engrossed with the blank view outside. With a small shudder, he snapped out of his reverie and turned to give her a tired smile. "We'll solve this. We'll find this creature and understand it and make sure we are safe."

"If it exists at all."

Mark hesitated. "Sure."

The pair stood in silence for a moment, contemplating the lazily floating motes caught in the dull glow from their viewing port. The ambient noise in the platform seemed to intensify. Miners moved about urgently, their conversations hushed and anxious. Abuya glanced around, realising that they were being watched by a couple of nearby miners. She could feel their fear tangibly, like an electric charge in the air.

Mark seemed to read her thoughts.

"They're just nervous Abs." Mark seemed to read her thoughts. "They think the commander and you surface lot know about this creature and are trying to hide it from them."

"I wish I knew anything worth hiding. It's the miners that seem to know something that we don't."

"Maybe. Maybe not." With a sigh, he turned and walked away towards his office, the crutch thunking against the floor with each second step. Abuya watched the retreating figure, his silhouette growing smaller until he disappeared around a corner.

Turning, she continued on her way towards the final ladderway and Cole's quarters, the low throbs of machinery and faint clanging echoes resonating in the corridors around her.

Suddenly as she ducked through a hatchway, one of the miners stepped in front of her, blocking her path. He was a slight man and she recognised him as one of the latest arrivals that had come with Jacob. He was clearly agitated, his hands twitching as if barely restrained from grabbing at her.

"Where do you think you're going?" the miner challenged sharply, his voice thick with anger and suspicion. The intensity in his tone hit Abuya like a wave, the aggression palpable and almost physical in its impact, making her chest feel constricted. She involuntarily took a step back, her heart pounding, as she faced the miner's accusatory gaze.

The harshness of his question and the evident hostility in his stance caught her off guard, causing her to falter momentarily. She struggled to find her voice, realising the critical need to defuse the situation quickly before it spiralled into something more dangerous. Her mind raced to formulate a response that could calm the rising tension, her usual confidence momentarily shaken by the miner's confrontational approach.

"The Doc sent me down to…"

"What fucking business is it of yours Abbott?!" Abuya jumped at the loud exclamation. She hadn't heard Wei-Yun approaching from behind her. He had not shouted, but in the confined space his firm voice had sounded like a gunshot. Abbott cringed back his eyes darting from one to the other. Abuya could see concern mingled with anger in Wei-Yun's eyes. He spoke more evenly, clearly trying to calm the man. "Come on Abbott, we don't speak to colleagues like that."

"She shouldn't be down here." Abbott hissed. "It doesn't want them here."

"*'It'* doesn't exist. There's nothing here! You've got to snap out of this. There is nothing here, no creature, no monster, no nothing." Wei-Yun's voice was exasperated and he clearly struggled to keep a level tone.

Abuya stumbled back to be closer to Wei-Yun as his statement unleashed a tirade from Abbott. The man's eyes went wild and she could almost imagine him frothing at the mouth as his fear and anger and hate poured from him in a torrential babble.

"I've seen it, it's real, its eyes, like stars, they see everything! It's out there, lurking, waiting. It knows our secrets; it knows your lies. It knows. She knows. In the water, in our minds, in our souls. She will come, claim us, claim you. Feast on despair, on terror, on flesh. We can't escape her, shouldn't escape her. The beauty, the horror, the glory. I can feel her, her power. In the shadows, the depths, the darkest recesses of our minds. She is hungry, she wants us, our souls, our devotion. She is beauty, she is fear, she is deliverance and she will feed!"

Abbot's final words seemed to be wrenched from him in a shrilling crescendo, fading into either sobs or laughter, Abuya couldn't be sure. He turned and fled down the corridor, heedlessly barging into protruding pipework before staggering round a corner out of sight.

Abuya was frozen in shock but Wei-Yun was already moving, dashing after the man, pausing only to shout into the nearest intercom panel. "Mark, somethings wrong with Abbott, he's headed down service corridor eighty-nine, can you send help PDQ."

Abuya was left with the clattering footsteps ringing through the floor beneath her. Any other miners who might have been nearby had melted away into the shadows and she was alone. She tried to bring her heart under control, tasting bitter adrenaline in her mouth. She wanted to turn and fly back towards the ladderway and keep running until she'd flung herself down on her cot. But Cole's dorm was just metres from her and she couldn't turn back without answers, not having come so far.

Hesitantly, she approached the hatchway and paused for a moment before cautiously pushing the hatch open. The room was nearly identical to the researchers' dormitory so far above her. Cots lined the walls in alcoves, two high, each alcove just wide enough to accommodate the narrow beds. Clothes rails, screened by thin, blue curtains, hung beside each cot, with small drawer units crammed beneath them. The walls were bare metal, with rivets and seams visible, giving the space a utilitarian and somewhat harsh feel.

Personal items were sparse, limited to a few trinkets and the odd picture taped to the walls beside the cots. A faint smell of metal and recycled air pervaded the room, a constant reminder of their artificial environment. The air was dry and cool, making her skin prickle. The room was quiet, save for the distant hum of machinery, heightening the eerie sense of isolation.

Abuya began her search, sifting through the few personal items to be found in Cole's alcove. She found some photographs, presumably of his family, stuck to the back wall above his cot, their smiling faces gazing down at her. Careful not to tear them, she gently pulled them from the wall and tucked them away into a pocket.

She turned her attention to the drawers, finding a few toiletries, a dog-eared engineering manual with handwritten notes, a game console with well-worn thumb-sticks. Nothing seemed out of the ordinary. At the bottom, she found a small tattered book of field notes and she sat on the edge of Cole's cot to flick through it.

She flipped through the pages, finding scrawled diagrams and notes, presumably about the maintenance of the spectrography unit Cole was responsible for. After leafing through the first few dozen pages however, she found the handwriting becoming shaky and erratic, the words almost illegible in places. The diagrams, previously concise, became more abstract. The labels and sentences around them becoming more meandering, making less sense. Turning slowly through the book, Abuya felt a chill as she saw the phrase

"I think I saw something in the water."

With trembling fingers, she turned through the pages, more phrases jumping out of tangled paragraphs at her as if glowing off the page.

"Elliot has seen it now"

"Mark doesn't believe us"

"We dream of her"

"Nightmares…creature watching…hungry…It's real…"

"I speak to her, she called to me"

"We can save them; I can save them"

"She will feed and we shall witness"

As Abuya sifted through the contents of the notebook, she found herself increasingly perplexed. Many of the phrases were disjointed, some even appeared to be in a language she couldn't identify, certainly not English. She turned through the pages slowly, trying to make sense of the erratic entries, but the more she read, the more baffled she became.

Taking a moment to pause, Abuya sat back on the edge of

the cot, closing the notebook. She let out a shuddering breath, trying to calm the whirlwind of thoughts swirling in her head. She needed a moment to step back, to clear her mind. She glanced around the small, cramped quarters, her eyes scanning the familiar, yet now somewhat ominous surroundings.

Her gaze drifted across the room, eventually settling on the hatchway leading into the main corridor. Something caught her eye —a pattern of scratches on the coaming above the hatch. Curious, she stood up and moved closer for a better look. The scratches formed some sort of X shape, with a few extra lines added, creating a distinctive design. Intrigued, she ran her fingers over the rough texture of the scratches, feeling their depth.

A nervous thrill coursed through her. She recognised the symbol. The same odd design had been scrawled on several pages of the notebook. She opened the book once more and now she was specifically looking for it, the symbol jumped off the pages, over and over again.

She began to pace up and down the confined space, forcing her mind to think and not just race away into anxious fretting.

As she walked over them, a collection of dark stains on the floor caught her eye. As she stepped closer to examine them, she saw similar stains on the curtain covering one of the clothes rails. Apprehensively, she slid the curtain across, unfurling it to reveal a patchwork of lurid brown markings.

She staggered back as, for a brief moment, her agitated mind thought they might be the stains of old blood before she recognised the yellow tint of iodine disinfectant. The curtain had the symbol again, an X shape with twin lines joining the top two arms at an angle. Around the sign were scrawled words, presumably daubed with someone's fingers. The largest phrase drew her eye immediately.

"We Shall Witness."

She whirled around at the sudden clanging of the hatchway and found herself phase to face with one of the miners, Tara. Presumably she was one of Cole's bunkmates. She looked shocked to have found Abuya here in her dormitory.

"Get out!" she hissed fearfully. "Get out before they see you in here."

Abuya didn't need a second prompting, she pushed past the woman, ducked through the hatchway and scurried back towards the ladder. Stuffing the notebook in a pocket, she threw herself at the rungs and pulled herself up as quickly as she could go.

Her mind raced with implications of what she had seen. Words from Abbott's rant and Cole's journal echoing in her mind, continually redounding back to the brown stained words, 'we will witness.' They echoed in her mind over and over, becoming like a chant from many voices.

She stopped suddenly, something felt wrong, but what. As she stood panting, holding her knees, her frantic mind finally caught up.

She was alone.

There were no miners, none of the normal bustle and to-ing and fro-ing of everyday operations. She looked about her, still trying to catch her breath and froze. There was a viewing port next to her, its shutter down and above it, the same symbol, written this time in a black marker pen, on the dark wall. She hurried away, knowing she was only a few more twists and turns and a single ladder away from the elevator terminus. Passing the next viewing port, she checked for the symbol and found it once again above the shutter and here it was on the edge of an intersection.

Still, there was no sign of another person and their absence unnerved her even further. As she finally came into the atrium containing the elevator terminus she almost sobbed with relief and she clattered the elevator grating open, nearly falling inside.

As the machinery grumbled to life and the elevator car started to move, she looked back along the corridor she had just exited. Someone was there now, standing at the end, watching her. His face was shadowed so she couldn't be sure, but as the elevator shaft blocked her field of view, she could have sworn that it was Mark, gazing coldly at her.

CHAPTER SEVEN

Frozen Discovery

TAURS Judicial Investigation Submission E.I.18: Excerpt From Research EVA Recording R382, Mission Day 587 (J-Cycle 168).

Transcript of suit camera feeds for Commander Scott Taylor and Specialist Alistair Dalton, beginning at timestamp 02:39:18.

[Video: Close view of Spectral Magnetometer H4. Commander Taylor and Specialist Dalton are attempting to free it of ice following recent plume activity.]

02:39:18 DALTON: Give us a moment would you Scott?

02:40:02 TAYLOR: We're nearly done.

02:40:21 DALTON: We've been chipping away at these bloody tin cans for hours though.

02:40:37 TAYLOR: They're your machines Al, but fine I'm pretty stiff too.

[Video: Specialist Dalton steps back and straightens. Commander Taylor briefly continues chipping at the ice before standing to join him.]

02:42:11 DALTON: Europa's really showing off today wouldn't you say?

02:42:18 TAYLOR: Quite a sight.

02:42:59 DALTON: And now there came both mist and snow. And it grew wondrous cold. And ice, mast high, came rolling by, as green as emerald.

02:43:38 TAYLOR: We don't have a mast.

02:43:56 DALTON: Philistine. You can't tell me this landscape doesn't stir something in you?

02:44:17 TAYLOR: What do you want from me man, it's ice.

02:44:44 DALTON: Well, you're the geologist, it's your job to find this stuff interesting.

02:45:06 TAYLOR: Yes but it's not your job to spout poetry when we should be freeing the equipment. Your equipment remember, not mine.

[Video: Specialist Dalton kneels and continues working to free Spectral Magnetometer H4]

02:49:38 DALTON: Well. Are you going to help or not?

02:50:14 DALTON: Scott?

02:50:24 TAYLOR: Come take a look at this.

[Video: Specialist Dalton stands. Commander Taylor points towards primary plume outlet. Visible to camera is a dark object protruding slightly]

02:49:38 TAYLOR: You seeing a dark lump at the rim there?

02:50:14 DALTON: Yes, now that you mention it, any thoughts on what it might be?

02:50:24 TAYLOR: Let's go take a look.

[Video: Commander Taylor and Specialist Dalton proceed towards primary plume outlet.]

03:04:02 DALTON: I'd say that's the corner of a packing case.

03:04:29 TAYLOR: We'll have to chip it out.

03:04:58 DALTON: Quite right. How could it have got there though, very odd.

[Video: Commander Taylor and Specialist Dalton chip away at the ice

surrounding the unidentified object.]

03:11:01 DALTON: It's a case of ration packs, Scott, look at the label. What the hell is it doing out here?

[Video: Specialist Dalton, having freed the object, turns it to bring label into view, reads: MRE Menu 4 - 25 portions]

03:11:22 TAYLOR: Let's get it inside and show the commander.

[Video: Commander Taylor and Specialist Dalton proceed towards pressure lock C7]

Excerpt Ends

• · · · ·

Abuya's thoughts still whirled as she rattled the elevator's grating closed behind her and made her way towards the researchers' dormitory. The long slow ride to the surface had done little to calm her and her mind raced through the implications of what she'd seen below. She needed a moment to collect herself, possibly a drink, and then she would report what she'd found to Commander Callaghan.

The recycled air on the surface levels was the same as the air down below, yet somehow, she felt like she'd stepped outside from a stuffy room. She filled her lungs gratefully, finally feeling her pulse begin to slow.

Entering the research dome, she nodded to Henning and

Delun, acknowledging their presence but avoiding any direct eye contact, not wishing to invite conversation. Her steps were quick and purposeful, her mind whirling with thoughts and emotions she wasn't ready to share or even fully acknowledge to herself.

She was about to make her way through to the dormitory, seeking solitude, when the hissing of the pressure lock door made her turn. Alistair and Scott were pushing their way through and Henning bustled over to help them de-suit.

"You have brought us something?" Henning asked, relieving Alistair of a black packing case.

Delun peered at the case over Henning's shoulder as he helped pull off Scott's gloves. "Menu 4, that's macaroni with beef and sauce. You… shouldn't have."

Alistair tossed his helmet to Abuya with a grin. "We found that out on the surface!"

Abuya was startled at the revelation, nearly fumbling the catch. "You're kidding. How the hell did it get out there?"

"Couldn't rightly say, but it was. Our illustrious leader here is flummoxed too, he's going to see what Commander Callaghan makes of it."

Abuya thought for a moment. It didn't make any sense. EVAs were never long enough to need rations and even if they were, you couldn't open up a meal pack and eat it while in a surface suit.

"Where did you find this?" Henning inquired curiously as he stowed the pair's gear for them.

"It was stuck in the ice on the rim of the plume hole," answered Scott. "My best theory is it was dropped in the water back when the base was being constructed and it's only just been uncovered.

Delun didn't look convinced. "Seems unlikely though."

"What else could it be?"

"Could have come up from the mining section, but I doubt Mark's letting them throw their meals out of the window." Delun chuckled at the idea but Abuya's brow wrinkled in thought at the suggestion. Rations were one of the items Cole has been loading into the pressure lock.

Scott finished the struggle out of his suit and took the case from Henning. "I'm heading to Commander Callaghan's office to report this," he declared.

"I'll join you. I need to tell him about what's happened down below."

Scott raised an eyebrow, yet he refrained from pressing her for further details.

Abuya, unease still gnawing at her, followed in Scott's wake along the corridors to the command centre and Jacob's office. She was a rational person, too intelligent to believe in monster stories, and she knew full well there couldn't possibly be any sort of horrific creature living in the deeps. Then again, Cole was rational and intelligent. So, presumably, was Abbot. There wasn't a person on the base who wasn't an expert in their field with PhDs, qualifications and so many other letters after their name it made email signatures look like a word jumble. What could they have seen to inspire such fear, such madness in them?

As they passed by the medical bay Annika stepped out, on her way to update the commander on Cole's condition. As she spotted the shaken look on Abuya's face, her smile turned to a look of worry.

"You ok kjæreste?" Annika asked with concern, her eyes filled with an odd mix of empathy and clinical detachment as she looked Abuya up and down for signs of an injury.

Abuya hesitated for a moment thinking what to say. "I had a bit of a scare in the mining section." She bit her lip, cursing the tremor in her voice. She'd wanted to reassure Annika, but the fears building in her mind wouldn't be denied.

Annika studied her for a moment before looping her arm into the crook of Abuya's and continuing after Scott towards the commander's office. "Whoever has scared you I'll beat them up!" she whispered.

Abuya snorted and grinned at her tiny, ferocious partner. She knew she was joking, but she also was pretty sure she wouldn't want to be the target of Annika's wrath in any case. "Thanks love." The three of them made their way down the last section of corridor to Commander Callaghan's office.

"How's Cole doing?" Abuya asked.

Annika shrugged. "About the same. I've got him sedated for now. His bloods came back, normal. White cell count ok. Normal erythrocytes. No unusual markers at all. He's physically healthy enough, or at least his immune system isn't fighting anything off."

"So, what does that mean?"

"I think it's something psychological, you can break from reality without a physical cause after all. I dunno, maybe stress of the job or just being six hundred million kilometres from home or something."

"So, in that case, it wouldn't be contagious, right?"

Annika shook her head. "No, it wouldn't be contagious. There are some rare instances of shared psychoses though. Think about the Salem witch trials—whole villages convincing themselves they were cursed. Or the dancing plague in Strasbourg in the middle ages.

"Dancing?" Abuya raised an eyebrow.

"No one knows why, but dozens of people danced in the streets for days. Some of them dropped dead from exhaustion."

They walked on for a moment in silence, Abuya digesting this oddity.

"So, it could possibly be contagious then, even if it was psychological?"

"I really doubt it. Probably would have spread quicker in that case anyway."

"Well, I'm afraid you may have to rule out the psychological theory. I just had an encounter with Abbott down below and he seemed to be going the same way as Cole."

Annika stopped dead in her tracks and looked at Abuya. Ahead of them Scott, who had been trying unsuccessfully to give them privacy and ignore their conversation, turned back to face them.

"What the hell happened with Abbott?"

Abuya really didn't want to go through everything twice. "I'm about to tell the commander, you can hear it all then. But Anni, if Abbotts caught the same thing that means there's something wrong with Cole that you're missing, right?"

Annika considered for a long moment, looking up at the ceiling as if for inspiration as she thought. "Almost certainly. It indicates that there's probably some underlying cause at the bottom of it. I'll just have to dig deeper."

She continued walking, deep in thought, as Scott hefted the packing case once again.

As they approached the final bend, the distinct, measured tones of Evans's voice filtered through the corridor. "Remember, if you're playing a king's Indian like this, you should aim to back it up with something like a fianchetto. You've left yourself very exposed right now."

Scott didn't stand on ceremony and pushed the ajar hatch open without knocking. He dropped the heavy case onto the desk, shaking a few pieces from their squares on the chess board as the two men looked up at him, startled.

"Commander, we need to talk."

CHAPTER EIGHT

The Oncoming Storm

The office was still and silent as Jacob considered the new information. Abuya had relayed her misadventures on the mining platform and Scott had just concluded his report, telling how he and Alistair had found the case of rations. The case itself sat on the desk, incongruously out of place in the otherwise orderly room. Its contents quietly dripped onto the papers below. Jacob was staring dully at it, absently rolling a bishop between his fingers as he processed the discovery.

Finally, just as Abuya felt she must speak, simply to break the tense silence, Jacob leaned forward with furrowed brows. "This is certainly concerning," he muttered, almost to himself.

"It confirms my suspicions though." Evans pointed out.

Jacob nodded slowly before turning to address Abuya. "You say the other miners seemed off to you as well, not just Abbott?"

Abuya paused for a moment, sorting through her memories of the mining platform and the peculiar behaviour of the miners. "It definitely didn't feel right down there." She hesitated before continuing. "Wei-Yun seemed to be his usual self. I guess Mark was a bit shaken or overwrought perhaps. Some of the miners seemed normal, just not cheerful. Some seemed upset to see me, maybe even angry."

Before Jacob could respond, Annika interjected. "Commander, I will need more time to assess Cole's condition thoroughly, but this new insight is particularly troubling. Abbot's recent outburst and the off behaviour from others indicate that this is more than just one man's unfortunate delusion."

"But your tests haven't found anything yet? No toxin, no bacteria?"

Annika shrugged unhappily and sighed. "Yes, but there's only so much I can test for. Even without the limitations of the resources at my disposal, there are any number of things that simply cannot be detected till it's too late."

"Okay," Jacob paused thoughtfully. He scribbled a note on the scratch pad on his desk. "Annika, I want you to take Cole off his sedation. Monitor him carefully and let me know as soon as he wakes. I want to try and talk to him."

Annika's lips pursed in evident disapproval. "I have to protest against that Jacob. Waking him at this point could be detrimental. I can't anticipate what risks there might be to removing him from sedation."

"Duly noted Doctor. Please proceed as ordered. I will note your quite reasonable objections in my report to TAURS."

Annika sighed, her shoulders slumping as she reluctantly accepted.

"Evans." Jacob nodded to the man, indicating he should

speak.

"The commander and I," said Evans in his soft voice, "were just discussing the significant drop-off in the osmium yield over the last few days. I had planned to discuss possible equipment failures with Mark, but perhaps the fault lies with the operators. The deficit may in fact be symptomatic of this problem."

Jacob let them consider this possibility for a moment. He leaned back in his chair, blowing out a long breath between his lips and gazing up as if for inspiration. The commander's office had a viewing port set into the apex of the dome through which the dull orange of the jovelight glowed. The planet was waning, with only a sliver of a crescent illuminated by the sun and yet still it filled much of the dark sky above them.

It was Scott who broke the silence, snapping them out of their contemplations. "I still don't understand what the ration packs have to do with anything."

Jacob and Evans exchanged glances, but there was no immediate answer.

"Maybe they don't, maybe it's just a coincidence?" Scott continued.

"From my understanding, Mark's encounter with Cole revolved around his loading various supplies into a pressure lock down below, including cases of ration packs. We can only assume he had the intention of jettisoning them." Evans's suggestion had occurred to Abuya as well, it was the only solution that fit.

"But he didn't manage it, right? Mark interrupted him in

time?"

"Indeed. So, we can only assume," said Evans levelly, "that this was not his first attempt. He, or for all we know another miner, successfully jettisoned supplies in the last few days and one of them happened to surface through the vent to be found by you."

"But… why?" insisted Scott. "It just doesn't make sense to throw supplies out into the ocean."

"Not much of anything makes sense right now." Jacob pointed out.

"A sacrifice." The realisation had slipped from Abuya's lips without her meaning it to, coming out as a breathy whisper, but nonetheless the whole room turned to look at her.

Evans nodded solemnly. "That is my best guess as well. Listen to what Cole had written, I think it fits Abuya's idea well."

He held up the book of field notes. Abuya had placed it on the desk for inspection and Evans had been slowly thumbing his way through it as they spoke. "They will not understand. She will be angry at them, angry at me, angry at us. She must be appeased or she will consume them. We can do it. We can save them; I can save them. She must be appeased. She will feed."

A collective shudder went around the room as Evans placed the book on the table and removed his reading glasses. Jacob fidgeted uneasily. He was a fine corporate leader, only the best would have been sent on this mission, but this problem felt beyond his scope to handle.

Scott was the one to propose a course of action, his voice

filled with determination. "I believe it's imperative that we head down to the mining platform to get to the bottom of this. We need to confront the issue head-on, understand just what the hell is going on down there."

There was an assenting murmur, but Jacob looked unsure. "I want to speak to Mark first."

He reached out and pulled his laptop closer, his fingers tapping lightly on the keyboard as he initiated the call. The room fell into a momentary silence, punctuated only by the familiar, almost cheerful jingle of the teleconferencing software as it began dialling through to Mark.

"What is it, Jake?" Mark answered the call without preamble. Jacob was clearly startled at Mark's appearance and terseness. Even Abuya, who had seen him in person only an hour or so ago, was taken aback. He looked haggard, as if he hadn't slept in days. Most concerningly, a nasty bruise stretched along his jawbone, mottling it with purples and yellows.

"Just checking in, I've heard things are a bit rough down there?"

"It's fine. It's under control." Mark's response was curt, rude even. "When can we have Cole back?"

Annika stepped forward. "He's still not well Mark, I've got him sedated right now for his own safety."

"You, have no right!" Mark growled the words out through gritted teeth. "I need him back down here, he's done nothing wrong, you don't have any right to hold him!"

"No right?!" Scott's outburst was loud in the confined office. "No right? He only stole supplies and attacked you

Mark, where the hell do you…"

"Major Taylor!" Jacob cut across Scott's burgeoning tirade firmly, using the man's erstwhile military rank to grab his attention. He gave him a long glance and then turned back to Mark's picture on the monitor. "I'll see to it that he's back below with you as soon as possible Mark."

His soothing tone appeared to do a little to calm Mark, but his features remained angry. "We noticed that the osmium yield has been down lately, might that have anything to do with your personnel issues?"

Mark's eyes flicked away from the camera momentarily and he appeared reluctant to divulge any information. "I don't have personnel issues," he protested sullenly. "The filter repairs we made a couple of weeks back didn't work out so we're restricted on intake. I've got the engineers on it now."

"Good to know," Jacob seemed almost cheerful, "well keep me up to date and come up for a drink when you can ok?"

His smile wasn't returned, but there was a noticeable easing in Mark's demeanour. He did seem somewhat pacified as he hung up the call.

As soon as the camera feed dropped, the smile slid from Jacob's face to be replaced by worried determination. "Sorry to cut you off like that Scott, I didn't want to play into to this 'them and us' idea that seems to prevail down there. You're quite right, we need to get down below and see for ourselves." He nervously pushed his hand through his hair and glanced towards Evans, apparently for reassurance. "I've known Mark since he was born and I've never seen him like that."

"No indeed." Evans agreed.

Standing, he strode across the room to the intercom panel and used it to call for Okoreye.

"Scott, I want you to come down with me and Evans. Abuya, if you're up to it I'd like you to come too."

"Will you need me, commander?"

"No Doctor, I want you to stay with Cole, make sure you're there when he comes out of sedation."

Annika's concern was evident as she interjected, "Commander, wouldn't it be wiser to delay awakening Cole until after your return?"

Jacob remained resolute however. "I understand your caution, Annika, but time is a luxury we don't have right now. We need every piece of information as quickly as possible to prevent this situation from escalating further. I trust your expertise to handle Cole's awakening safely and efficiently in our absence."

Any further protest from Annika was interrupted by a voice from the hatchway. "You called for me commander."

Abuya felt immediately more confident on hearing Okoreye's deep voice behind her. She flashed him a small smile, although in her current mood, it likely came across as a grimace. "Gathii, I need you to look after things up here for me while I go and investigate down below. The doctor can get you up to speed on our discussions."

He was already pushing through his now quite crowded office, heading towards the hatchway. "You have the conn."

"He watches a lot of Star Trek," explained Abuya in response to Okoreye's confused expression. Then, pausing only to squeeze Annika's hand for reassurance, she hurried out in the wake of Scott, Evans and the Commander.

CHAPTER NINE

Descent Into Madness

The elevator clunked and rattled through its slow descent. The metallic walls vibrated subtly, responding to the motion of the journey. The air in the shaft made odd moaning sounds as it was forced passed them, as if the elevator car itself were acting like a piston head moving within a cylinder. Abuya, standing as she was in the midst of the other three, all of whom were taller than her, felt the closeness of the confined space more than ever. Her heart raced, each thud seeming to echo loud in her ears. She tried to suppress her growing unease, focusing on anything other than the task at hand. Her gaze shifted to the dull, aluminium walls of the elevator, but the reflections she caught in the dim overhead light held nothing but her own worried expression.

The elevator's halt, when it came, seemed sudden, sending a startled ripple of exclamations through the group, revealing their collective tension. As Scott slid the grating open, the warren of the mining section was revealed. Keyed up as they were, the sight before them was unnerving. They stepped out into the relative expanse of the terminus, greeted only by an eerie, empty silence.

The mining section should have been bustling with activity at this hour, but instead it was deserted. There was not sight or sound of another soul. Abuya exchanged glances with her companions, her own confusion mirrored in their eyes.

She realised that some of the corridors reaching away from them were reduced to red emergency lighting, causing dark shadows to stretch away down their lengths. Her mind imagined she saw shapes at the end, now staring, now turning and vanishing leaving behind the faint echo of footsteps on metal grating.

"What the hell is going on down here?" Jacob hissed, his voice, barely louder than a whisper, breaking and cracking. The white knuckles clenched at his sides betrayed the rising panic he was trying to conceal.

Evans, ever analytical, examined their surroundings. "This shift rotation should have at least twelve operatives on this level of the mining platform."

Apparently unaffected by the uncanny atmosphere about them, his voice was level and measured, its normal volume seeming like a shout. "Other than a major equipment failure, or some sort of emergency, I'm not aware of any reason that they would have been stood down."

"Clearly something is very wrong."

Abuya couldn't agree with Jacob more. She had made dozens of trips to the mining section during her time at the base and the emptiness was disconcerting. The miners were a boisterous community and even during off-hours, the corridors were typically alive with laughter and conversation. Even in the few hours since she had fled back to the surface the atmosphere seemed to have thickened, a heaviness she could not explain hanging in the air and filling her lungs.

Scott spoke up, "So what's the plan, Jacob? We can't just report back to Earth that the mining platform got creepy on us and leave it at that."

Jacob didn't look at him, his eyes flitting from corridor to corridor. His tongue flicked out to moisten dry lips before he answered. "You're right of course. Let's take advantage of being alone and take a look around."

With a visible effort to calm himself, he turned to look at Abuya. "You've been down here more than us Abs, how should we work our way quickly around the whole ring?"

Abuya thought for a moment. "The ring has three concentric circles off this hub. There are corridors going out like spokes and rooms in between, offices, control rooms, that sort of thing." She turned, getting her bearings."If we start down corridor one over there we can go up and down the spokes and work our way round till number twelve. The ladderway down to the second ring is at the end of twelve."

Jacob nodded, "I want to cover the ground quickly. Scott you and Abuya start at seven and work up, Evans you and I will work down from six."

Abuya was reluctant to split up, not wanting to lose the safety in numbers, but she trusted Scott's competence. Jacob on the other hand was concerning her, he seemed jumpy, panicky. Evans by comparison seemed entirely at his ease, as if he were simply here for a mildly interesting tour of inspection.

Evans led the way as he and Jacob headed down their first corridor. Abuya and Scott ventured cautiously into their own, thankfully one which still benefited from its standard lighting and had not been reduced to the dully glowing emergency strips along the floor.

Abuya couldn't shake the feeling that they were walking through a ghost town, an abandoned relic of a once-thriving operation. She knew first-hand that there had been miners working in these rooms only a handful of hours ago, but she could have readily believed that she and Scott were the first to uncover a ruin that had gone unpopulated for decades.

They turned a corner and Abuya noticed the now familiar, peculiar symbol painted on the wall. The X-shape joined at the top with a diagonal slash. She pointed it out to Scott. "That was in Cole's notes and on the curtain in his dorm."

Scott peered closely at it. "Doesn't look familiar. Maybe it's a shibboleth. Something Cole's little conspiracy used to communicate."

Abuya raised an eyebrow at 'conspiracy' but didn't comment. For all she knew, that was indeed what was going on. Now that she was looking out for it, the symbol appeared again and again as they continued their sweep. It was marked above most of the hatchways into the various control rooms, laboratories and work areas they passed. Sometimes it looked to have been scratched into the metal, sometimes drawn in marker. One even had simply been scrawled on a post-it note.

As they reached the outermost circle, Scott paused, leaning on the rim of a viewing port. It too bore the symbol, this time drawn directly onto the inches thick perspex in sharpie. Scott gazed past it, out into the void of dark water beyond. Abuya stood at his shoulder and gazed out too, thinking about the crushing pressure and the water so cold it barely stayed as a liquid.

Nothing, Abuya was convinced, could endure the harshness outside. Her mind contemplated the immense pressure that could crush anything unprotected and the water so frigid it teetered on the edge of freezing. The thought that any form of life could exist in such an extreme, unforgiving environment seemed beyond belief.

Scott had resumed his slow progress along the ring and she turned away to join him, but as she did, out of the very corner of her eye, she could have sworn a patch of the darkness moved. She whipped her head back and stared again, nothing but dark water. Her imagination? A braid of her hair swinging as she turned her head? Or possibly, just possibly, something in the water.

"Scott I…" She was cut off abruptly as the intercom panel at the nearest intersection crackled into life, making them both jump.

"Scott, Abuya, are you there?"

Scott strode over and thumbed the button for ring one. "We hear you, Commander."

"We've found something. Come and meet us at the pressure lock."

Scott shared a glance with Abuya and then the two of them set off along the outer ring. Scott made a quick check of each room they passed while Abuya peered through each viewport, hoping desperately to see nothing but inky black water.

Coming to the pressure lock vestibule, they found Jacob pacing, his hand tugging at the hair at the back of his head. Evans was standing calmly to one side, engrossed in the pages of Cole's notebook. Before Scott could even voice a question, Jacob gestured over his shoulder, pointing to the hatchway of the pressure lock itself. It was a solid slab of metal, studded with rivets and inset with a thick perspex window. The pressure lock allowed ingress and egress of personnel and equipment and had to tolerate the huge changes in pressure resulting from the freezing water beyond. Abuya saw the symbol once again, daubed two metres tall across the hatch and its surrounding coping in a dark, reddish brown.

It was blood.

She didn't know why she was so sure, but she was certain the symbol had been smeared across the metal by fingers coated in blood. Looking down at the floor, she saw further stains and looking back at Jacob's face she knew she'd guessed correctly.

Jacob's expression was grim. "We found this symbol everywhere," he said, his voice a hoarse whisper. "Always above the hatchways or viewports."

Abuya nodded, a knot of dread forming in her stomach. "We found the same, always a hatchway. I thought it might be a warning or some kind of protective sigil, something to try and keep the creature out."

"Or indeed, to welcome it in." Even Evans didn't sound quite his usual placid self. His words made Abuya shudder.

Jacob cut short their discussion. "Regardless of what it

means, we need to stay together from now on. Clearly, at least one person has been hurt, I don't want to add to that number."

"We've seen enough." Interjected Scott, "We need to find Mark, find the people and confront them, find out what the hell they think they've been doing."

Without waiting for Jacob's assent, he turned on his heel and strode toward the ladderway that would take them down to the second ring of the mining platform. Abuya's hands felt weak as she gripped the cold metal ladder, her feet questing tentatively below her for each rung. She tried desperately to get a hold of herself, focusing on breathing slowly through her nose, urging her heart to settle.

Stepping out of the ladderway onto the second level, Abuya froze. At the end of the next corridor were two miners. Abuya recognised them, one had joined the expedition in the recent arrivals. The other was Tara who had been here as long as Abuya herself. They'd played Scrabble together only three weeks ago. As soon as Abuya's group was recognised, the miners froze. Fear was etched across their faces and they exchanged quick, anxious glances before hurrying away.

"Tara Wait!" Abuya called out, but her words fell on deaf ears. The miners vanished around the curve of the outer corridor, casting nervous glances over their shoulders.

Scott and Jacob pushed past Abuya, pursuing the receding footfalls of the two miners. As they ran passed, Evans stooped to pick up a box, dropped by Tara. It contained an odd assortment: bits of cable, spare processor parts, a couple of books. There was no pattern to it, nothing they could wring sense from.

The chase led them right across the second level to the next ladderway. As they approached, they saw Tara's head disappear below the deck.

Abuya called out to her again, "Please, wait! We're here to help." But to no avail.

Reaching the ladderway, Jacob hurled himself down, taking the rungs two at a time, almost frantic now he had overcome his timidity. Abuya was last down the ladder and reaching the bottom, she found herself surrounded on all sides. Three corridors led away from the ladderway and in each was a small knot of miners. They looked at her with a mix of fear, hatred, confusion, even haughty derision. They all carried some burden. Crates like Tara's or packing cases; one of them even had a huge coil of cabling slung about his shoulders which he clearly struggled to even walk with.

Mayumi stepped forward, looking more haggard than she had at their meeting. She had the same wild, accusatory look in her eyes, staring them down defiantly. She spoke in a venomous hiss. "You shouldn't be here."

Jacob spread his palms and spoke as calmly as he could. "We're just here to help. We need to know what's going on."

"We don't need your help. You shouldn't be here. You're not wanted here." Mayumi's hiss rose to a shriek with this last sentence and Jacob couldn't help stepping back a pace in alarm.

Another miner, a young woman with wide, frightened eyes, spoke. "You need to leave while you still can. The creature...It's not safe."

"What creature? There is no creature." Jacob pressed.

The woman shook her head and Mayumi muttered something to those nearby. They looked fearfully at Jacob and began edging away down the corridor.

Abuya exchanged alarmed glances with her companions. The situation was grimmer than she had imagined could be possible.

Jacob remained determined. "We are not leaving without answers. Lead us to where this creature is. We need to understand what we're dealing with."

There was no answer as more and more of the miners turned to leave. Eventually, only Mayumi was left, glaring daggers into Jacob before she too turned on her heel and hurried away.

The group followed Mayumi through the maze of corridors, their echoing steps joined by a murmuring susurration from up ahead. Mayumi kept her distance, casting frequent backward glances, her eyes flashing with anger.

As they traversed the ring, Abuya saw the symbol repeated again and again. In some places, it was hastily scribbled, the lines jagged and uneven. These contrasted starkly with the instances where the symbol was carefully crafted, its lines straight and precise as if laid out with a ruler or a straight edge.

Finally, Mayumi turned to duck through the hatchway to this level's pressure-lock vestibule. As they rounded the same corner, they were struck by the loud babble of voices.

The chamber was crowded with miners, nearly twenty of them. The room heaved with most of the mining platform's complement. The pressure lock was wide open and a stack of supplies was being loaded inside, miners jostling their way through to add their own armfuls to the pile.

Jacob's face darkened as he comprehended the situation. He grasped Mayumi's shoulder, his voice firm. "What are you doing with these supplies? Are you planning to jettison them again?"

Some of the miners shouted angrily, while others appeared abashed and fearful. Mayumi shrank away from the touch but some of the others pushed forward, looking ready to leap on Jacob. Their eyes were filled with hatred and desperation.

A fight seemed inevitable. Just as Scott was trying to push Abuya behind himself and make ready to stand with Jacob, Mark's voice cut through the tension. "What the hell's going on here?" He appeared at the other side of the throng, using his crutch to push miners aside as he limped towards the open pressure lock.

The miners, at the sight of Mark, seemed to grow sullen, scattering and dispersing. Mayumi and a small cadre of the most determined gathered around the pressure lock's hatch, as if to defend it.

Mark turned slowly on the spot, taking in the entire scene. He made a gesture to Mayumi, who seemed cowed, before coming to face Jacob, leaning heavily on his crutch. "I don't know what's been happening here Commander, I don't know what they're doing, but I'll make sure they get back to their duties."

Jacob was far from satisfied. "I want to know what's happening down here. I want to know why they are trying to jettison supplies and I want to know why the fuck there's blood on the top level."

He stepped close to Mark as his voice rose to a full shout. Mark faced down his brother and held his ground.

"I will sort this out Jake, there's a situation here but I've got it under control. We can fix it, but please, get back to the surface. You're not helping right now."

Jacob stood rigid, his face a mask of barely contained fury. His jaw clenched and unclenched silently as he bore down on Mark with a glare that was both angry and frightened. He seemed on the verge of another outburst when Evans gently placed a hand on his shoulder.

Jacob deflated visibly, the tension in his shoulders easing as he took a deep, controlled breath. It looked to Abuya like this was far from the first time Evans had prompted him to find his calm in their long career together.

Mark, taking advantage of this opportunity, stepped closer, his voice low and earnest. "Trust me, Jake. Please. I can fix this."

Jacob wasn't mollified by Mark's plea, but before he could argue further, the intercom panel crackled to life and Annika's voice came through. "Commander, there's an emergency in the medical bay. Please, come at once!"

The panic in Annika's choking voice made Abuya's blood run cold. For one long second, she was frozen to the spot and then she turned and sprinted back towards the ladderway, adrenaline lending her speed. Scott called after her and then followed at a run, unwilling to let her navigate such unfriendly territory alone.

Cursing under his breath, Jacob gripped the front of Mark's shirt.

"Fix this damn mess." He growled.

He could not help but mistrust Mark's words, the man seemed to be relieved that the emergency was calling them away, but he had no choice.

He turned to Evans, quickly coming to a decision. "Evans, stay below and support Mark. Keep an eye on things here. I'm heading back to the surface. I want regular reports."

This last comment was shouted over his shoulder as he too dashed for the ladderway.

CHAPTER TEN

In Jupiter's Light

Abuya wrenched the metal grating aside the moment the elevator clattered to a halt at the surface level. She burst out, colliding with Delun who had been standing just outside. The impact sent them both tumbling to the ground in a tangled sprawl of limbs. Scott reached down to disentangle the pair, pulling them to their feet. The pit of dread in Abuya's stomach was only worsened by the look of fear and confusion on Delun's face.

"What's happened, what's going on?!"

"I…I…I don't know." Delun was clearly shaken. "Henning burst into the mess and said there was an emergency. He said Cole was missing and he sent me here to make sure he didn't get down the elevator."

"Annika, where is Annika?" Abuya almost screamed the question.

"Henning sent Alistair to medical to go help her. That was a while back though, I don't know what else is happening now."

"Ok, we need to.."

Abuya was already streaking away and didn't hear the rest of Jacob's words. She sprinted along the corridor leading towards the medical bay, heedless of anything else that might be happening. Her rapid footsteps echoed off the metallic walls as she dashed through the main command dome, weaving around obstacles. Down the last corridor and the medical bay's entrance loomed ahead. With a final burst of energy, she reached the entrance, throwing herself against the wheel which cranked the hatch open.

Shoving her way through the hatchway, Abuya burst into the medical bay, her heart pounding right through her chest. With a rush of relief that nearly made her knees buckle, she saw Annika—looking scared and shaken but very much alive. Her love was sitting on the white bed, face ashen, nursing her throat with one hand. The other hand was being held by Alistair who was carefully dressing a slash across her fingers. He looked up, his expression grave and his eyes met Abuya's. She wasn't sure she had ever seen him look so serious before. His solemnity added an unsettling element to the already tense situation.

Abuya started forward to comfort Annika, but her eyes caught something between them that stopped her in her tracks. A white sheet on the ground, stained with blood. Her breath caught and the world around her seemed to stop. A lump formed in her throat as she realised the only thing that the huddled mass beneath the sheet could be.

"Is that… is that Cole?" She wanted to seem strong and assured for Annika, but her voice came out as a whimper.

Annika's eyes welled with fresh tears and she dropped her chin to her chest. Alistair looked up from his careful bandaging. "No." He let out a long sigh. "I'm afraid, that is Commander Okoreye."

He lowered his gaze back to his work, not wanting to meet her eye. The news rocked Abuya like a blow. She had known Gathii since she was fifteen. He had been under her father's command when he was just a midshipman in the Kenyan Defence Force, something of a protégé of his. When she'd first arrived at the Olapo spaceport for her mission training, she had been delighted to find him there. He had taken her under his wing and seen her through some of the most arduous times of her life and now—here his body lay on the ground before her, slowly cooling in the chill air.

The sound of hurrying footsteps and Scott's loud voice came down the corridor behind her. "How the hell can he be hiding; this place is smaller than a damned tuna can!"

Scott's voice stopped abruptly as he came through the hatchway and was confronted with Okoreye's covered form. Henning who came in at his shoulder must have told him the news but the reality still clearly shook him.

"She will be alright?" Henning directed his question to Alistair.

"Nasty cut here, and her throat is going to hurt like mad, I'm sure, but nothing lasting I think."

Whether through physical injury or mental anguish, Annika couldn't seem to speak, but she looked up and nodded painfully.

Scott turned to Abuya. "Abs, I'm sorry, but we need

everyone to search. We still haven't found Cole. I've only got half a dozen people to do a sweep and I don't want anyone going alone."

Abuya was about to object when Annika croaked. "Go. Please. I'm worried about him."

Gathering all her self-control, Abuya nodded. She stepped gingerly around the object in the middle of the room to quickly clasp Annika, kissing the top of her head, before hurrying to Scott's side.

"Go with Henning," he ordered. "Check the research dome and be very careful; he is clearly dangerous and he may still be armed."

"He dropped his knife when he ran." Alistair indicated a bloody scalpel lying on the ground with a jerk of his head.

"Even so. Treat him as armed until we know otherwise. Report in on the intercom every ten minutes."

With a nod, Abuya and Henning ducked through the hatchway and the pair moved off down the corridor towards the research dome, checking every possible nook and cranny that could conceivably conceal a person. Abuya tried hard to focus on their task to the exclusion of all else but it was an impossibility. With panic, anger or grief threatening in turns to rise up and overwhelm her, she was struggling to keep her mind focused.

Carefully, they made their sweep through the researcher's dormitory, the various laboratories and workspaces that the researchers occupied, and the storage lockers that supported them. Their efforts yielded no sign of the missing patient although they both felt uneasily as if the man was somehow watching them from the shadows. They worked grimly, without speech and the silence between them was punctuated only by the soft sound of their breath and the occasional creaking of the station itself.

Abuya found herself caught in a maelstrom of emotions. Each thought tugged her in different directions, but all urged her to find the fugitive as quickly as possible. Her natural compassion and concern for a sick man battled against the fear or the harm he might inflict.

Yet, simmering beneath this, a fierce anger burned, fuelled by the terror she'd seen in Annika's eyes and the memory of Gathii's lifeless body. Every step was a struggle to suppress the vengeful urge to confront Cole and hold him accountable for the chaos he'd caused.

She remembered something her mother had always said: that holding anger was like holding a smouldering coal—it only burns you. Drifting in the cold of space on this speck of ice, some extra warmth was dangerously appealing. Casting the coal aside was not something she could manage just yet.

As they moved into the rover hangar, at the far side of the research dome, they finally discovered the first clear sign of their quarry. A bloody handprint was smeared along the edge of one of the suit lockers. The crimson stain stood out starkly against the white painted metal, sending a shiver down Abuya's spine. Henning, with a grim expression, pointed towards it. They exchanged a tense look.

Their approach towards the locker was slow and deliberate, each step measured to avoid any sudden noise. The silence of the room seemed to amplify with their every movement.

Abuya felt sure the beating of her heart must be audible—its frantic drumming spiking and erratic.

Abuya reached out, her hand hovering momentarily over the handle, slick with the remnants of the bloody print. She glanced at Henning. He gave a curt nod.

With a deep breath, Abuya grasped the handle firmly, bracing herself. She positioned herself to the side, allowing Henning a clear path to lunge at the man inside and smother him in his huge arms.

Her muscles tensed as she wrenched the door open in one swift movement, leaping back as she did so.

But the locker was empty.

They both stood, breathing heavily, feeling almost giddy at the release of tension. The suit inside the locker had been crushed onto the floor. That and the further red smears, indicated that Cole had indeed hidden there at one point.

Suddenly unable to hold herself steady any longer, Abuya leaned against the wall. She slid slowly down it to the floor, needing a few moments to gather herself. The build and release of tension, the keying up of her muscles and the constant fear of assault by a madman had taken their toll and she felt utterly spent.

As she sprawled, her gaze aimlessly drifted around the room, taking in the familiar yet now somehow distant features of the hangar. The tools neatly arranged along the walls, the subtle hum of the station's life support systems and the soft glow of emergency lights created a sense of surreal calm.

Her eyes eventually settled on the airlock embedded in the bulkhead of the opposite wall. Something about it seemed amiss, but her tired and muddled brain struggled to piece together what it was. She stared at it, trying to make sense of the nagging feeling in the back of her mind.

Suddenly, with a sharp jolt of clarity, it clicked. The status lights on the control panel were flashing amber. The airlock was in use.

The realisation coursed through her, washing away the fog of fatigue. The hair on the back of her neck stood on end as she scrambled to her feet with quick, urgent movements.

She waved frantically at Henning, trying to catch his attention. Each second seemed critical.

Carefully, she moved toward the airlock door. She realised that she had been unconsciously holding a breath and she eased it out in a long sigh, trying to control herself. The heavy inner door of the airlock had an inset window and she cautiously lifted the shutter to peer through. What she saw sent a wave of unease down her into her stomach and brought hot tears back into her eyes at the thought of what the man had done. Cole was inside the airlock. He was kneeling on the hard floor in his thin medical gown, leaning against the outer door and gazing upward through its window. His hands were pressed tightly against the door and he seemed to be trembling, even swaying as the rust-coloured light of Jupiter bathed his face in its lambent glow.

Henning and Abuya exchanged a wordless glance, each unsure how to proceed. Cole was oblivious to their presence, his focus locked on something beyond their sight. Muffled through the heavy metal of the door they could just make out some sort of incoherent babble coming from the supplicant form.

Hesitantly, Abuya raised a trembling hand and tapped on the perspex of the window. At the sound, Cole sat bolt upright as if electrocuted. Slowly, he clambered to his feet, turning as he did so until he faced Abuya. His wide-eyed stare held her rooted to the spot, the eyes seeming both vacant and burning at the same time, the dark pupils blown out to leave only the smallest sliver of iris. Even with the thick metal door between them, the man standing barely six feet from her froze her limbs and filled her with dread.

And then he smiled.

He smiled beatifically like a man seeing the sun after a long night. His lips stretched so wide that they almost seemed unnatural and a tear rolled down his cheek. Raising a hand, he beckoned to her through the window, beaming all the while, urging her to open the door and join him. Abuya was held transfixed by the sight. It was a tremendous effort just to jerkily shake her head, 'no'.

With her rejection, the smile faltered a fraction, but then the man shrugged and spread his hands before turning back to the outer door. He stood for a moment, gazing once more through the window at the ruddy sickle of the planet beyond. Slowly, calmly, his hand reached out towards the door's control panel. He pressed a button.

Abuya let out a wordless scream as she watched the rapidly venting air whip the medical gown about Cole's body. Behind her Henning bellowed like a bull and tried to wrench at the inner door, but the pressure difference was already far too great for it to budge. Cole dropped to his knees, still with his face and palms turned towards Jupiter's light, before he tottered and began to keel sideways—the sudden cold and lack of air overcoming him.

Forcing herself out of her shocked stupor, Abuya leapt for the control panel and tore the cover off the controls. As she wrenched the emergency pressurisation handle down, she heard, amid the sudden blare of klaxons, the banging of opening valves like gunshots and the torrential rushing noise as the system dumped as much atmosphere as it could into the confined space.

Suddenly relieved of the differential pressure, the door gave way to Henning's desperate strength and rocketed open, sending him sprawling to the ground and releasing a wash of frigid air over them both.

Abuya scrambled into the airlock and dragged at Cole's shoulders, frantic to get him into the warm air of the base. Heaving him bodily over the airlock's coaming she cradled him on her lap and put her ear down to his mouth.

A shuddering breath, barely audible told her he still clung to life and she tried desperately to hold his body close to hers and give him what little warmth she could.

Henning had sprung to his feet and dashed to the intercom, calling for help before hurrying back to her side—vigorously rubbing the unconscious man's shoulders and legs to try and bring a flush to the waxy, frozen skin.

Abuya heard as if at a distance the clattering sound of help arriving. Her entire attention was held by Cole's frozen eyes and the faint smile that still lingered on his blue-tinged lips.

CHAPTER ELEVEN
Unravelling

Abuya knelt alone.

Henning had borne Cole's limp form away, Scott sprinting ahead of him to warn Annika and help her prepare for the emergency arrival. The base's warning lights flashed overhead in time to the still-sounding alarm, casting an eerie glow on the walls and corridors. Only Abuya remained, huddled on the floor of the dimly lit hangar, the swirling maelstrom of her emotions receding into a grey fog of numbness. The events of the past day had overwhelmed her. Overwhelmed had been a long time ago. She had barely slept, and the waking nightmare of the day's events replayed in her mind with cruel precision until they, like everything else, were blanketed by the fog of nothingness that was creeping over her.

Eventually she stirred, rising unsteadily to her feet, vaguely conscious that she should follow the two men. She felt like a phantom, a wraith-like figure moving through the base. The walls seemed to close in on her as she followed the receding echoes of footsteps. She reached out to the bulkhead to steady herself as the world around her swayed. Sounds were at once sharpened and muffled and the flashing warning lights flared at her like sunbursts. Her brain refused to cooperate and her surroundings appeared through a hazy, dreamlike filter. The base, once familiar, now felt alien—a place where reality blurred into the surreal.

As she walked, her eyes flitted over the intricate details that would usually be beneath her notice. The tiny web of pits around the welded aluminium of the bulkhead she touched stood out in perfect detail, the metal itself appearing otherworldly. It was as if her senses were heightened and yet not enough to allow her to put one foot before the other and keep a straight line down the corridor without the greatest of care.

After a journey of seconds or of hours, she could hardly tell which, Abuya staggered into the medical bay and trudged unsteadily to stand with Henning. He was helplessly watching as Annika worked in a frenzy around the prostrate Cole. Reaching his side, Abuya gripped at his arm, seeking a solid anchor. He glanced down and placed his warm hand on hers, grounding her in place, at least somewhat. The pair stood and watched together as the doctor moved with a graceful urgency, her hands expertly navigating the medical equipment. She intubated her patient, forcing high-flow oxygen into his hypoxic system. Her white-blond hair flashed and swirled through the room as she flitted from station to station, setting up monitors for the man's vital signs, attaching heating pads to his extremities and fitting IV tubes to the cannula already embedded in his arm.

Abuya watched the incredible woman work in a blur. Her focus was consumed by the tableau playing out before her, her mind dissociating and retreating from its own pain and emotion. The world seemed to rush past her, like a time-lapse of quick jerky movements. Henning disappeared from her side and walked through her field of vision in a blur as he excused himself and left to relieve Delun. Abuya barely noticed as time stretched around her, swaying gently on her feet. Others came and left, some standing in silence, some trying to engage her, but she was, for a time, lost.

Finally, the world began to slow to its normal speed. Annika had done everything she could for Cole, and now she slumped against the table, her features drawn and exhausted. Abuya's mind grudgingly gave up its racing detachment and she forced herself into action. She stepped forward with a lurch, wrapping her arms around Annika and holding her close. She felt tears on her cheek and could not be sure if they were her own.

Cole lay unconscious on the medical table, still with that inexplicable smile on his face, now frozen in a rictus grin by his ordeals. His flesh was starting to blister from the exposure to the vacuum and the cold of the airlock. The underlying pallor of his skin was mottled with purple storm clouds of bruising. Restraints held him solidly to the table.

Alistair slipped in at that point and stood quietly by, looking down at Cole. He was silent, his gaze fixed on the injured man. He gave Abuya a solemn nod, indicating that he would take over monitoring Cole, allowing Abuya and Annika a moment of respite.

With great effort, Abuya pulled Annika to her feet and away from her charge. She feebly tried to resist, drawn by her duty to stay with her patient, but eventually succumbed, leaving the man to Alistair's care. Together, they stumbled toward Annika's quarters, exhaustion weighing on their shoulders like lead, each doing their best to prop up the other.

They collapsed together onto the narrow cot, clinging to each other tightly as sleep finally overwhelmed them, hammering them from consciousness. The base continued to hum with its muted mechanical symphony, indifferent to the struggles of its inhabitants and the pains of the two women, lying dreamlessly, protecting each other from the world.

· • · ·

"Aufstehen, meine Kleinen."

Abuya's consciousness swam back to the surface as she felt the hand gently her shoulder. It was Henning and the sudden intrusion of his voice and touch startled her awake. Her eyes blinked open and the harsh lighting of the room, that they hadn't had the wherewithal to turn off, stung her vision.

Next to her, Annika awoke with a start, her hand flying to her throat as she gasped for breath. Her wild eyes darted around the room, scanning for signs of danger before remembering where she was.

"Cole," she croaked, coughing against the swelling. "How is Cole?"

"He is stable and being monitored. You have been out for nearly twenty hours. Alistair says he has remained unconscious and his frostbite is more pronounced, but otherwise no changes." Henning spoke soothingly, clearly hoping to calm her.

Annika didn't seem to hear him, remaining agitated. She leapt up from the cot, hastily shrugging off her jumpsuit and casting it aside before frantically clambering into a fresh one, her nimble fingers working with practiced efficiency on the buttons and zips. The sight of the immodest change in attire left Henning mortified. He turned beetroot red, hurriedly averting his eyes and causing Abuya to burst into peals of laughter. The laughter felt wonderful after the nightmares she had been having, more refreshing even than the long sleep had been. Quickly though, it threatened to turn into something manic as the events of the past days rushed back into her mind. The absurdity of it all—the chaos, the danger and now poor Henning's flustered face—bubbled over and Abuya found herself cackling uncontrollably.

She stopped abruptly when she saw Henning and Annika looking at her, concern evident in their faces. The laughter had been a brief escape from the suffocating grip of their recent traumas, but it also revealed the fragile state of her mind, both to them and to herself.

Henning cleared his throat, still avoiding eye contact with Annika. "Jacob has called a meeting. You have a few minutes Doctor if you wish to check on Cole."

Annika nodded and rushed out of the room, her hurried footsteps echoing down the corridor. Abuya followed her with her eyes, she wondered at Annika's fierce determination to save the man who had tried to kill her. She felt a warm swell of pride and turned back to Henning with a small smile.

"We should head to the meeting also," he pointed out.

"Yes." She stared pointedly at him for a long moment.

"Well unless you're planning on watching ME get changed as well, why don't you step outside and I'll be with you in a moment."

The tips of Henning's ears flushed again and he stropped out, muttering something in German under his breath.

Abuya soon joined him in the corridor and the pair walked abreast, nearly two of her strides needed for Henning's one.

"Did I miss anything?" she inquired, a hint of guilt in her voice for having rested while the others continued their work.

"Not so much," Henning replied, shaking his head slightly. "We have just been sorting out the aftermath."

"Sorry," was all Abuya could muster and they proceeded in a companionable silence for a time.

"It seems to be ages since we had the movie night, does it not?"

Abuya gave a nod, her mind drifting briefly back the shockingly few days to when something so trivial had seemed to matter.

"I really liked that monkey," Henning remarked casually.

His offhand comment caught Abuya off guard and a spontaneous snort of laughter escaped her. She pictured Henning, laughing thunderously at Mona the monkey's antics on the screen and couldn't help feeling a small flicker of amusement.

Glancing up at the man, she noticed him watching her sidelong. It was clear he'd been trying to lighten her mood.

She returned his effort with a small, appreciative smile and he nodded in quiet satisfaction.

Rounding the final bend, they spotted the meeting room's hatch slightly open, protruding into the corridor. Muffled voices floated out, signalling the meeting had already begun. Quickening their pace, they hurried through the hatchway.

The meeting room was already half full. Scott, unusually, was sitting at the head of the long table, his expression serious and his fingers tapping rhythmically on the tabletop. Jacob sat on the opposite side, gazing distractedly into space, his face bearing the weight of recent events. He chewed at his fingernail, a nervous tic Abuya had noticed a few times in the last few days. Delun sat a few seats down, looking equally worried, while along from him were Tomas and Lena, the two maintenance engineers that made up the rest of the surface crew's small complement. They were soon joined by Annika and Alistair. The entire population of Europa's surface, all nine of them, were now in the room.

As Annika entered, Scott looked up, "All secure?"

Annika nodded sadly, "Sedated again and restrained."

Scott nodded to her and cleared his throat to begin the meeting. Abuya wondered at Scott taking the lead, looking curiously at Jacob who was sat to her left. He appeared distant and distracted, his gaze unfocused. She suddenly realised she could smell alcohol on his breath. The realisation made her uneasy.

She returned her attention to Scott who was outlining their misadventure on the mining platform for those who had not been there. He ended the story with the urgent message from

Annika across the intercom and turned to face her. "Please would you give us your account of... of the incident in the medical bay Doctor."

Annika nodded, looking down at the table as she collected her thoughts and mentally braced herself.

"At eleven hundred hours yesterday, I ceased administration of phenobarbital to Nathaniel Cole. Until this point, I had kept the patient sedated. At approximately fifteen hundred hours the patient showed signs of waking, coming to be fully conscious over a period of about an hour." Annika swallowed painfully against the fresh memory.

"Upon speaking to him, he appeared to maintain his delusional beliefs, however less agitatedly than before. He asked several times to be allowed to return to the mining platform, stating that 'she' was calling to him however he was not restrained and did not attempt to leave against orders."

Until this point, Annika's previously clinical account could have been read directly from her official logs. Now though, it took on a more anxious, pained tone. "I decided to administer a dose of lorazepam to help control his agitation. I turned to the storage unit to obtain the medication and, without warning, he leapt on my back. We tumbled to the ground and his hand closed on my throat."

Here she gently fingered the mottled bruises that covered the left side of her neck. "He held me so tightly and with his other hand, he scrabbled at the shelves of the storage unit, finding a scalpel. I grasped his wrist desperately and tried to keep the blade away from me."

Tears came rolling down her face now. The room about

her was held in horrified silence. "Suddenly, I heard a yell and his weight was gone. Gathii had run in and dragged him away and then."

She swallowed painfully again, brushing the tears from her eyes with a jerky movement. When she continued it was in a dull, flat monotone. "And then Cole twisted round—slashed the scalpel across his neck. As Gathii fell, Cole fled."

She paused and continued in a bare whisper. "I tried… I really tried.. but.. he bled out." Silence filled the room as Annika's grizzly account tailed off. Jacob rocked gently back and forth in his seat. Abuya reached a hand across the table to Annika, wishing she could offer more than a reassuring squeeze.

Scott let out a long sigh. "Commander Okoreye's body will be returned to earth for proper burial. In the meantime, he will be moved to cold storage Alpha-Two on the surface. Myself and Henning will attend to that at eighteen hundred hours at which time I invite anyone here to come and pay their last respects in the hangar."

Nods and murmurs came from around the room.

"Now though, we need to discuss the current situation. As you all now know, there seems to be a serious problem with the mining personnel. We can't say why, but they seem to be operating under the delusion that there is some sort of creature, some monster in the ocean. They believe it's out to get them."

"Do we actually know that it's a delusion?" As a room full of incredulous faces turned to him Alistair hurriedly expounded. "Not a monster of course, but something? No smoke without fire and all that."

Abuya was almost surprised to hear her own voice chiming in. "I thought maybe I saw something."

She looked around the room almost guiltily and spoke louder. "I felt like I saw something when we were down there. I was looking through a viewing port and I thought maybe there was a dark shape."

She flushed and looked down at the table, suddenly embarrassed by the attention. "Maybe I just imagined it, it doesn't make sense."

"Perhaps, we should go down once more in strength, try to determine what is really true." At Henning's words, Jacob jerked in his seat.

"No!" it was almost a yelp. "No one goes down, we can't risk it, we have to keep everyone safe."

Scott looked at the Commander, quiet disapproval mingled with concern. However, he agreed with the sentiment if not with his outburst. "Strength isn't an option Henning, there's nine of us up here and only the two of us have ever served. There are over thirty miners. More importantly, though, I just don't care. I don't care if there's a creature and I don't care to find out what the hell the miners think they're playing at. All I care about right now is keeping our people safe."

"I," he broke off briefly and glanced at Jacob. "The Commander and I," he continued, "have prepared a report to send back to TAURS control with everything we know. We are currently in the shadow of Jupiter and so the report will be sent out when Earth is back in line of sight at the end of the current J-cycle." He checked the watch at his wrist. "That's approximately 57 hours from now. Allowing for about an hour's transmission each way and a few hours of the ground team arguing about what to do, we can expect to receive orders three days from now. Until then, we need to contain this situation."

"The elevator to the mining platform will remain offline. So far no one from below has tried to call it down. If they do, we'll tell them it's under emergency maintenance. No one is to communicate with anyone below without authorisation. We sit tight here and wait. Got that?" He looked around the room, locking eyes with them each in turn to be sure his message had sunk in. His manner was so authoritative that Abuya raised her hand rather than speak out of turn.

"What about Evans? He's still down there isn't he."

Scott nodded."Evans has been in contact twice. He does not believe he is in immediate danger from anyone down there. He tells us that Mark exhibits the same erratic behaviour but he does believe there's a chance to steer him back to rationality given a little time."

"Evans will fix it." Jacob seemed to mutter this more to himself than anyone else, looking desperately for reassurance.

Scott ignored the interruption. "He's due to report again late this evening. Hopefully, he'll have some good news for us then. I'll let you all know when that happens. In the meantime, go about any essential duties you may have and try to remain calm."

With that, the meeting broke up, the group separating into ones and twos. As Abuya turned to leave with Annika, she was clapped on the shoulder and turned to face Alistair who had interposed himself between the pair.

"Mess hall for you two!" It wasn't a question. "In my expert opinion as the base's back up emergency medic, I'd say the pair of you are looking decidedly peaky and in need of a hot meal."

Abuya wasn't in the mood for Alistair's usual ebullience but Annika gave him a weak smile. "An excellent diagnosis. Come on Abs, let's go take our medicine."

Abuya scowled and Alistair leaned in close to whisper conspiratorially in her ear. "Must keep cheerful, put on a good show for the troops."

"What troops?"

"That's the ticket!" he exclaimed absent-mindedly, steering the baffled pair out of the room and chivvying them along the corridor.

CHAPTER TWELVE

Cold Farewell

"As the stars that shall be bright when we are dust,
Moving in marches upon the heavenly plain;
As the stars that are starry in the time of our darkness,
To the end, to the end, they remain."

The grave atmosphere in the hangar weighed on them all as Scott, solemn and composed, finished his eulogy, his words heavy with the gravity of the situation. The commander's lifeless body was wrapped in canvas and laid out on an improvised litter, bathed in Jupiter's eerie light as it shone through the viewing port. There were no proper flags on the base, but Abuya had carefully removed the embroidered patch from the shoulder of one of her own jumpsuits and the tiny flag of Kenya now lay upon her friend's breast.

Solemnly, Henning, Scott, and Abuya donned the helmets of their surface suits, moving with a sense of purpose and feeling the weight of this unhappy duty. Together, they approached the commander's body and stooped to lift him between them. Carefully, they moved toward the airlock door, Henning and Abuya trying hard to put from their minds the memories of their encounter with Cole in that very same airlock.

The trio, each burdened with their own thoughts and reminiscences, moved in unison as they carried the commander's body toward the airlock. Abuya thought of the man she had known, once so full of life and purpose, now reduced to a lifeless form in their arms. The airlock's heavy door awaited them, a gateway between the bleak, unforgiving environment of Europa's surface and the relative safety of the base.

They manoeuvred the commander's body into the airlock, the door was sealed behind them and the depressurisation cycle initiated. The sound of whirring machinery filled the enclosed space as the airlock prepared to open, exposing them to the harsh exterior. Abuya couldn't help but glance back at the viewing port, thinking of Cole—of his blistered skin, of the beatific smile stretched over his face. Angrily, she pushed those memories aside and focused on the solemn work before her.

As the airlock door opened, the frigid cold of Europa's surface rushed in to greet them, kept at bay by their surface suits. The desolate landscape stretched out before them, bathed in the eerie glow of Jupiter's distant presence. In silence, they loaded the commander's body into the rover, each movement deliberate and respectful.

Once everything was secured, they climbed into the rover and set off towards the offsite storage facility. The journey was a quiet one, the only sounds being the hum of the rover's engine and the squeaking crunch of ice beneath the wheels.

Abuya couldn't help but reflect on the fragility of life, the pronounced disparity between the vast, unforgiving expanse of Europa's surface and the warmth of the base. She thought about just how fragile the base really was. It was nothing more that some thin sheets of reinforced canvas fighting to keep the harsh environment at bay, as delicate and vulnerable as an eggshell. Vulnerable she reflected, not only to Europa, but now it seemed to the people within.

The small dome of the offsite facility loomed ahead of them as they rounded a jutting shoulder of ice. It contained the base's power reactor and served as storage for anything too hazardous to be kept within the main facility. The dome was not heated and Abuya shivered as they approached it, knowing that Gathii would lie undisturbed in this cold tomb until he could be taken back to Earth, preserved by the frigid temperatures.

Having driven at a slow, dignified pace, the rover finally rolled to a stop and the small group disembarked from their vehicle. The barren landscape, always still, seemed to grow even more so, as if paying its own respects to the moment. With great reverence, they carefully unloaded the commander's body and lifted the litter onto their shoulders. Henning and Scott bore the load while Abuya paced ahead of them to cycle the hatchway and allow them inside.

As the two men stepped through, she cleared a space among the crates and bundles. Finished, she stepped back and allowed them to gently set the body to rest.

Her heart laden with grief, she knelt beside her dear friend. She had not turned on her inter-suit radio and so all she could hear was her own sniffles, reverberating around her helmet.

She placed her hand tenderly on her friend's broad chest and whispered "Udongo unaiita. Kwaheri mpendwa wangu." A final farewell.

A small, choking laugh broke through her sobs as she thought of how Gathii would have rolled his eyes at her pronunciation.

She stood and, turning her back, walked back towards the hatchway past Henning and Scott who had been standing at a respectful distance. Turning as she passed, they fell into step behind her and the three of them left the dome.

The rover hummed softly as it carried them back toward the base, its wheels crunching over the icy surface. The shadow of their recent duty lingered in the air and none of them felt the need to break the silence. Their thoughts were consumed with the memory of their fallen comrade as the vast, icy expanse of Europa's surface stretched endlessly around them.

Left to her thoughts, Abuya sat in the rover's cabin, absent-mindedly swinging her helmet between her hands. Her mind wandered, torn between conflicting emotions that churned within her. She found herself alternating between seething anger and profound pity for Cole. The jarring contrast between the quiet, personable engineer he had been and the madman who had attacked her love and taken the Commander's life was almost too much to bear.

Her fingers clenched around the edge of her seat as she

grappled with her conflicting emotions. However, the anger was shot through with a deep sense of pity. Abuya couldn't help but feel a deep sadness for the man who had fallen so far from the bright, smiling person she had once known. She had seen the fear and confusion in his eyes. The delusions that had consumed him had transformed him into a stranger, lost in the darkness of his own mind. It was a darkness whose grasping tendrils seemed to flutter at the edges of her own mind, seeking a purchase to pull themselves deeper into her soul.

Disembarking near the entrance hatchway of the facility, they mechanically went through the usual procedures of fettling the rover, ensuring it would be charged and ready for its next use. Finally finished and back within the warmth of the base, Abuya wasted no time, she knew what she needed to do. Leaving Scott and Henning to stow the three surface suits, she made her way to the medical bay, quickly at first, but slower and slower as the fear and memories acted like a sucking quagmire at her feet.

Cole, still strapped to the medical table, lay motionless, a pale and frail figure under the harsh, clinical lights. He was still under the effects of sedation, but she could see signs that he was starting to stir, his eyelids fluttering as he began to regain consciousness, the eyes beneath darting to and fro in some fretful dream.

Abuya stood at the foot of the table, her gaze fixed on the man before her. The anger inside her churned and threatened to boil over. She wanted to confront him, to demand answers for his actions, to make him understand the pain and loss he had caused. But she also felt an unbidden rush of sympathy, her eyes falling on the bruises, scratches, welts and blisters that mottled every inch of the scrawny body.

As she watched him, the anger within her built and swallowed the pity, each passing moment intensifying her desire to confront him. She struggled to find the words, to express the anguish that had been gnawing at her insides. She wanted to make him understand the enormity of what he had done, to make him feel the weight of their grief, to grab him and shake him and wake him out of his delusions.

But then, as her anger reached its zenith and she felt she could no longer contain it, Cole's eyelids fluttered open. His gaze met hers and for a moment, they locked eyes. Abuya saw fear and vulnerability and an awful confusion. A tear rolled down his cheek.

"Help," he whispered, his voice weak and trembling.

At that moment, Abuya felt something inside her break. The anger that had consumed her was suddenly replaced by an overwhelming sense of compassion. She saw the man before her not as a monster, but as someone who had been lost, who had succumbed to delusions and madness. She saw the tears in his eyes, the flicker of humanity that remained.

Tears welled up in Abuya's own eyes as she stood there, locked in a gaze with Cole. The weight of her grief and sorrow came crashing down on her and she couldn't hold back any longer. She collapsed to her knees at his bedside, her body racked with sobs.

She knelt there for a long time, neither of them speaking, as she wept. Wept for Gathii, wept for Cole, wept for the trauma and pain she had seen in Annika's face. Burying her head into the edge of the thin mattress, her fingers found Cole's restrained hand and she grasped it, feeling a tentative, weak return of her grip. She had no idea how long she stayed like that, the two of them engulfed in their small, isolated world until Annika came and gently helped her to her feet. By this point, Cole's had drifted back into unconsciousness and his hand had once again fallen limp.

Annika held her then, comforting her and sharing her strength. Together, the two slowly shuffled out of the room, heading for the mess hall and what little reprieve could be found in a hot mug of tea.

· • · ·

As always, Annika could bring joy back into her heart and before long she was laughing along with her as, over steaming tin mugs of milk tea, they swapped stories of their fallen friend. The warmth of the tea seeped into Abuya, easing the cold she felt from the outside world and from the chill that had settled in her bones. Sharing memories had a therapeutic effect. Each story they told seemed to bring Gathii's stoic, subtle humour and his endless vitality back to life.

Their laughter and their tears were intruded on by a confused looking Scott—his head peering around the hatchway to discover who could possibly be laughing. "Evans is due to report in," he said with a gruff clearing of his throat. "I'd like you there Doctor if you don't mind—your medical perspective may be needed."

Annika turned to Abuya. "You coming?"

Scott seemed on the verge of objecting but kept his peace as he turned to lead the pair away towards the meeting room.

They walked in silence, their steps resonating in the narrow corridors, reaching the familiar room where Jacob was already present. He sat hunched over a laptop, his eyes not lifting to meet theirs as they entered. The weight of depression around him was palpable, like a dense fog that threatened to swallow them too if they lingered too close. He didn't respond to their greetings, barely even looking up to acknowledge their presence.

Scott moved to the console and initiated the call. After a short series of beeps and the whirl of static as the connection stabilised, Evans's image flickered into existence on the screen at the end of the room.

His uniform, once pristine, now showed signs of a sleepless night, sweat-stained and neglected. Strands of hair had fallen out of place, framing a face creased with concern and shadowed with stubble, evidence of his relentless pursuit of answers.

But it was the expression in his eyes that held them transfixed, revealing the depth of the ordeal he had endured. His eyes, weary and red-rimmed, bore the marks of a bone-deep exhaustion, as if he had been staring into an unyielding abyss. Despite this, there was a sharp intensity in his gaze, a piercing fervour that suggested more than just sleeplessness. It was as if Evans had glimpsed the answers to the world's deepest secrets, igniting some ember of revelation or madness —or perhaps both.

The image flickered gently on the screen as those in the room took all this in, wondering what could have so changed a man usually in possession of such self-control.

Scott's voice was firm, but the underlying tension was clear. His apparent confidence wavered as he faced Evans on the screen. "Good to see you in one piece Evans, what do you have to report?"

His words were measured, but the edge of worry was unmistakable, mirroring the anxious looks exchanged around the room.

Evans's eyes seemed to search the room through the screen as if making sure of an unseen presence. There was a pause, thick with anticipation before he finally broke the silence, his voice slow and measured.

"There is a creature in the ocean."

CHAPTER THIRTEEN

Stirrings Below

A heavy silence filled the cramped meeting room. It was as if the air had been sucked out, leaving the crew gasping at this insane revelation. Abuya's chest tightened, a primal reaction that caught her off guard. Her rational mind strove to dismiss the statement, but somewhere, in the hidden recesses of her hind brain, the twin instincts of fight and flight reared up and grappled with one another.

Evans, whose haggard face still gazed down at them from the monitor, misread the collective stillness as scepticism. He pressed on, urgency creeping into his voice. "I've seen it, undeniable dark shapes moving through the water outside the viewing ports. Not just shadows, not ice. Something... substantial. Something alive."

He paused, a frown etching deeper lines into his already creased face. "Mark showed me...evidence. Scratches on the outer hull, patterns that can't be random—too systematic, too...deliberate."

For a long moment, no one dared speak.

Eventually Scott cleared his throat, his arms folded tightly as if to physically hold back the tide of absurdity. He responded with a sceptical arch of his brow. "Evidence? Evans, you're talking about scary shapes in the dark and reading meaning into some random scratches."

Evans acknowledged the point with a slow nod. "Yes, Scott and I would agree under any other circumstance. But what I've witnessed defies a simple explanation. The miners' superstitions are one thing, their behaviour is clearly erratic, but there's an undeniable anomaly occurring here and we can't afford to ignore it. You can't afford to ignore it."

Jacob, who was sitting sprawled across his chair like he had been thrown there, interjected, his voice weak and quavering. "And Mark? What's his…How has he…How's he doing?"

Abuya could hear the concern and fear in Jacob's voice. Her heart went out to him.

The speakers crackled momentarily as Evans exhaled over the microphone. "Mark is...He's as bad as the rest. He's wrapped up in the same delusions. He speaks of the creature needing tribute as if we're characters in some ancient myth. He's convinced it will annihilate us unless appeased; it's extremely unsettling to see him like this."

Jacob's voice was a raspy whisper. "We've seen the destructive power of these delusions first-hand, Evans. The threat they pose is all too real."

"I'm aware," Evans replied, his gaze flickering away as if checking he was still alone before flitting back up to the camera. "That's precisely why I'm calling. We're on the cusp of a crisis, we need to take decisive steps now, before the situation deteriorates further."

The room erupted into a cacophony of murmurs, a turbulent sea of ideas and plans clashing against each other. Scott stood firm in the midst of it, the rock against which the waves broke. "We wait for orders," he stated, his voice the anchor in the storm. "No rash actions. Panic will only make things worse."

Abuya's curiosity, her scientist's urge to explore and understand, clashed with Scott's cautious approach. The notion of an undiscovered life form, however improbable, however impossible, gnawed at her with a ferocity that was visceral. She pushed back, her voice tinged with the heat of a newly brewing obsession.

"If there's something out there, we need to understand it. Scott, this could be the most important discovery of the millennium. Imagine the implications—there could be life beyond Earth. Think of the scientific breakthroughs, the knowledge we could gain. Our mission is to explore and discover, isn't it?"

Scott met her fiery gaze with a look of steel. "No one goes down to the mining platform, Abuya. Not until we have a clearer understanding. We can't risk further exposure to whatever's causing these...episodes. Besides, if there's life beyond Earth today, there will be life beyond Earth in a few days' time when we're back in contact with TAURS control."

Jacob, who was still visibly cowed by the tide of events nodded feebly. "Scott's right. We exercise caution now, or we risk everything."

Seething with frustration and thwarted curiosity, Abuya

conceded with a reluctant nod. Logic dictated caution, she knew that. Yet every instinct in her body rebelled against the forced inaction. Answers were down there, she knew it, and she felt an overwhelming compulsion to seek them out.

Scott held her gaze for a moment until he was sure there would be no further outbursts and then he began to lay out his plan, the monitor casting a bluish light over his face. "We need to maintain order and keep the crew safe," he said firmly. "Evans, you're on the ground; we need you to act as a stabilising force. Play into their beliefs if you must, but try to curb their worst behaviours. Do whatever you can to prevent panic or violence."

Evans, a weary sentinel standing guard over the descent into chaos, nodded in understanding. "I'll do what I can," he assured them, though the ghost of something like trepidation flickered across his features. "I'll affirm their fears where it's harmless, but I won't encourage this madness. I still believe we can find a rational explanation for these...sightings."

Jacob suddenly spoke up again. His voice carried the fragility of glass on the verge of shattering. "Evans, look after Mark, please. He's not...He's not himself."

Abuya felt a pang of pity for Jacob. She had a kid brother too back on Earth and she couldn't imagine how she would be feeling in the Commander's position. She did hope, however, that, in spite of everything, that she wouldn't have fallen apart to quite the extent Jacob seemed to have done.

Evans's expression softened, a human moment breaking through his facade of control. "I'll keep a close eye on him, Jacob. I promise," he replied.

With that, Evans reached out to the keyboard below the camera's view and struck a key. The transmission ended, leaving the room in a state of contemplative silence. Scott turned to the others; the mantle of leadership Jacob had dropped clearly weighed on his shoulders. "We'll monitor the situation closely. TAURS control should have a response for us in another day or two. Until then, we hold the fort and keep our heads."

Abuya was still struggling with her own mix of scientific zeal and creeping dread. Yet, she recognised the wisdom in Scott's caution. The risk of escalating whatever madness had taken hold of the miners was too great. The safety of the crew was paramount to her own curiosity.

The weight of the situation seemed to press against the walls of the base itself, a reminder of how fragile their existence was on this distant moon. The crew dispersed, each to their own sanctuary within the base. Engrossed in her own personal musings on their situation, Abuya found herself unconsciously following Annika's coat tails towards the medical bay. Perhaps Cole might be able to shed more light on the enigmatic creature that now felt all too real in her mind.

She increased her speed to walk abreast with Annika and slipped her fingers into the woman's cool hand. As they reached the hatchway to the medical bay and clattered it open, Annika stepped away to examine the wall of monitors. Abuya approached the examination bed, her footsteps loud in the quiet of the room. Reaching the sickbed, she gazed down at the piteous form.

Cole lay still, a pale shadow of the man he once was, his chest rising and falling with a rhythm that belied the turmoil she knew roiled within him. Each feeble breath wheezed in and out like air from a broken bellows. Wires crisscrossed his body like a spider's web, clinging to his chest and skull through adhesive pads.

She leaned forward, her shadow falling over him like an omen. Cautiously, she reached out, her hand trembling slightly as she touched his shoulder.

The man's eyes snapped open with a wheezing gasp. His eyes were clouded and distant, the pupils blown out to dark pits, before slowly his focus seemed to draw to Abuya's face. His mouth worked silently, opening and closing as if to scream or to beg.

Abuya forced herself to smile down at him reassuringly. "Hi Cole, It's Abuya."

There was the slightest flicker of recognition, quickly overwhelmed by fear. She pressed on. "Tell me about the creature, Cole."

Her voice was gentle yet insistent, the words spilling hurriedly into the sterile air. There was no answer as the man's eyes roved wildly about the small room, his limbs tugging feebly at his restraints. "Tell me… Tell me about Her."

Abuya stressed the word, repeating Cole's own language in an attempt to draw him out. In response, he let out a long, shuddering breath.

"Abs." Annika's voice was cautionary, but Abuya waved her off. She persisted. "Abs he's very weak. His BP is down, his oxygen levels are down; I doubt he could understand you and he certainly couldn't give you a straight answer if he did."

But before Abuya had a chance to respond, Cole spoke.

"She…" The word came out as a long, soft sigh, almost reverential in its tone. "She is… beautiful. She comes from the depths to find us and she will not be denied. We shall witness."

The voice, as feeble as it was, rose in vigour until Abuya felt compelled to rest a soothing hand on the man's shoulder.

"But what is she, Cole? What manner of creature is she?"

"She is darkness and hope. She is beginning and she is ending. She is the ending of us all."

The bright blue eyes, horribly bloodshot from their exposure to the airlock's vacuum suddenly locked onto Abuya's, forcing her to step back in alarm at their intensity. "She is the ending of us all, she will be your end. She will FEED and we shall witness."

The voice continued to crescendo as Cole's voice became more frantic, gabbling past his swollen tongue and blistered lips, spittle flying. "She...she is the whisper in the dark, the murmur of the void." His voice was a thread of sound that might snap at any moment. "She swims in the light of the great eye, it...it watches us, but she...she is its shadow, its disciple."

His restrained hands clawed at the air at his side, as if trying to sculpt his thoughts into coherence. "She dances in the light of the great eye, twirling, twirling, so graceful amidst the chaos...but she brings the chaos, she is the chaos! The great eye blinks and she moves closer, a phantom draped in the shroud of infinity."

Abuya could only watch, her heart pounding a frenzied rhythm, as Cole's speech became a litany of madness.

"The darkness, it's alive! Breathing and seething with her hunger. She is the end, the end of warmth, of light, of us!" His voice broke, a jagged sound that scraped against the walls and the inside of Abuya's skull. Beside the bed, the sound of the heart monitor accelerated wildly, keeping pace with the rhythm of the declamations.

"She is the cold embrace, the final grasp before the void claims us!" Cole was shaking violently. "The great eye, it sees all, it knows! It casts its gaze upon us, but she...she devours its light! She is the mouth of oblivion, the teeth of the cosmos!" His voice rose into a wail of despair.

"She will FEED! The great eye weeps for us, for it cannot save us from her insatiable feast! We are but dust to her, scraps to consume, she will feed and she...she is coming!" He thrashed against his restraints now, his back arching until Abuya thought it might break.

Annika had dashed for her storage closet and was returning, syringe in hand.

And then, as suddenly as it had begun, the storm broke. Cole's voice dwindled to a whisper and lapsed into an intermitent giggling. His body slumped, the energy that had fuelled his mad soliloquy spent. His head fell back against the pillow, his gaze still fixed on some distant point beyond the walls of the base, beyond the confines of sanity.

Abuya stumbled back against the wall, her hand clutching at her mouth, horrified at the ravings her questioning had unleashed.

Gently placing an arm around her shoulders, Annika murmured into her ear. "That wasn't you. He's done that pretty much every time he's come to. He rants and thrashes, uses up all his energy and then lapses again."

The pair approached cautiously. Cole's eyes were still open, roving wildly about the room, apparently without any recognition. The remnants of his recent delirium seemed to be fading into a profound sadness and an overwhelming fatigue. His breathing was laboured, each inhalation an effort as his chest heaved. Beside him, the heart monitor beeped steadily, a calm reprieve to the chaos of moments before. He looked up at them, his gaze piercing despite its weariness. A tear rolled down his cheek as he spoke in a whisper that barely brushed the air.

"I want to go home."

As the words dissolved into silence, the steady rhythm of the heart monitor faltered, becoming suddenly staccato and irregular.

"Arrhythmia." The machine's alarm blared dispassionately, the once orderly peaks and troughs of Cole's heartbeat now a chaotic scramble on the screen. "VFib."

Annika, with practiced urgency, sprang into action, her hands moving with precision borne of countless emergencies. She shouted for the defibrillator while her other hand snatched up a syringe of epinephrine. Abuya, caught in the sudden flurry, snatched the auto-defibrillator from its bracket on the wall and handed it to her before stepping back, giving her space to work.

Annika tore open Cole's shirt, exposing a chest marred by the bruises of past hurts and the icy kiss of the airlock's near-vacuum. She applied the AED's pads to his chest, the machine's calm electronic voice providing a stark counterpoint to the urgency of the moment.

"Analysing rhythm," it intoned and for a brief, hopeful moment, there was silence save for the machine's inner workings. "Shock advised."

At the automated voice's statement, Annika braced herself, pressing the button as the machine delivered a jolt, causing Cole's body to jerk once, violently. The monitor's line jumped and then returned to its erratic dance.

"No response, starting CPR," Annika spat, her hands moving in swift, precise compressions. Abuya could swear she heard the crack of a rib.

In the background, the defibrillator recharged, its capacitors whining as they prepared for another shock. Between compressions, Annika injected the epinephrine directly into Cole's IV line, hoping to kickstart his heart into a normal rhythm. But the green line on the monitor continued its erratic spike and fall.

"Come on, Cole," she urged, each crushing thrust against his rib cage a desperate bid for him to hold on.

The AED signalled readiness and once more, Annika delivered a shock. The heart monitor emitted a brief, hopeful series of beeps before falling back into disarray.

Despite the technology, the drugs and her relentless determination, Cole's struggle was fading. The monitor's squawks became more frantic and then, with a long, drawn-out beep, fell silent.

"Asystole," the machine declared—no electrical activity in Cole's heart.

Annika's resolve didn't waver following the monitor's grim announcement. She initiated one last, determined round of CPR. No longer needing to keep clear of shocks, she scrambled onto the table, straddling her patient's chest in order to bring her full weight to bare in the weak gravity.

Abuya stood by, helpless, her eyes wide and overflowing with silent tears. For her the moment seemed to stretch into eternity.

The heart monitor's steady whine continued without a single individuated beep. Annika pushed more epinephrine into the IV tube and continued pounding at the man's chest, but the line remained starkly, unyieldingly, flat. Finally, her shoulders slumped and the world seemed to shrink about Abuya as she realised there was no more the doctor could do.

Annika, her face a mask of controlled grief and frustration, clambered down from the table slowly and stiffly. Her chest was heaving with the physical exertion and she was trembling. Reaching down, she ripped the AED pads off Cole's still chest and, in a rare moment of raw emotion, she hurled the defibrillator across the room. It hit the ground with a crash, the sound echoing like a gunshot in the silent bay.

She drew in a deep breath, the air shuddering in her lungs as she sought to reclaim the composure her profession demanded. With numb, mechanical movements, she turned and strode across to the intercom panel, her voice steady but weaker than before. Thumbing the button for Jacob's office she pronounced.

"It's happened commander. Time of death, nineteen thirty-two."

CHAPTER FOURTEEN
Grave Silence

Abuya sat silently in the back of the rover, her gaze fixed on the jagged horizon. Once again, they were driving away from the offsite storage facility, this time having left behind the lifeless remains of Cole. Now Okoreye lay in state beside his killer. The impropriety of their final proximity was not lost on Abuya, but what else could they have done?

Her mind was consumed, not just with grief but with an unsettling guilt. Unbidden, the moments leading up to Cole's final outburst replayed yet again in her mind's eye. She couldn't help the suspicion that her questioning had been the trigger that had tipped his fragile psyche into the abyss. Annika, along with the others, had assured her that she was not to blame—that Cole's death was a tragic but inevitable endpoint of his condition. That no one could have prevented what had happened.

"He was holding onto a thin thread of life," Annika had said. "It was remarkable he held on for as long as he did."

Abuya's thoughts drifted back to the medical bay, to

Annika's post-mortem examination. The doctor had worked with what she had, employing the station's diagnostic equipment to its full capacity. She could picture Annika's face before her, set in concentration as she relayed her findings. "His dopamine levels were off the charts," she had explained, pointing to the readouts on the medical monitor. "It's not definitive without a tissue analysis, but every sign points to dopamine toxicity. His symptoms align: the manic energy, the delusions, the convulsions."

She remembered Annika pulling up the scans of Cole's brain, the images highlighting areas of hyperactivity that were consistent with a flood of neurotransmitters.

"See here." Annika had pointed to an area flagged with orange and yellow markers. "These areas should not be this active. It's as if his brain was in overdrive, unable to regulate the dopamine surge. This would induce extreme stress on his neural pathways, likely resulting in the psychotic episodes we witnessed."

Not able to perform an autopsy with the station's facilities, Annika had made do with her scans, piecing together a picture that was compelling if not complete.

"But do you have any idea what could have caused this in the first place?" Scott had persisted in trying to wring some answer, some sense out of the situation.

"We can't know all the details, but the evidence we have points to a catastrophic neurological event. The human body has its limits and whatever happened to Cole pushed him far beyond them. I can't say what triggered it, but look here and here, the brain has shrunk away from the meninges. I can't say if that is a symptom or a cause, but the problem was physical as well as chemical."

Abuya shuddered to recall the images of the brain. They had reminded her of dementia case studies she had reviewed in neurology modules at university. It had seemed withered to her eyes, like it had been eaten away at by some malicious swarm of insects, robbing the man of his consciousness, of his sanity, of his self.

A larger than normal jolt brought her back to the present. She felt relieved to have the memories dispersed. Henning twisted in his chair and smiled back at her, clearly trying to be reassuring and buoy her spirits.

"You were somewhere else I think?"

"Just thinking about Cole."

"Not a good place to be right now."

She gave him a small, tired smile and shook her head.

"How about a game, a road trip game."

"Not just now Henning."

"Come on. I spy, with my little eye."

"Henning."

"Well what else do you want to do? You want just be miserable?"

"Yes." She pouted at him and then pointedly turned to look out of the window.

Henning paused a moment, then barrelled ahead anyway.

"I spy with my little eye, something beginning with 'I'"

"I'm not playing Henning."

"It's ice." Scott broke in without taking his eyes off the terrain he was navigating. "Now leave her be Henning."

"Sehr gut Scott! You shall go first the next time."

Abuya couldn't help but smile at the man. She knew what he was trying to do.

"Thanks," she mouthed to him and received a wink in return before the two settled back into their seats and set themselves to wait out the remainder of the journey.

Their route took the rover passed the long crack of the plume vent. Its jagged, maw like appearance was a reminder of the huge forces at play beneath the moon's icy crust and of how the seemingly dead landscape could roar to life at a moment's notice. Abuya couldn't help but gaze glassily at the vent, remembering her misadventure earlier in the mission. It was an eerie sight, a dark void in the brilliant blue and white surroundings. There had been a large plume the day before and so the risk of another was very low, making it safe to drive this close and shorten their journey back.

Breaking the silence, Henning pointed through the window and jostled Scott's shoulder.

"Schau mal!" he exclaimed. "Look, there are more things about the rim."

Following the line of his finger, Abuya could see a dark lump, and casting her gaze wider, she realised there were several similar masses scattered about.

Scott grunted and manipulated the controls to bring the rover to a halt. The wheels came to rest with a soft crunching of ice and the gentle hum as the vehicle's six motors faded away to nothing.

With efficiency born of long practice, he reached for his helmet, securing it in place tightly before activating the seals with a hiss of pressurisation. Abuya and Henning quickly followed his example, double checking each other's dials and read outs, trying not to hurry through the important rituals of a safe extravehicular activity.

They disembarked from the rover, the crunching sound of their footsteps transmitting up through the suits' fabric to fill their ears. They traversed the short distance at the odd scampering trot that the stiff suits and low gravity demanded of them, leaving shallow impressions and scuffs in the surface frost.

Reaching the site that Henning had indicated, Scott knelt down beside one of the dark bundles. The black fissure of the plume vent nearby was rimed with superficial ice. Abuya could see further bundles resting on its surface, marked by the increased build-up of ice about the nucleation sites they provided.

Scott's gloved hands, bulky and clumsy in their protective layers, brushed away the loose ice crystals that clung to the object's surface.

"More ration packs." His voice crackled onto their suit-to-suit radio.

"A medical kit over here." Henning called out in reply as he extricated a second object, breaking it free and holding it aloft for the others to see. "More of these so-called sacrifices you think?"

"I'd wager so," replied Scott. "Could be new or could be from before, the plume will have brought things up that were floating around below."

The two men looked at each other, their features only

barely visible through the visors of their helmets.

"This is not good Scott. This is much more than last time."

Scott grunted his agreement and stood, at something of a loss, casting about himself to identify more of the bundles.

Without warning, sudden pain shot through the men's ears as Abuya let out a terrible wailing scream. It reverberated through their suit radios, grating and crackling as the speakers in their helmets were pushed beyond their limits. The two spun around to see Abuya scrambling on her hands and knees towards the rim of the vent. They raced after her, their boots kicking up showers of ice particles in the low gravity as they loped towards her with long lumbering strides.

They approached the silhouette of Abuya's body, now hunched over a dark mass. She was fixated, her gloved hands frantically moving over the object as she scooped away the loose frost deposited by the last plume. Reaching her, they peered over her shoulder. Beneath the woman's scrabbling fingers, a starkly defined shape began to resolve – the unmistakable outline of a human hand. It was flung upwards in a silent, frozen plea towards Jupiter, as if begging for mercy from the cold void. The fingers curled grotesquely, as if in agony or a final attempt to grasp at the life that had long since fled.

Scott's breath caught in his throat and he exchanged a grim look with Henning. They stood over Abuya, their suit lights casting a harsh glow over the scene. She continued to brush away the ice crystals that clung to the body with a tenderness that contrasted sharply with the brutality of the situation. Finally, as a face began to emerge, they heard her strangled voice through the radio.

"It's Wei-Yun," Abuya gasped, her voice breaking with grief and shock. She had partly uncovered the face and rocked back on her heels as the realisation hit her.

Wei-Yun's body was a disturbing sight. The vacuum of space, the frigid temperatures and the crushing pressure of the water below had not been kind to the fragile scrap of flesh she had once known. However, the effects of the harsh environment were not all that had disfigured the man. His torso, inexplicably bare against the elements, was marred with the clear signs of deliberate cuts. The edges of the wounds were roughened by ice crystals, the flesh beneath discoloured by the unrelenting cold. They gaped open bloodlessly, the frozen fat and muscle glinting dully underneath like freezer burned meat.

Scott knelt beside Abuya, his protective instincts kicking in, even as he felt a wave of nausea at the sight. He reached out a hand to steady her, but his eyes were drawn inexorably to the macabre cross on the man's chest.

"It's the same symbol," she stammered, her fingers hovering just above the mark, afraid to touch as she traced the lines. "It's the same one we saw on the mining platform. They...they cut it into him." The three stood frozen, stupefied by the sight before them.

Scott finally spoke, his voice of command snapping them out of their shock. "We need to move him. We can't leave him out here like this."

"The Doctor should examine him also," agreed Henning.

Gently pushing Abuya to one side, the two men knelt to set

about their grizzly task. They steadily chipped away at the encasing ice, each strike producing a dismal tinny note, their two rhythms syncopating jarringly. They worked methodically, trying to detach themselves from the horror of the scene, to view it through the clinical lens of duty rather than the raw, emotional reality.

Abuya, stumbled a few paces back, watching their progress numbly. The sight of Wei-Yun, reduced to a frozen, lifeless husk, was almost too much to bear. She felt unsteady, her legs wobbling as if the solid ice beneath her was giving way. She turned, distancing herself from the scene, needing a moment of respite. Pulling her focus from the grim tableau, she reached for the radio controls on her cuff, her fingers trembling slightly as they found the switch to mute the inter-suit channel. The grunts of effort and muttered curses of the two men working were cut off. The soft scuffling sounds of their gouges into the ice continued strangely, transmitted to her through the ice and into the soles of her feet. It made her think of fingernails scratching at the lid of a coffin—an unnerving soundtrack to the tragedy.

As she keyed in the frequency for the base command, she braced herself for Jacob's response. His recent demeanour, clouded as it had been by a growing despondency, made her apprehensive. She worried this news might be the final straw, the one to break his already faltering spirit.

When his curt *"What?"* came back to her hail, she could hear the misery and despair in its timbre, to say nothing of the slur of alcohol.

She reported their discovery, as clinically as she was able, glossing over the gruesome detail of the scene unfolding as Wei-Yun was steadily exhumed. There was a long pause on the other end of the connection. She could hear Jacob breathing heavily and was startled by a sudden loud crash as if he had struck his fist on the table or hurled some object across the room.

When his voice once again crackled through into her helmet, it carried an unexpected steel. Gone was the desolation, in its place was a hard, flinty resolve. "Bring him in," Jacob's voice commanded, its newfound steel cutting through the static. "I will not let this continue."

The words were more than a directive, they were a clear declaration, a line drawn in the sand. There was a firmness in his tone that gave Abuya hope, a resolve ignited by the brutal reality of their situation. It was as if the discovery of Wei-Yun's body had lit a fire within him, driving the need to seize control of the spiralling events that he had previously allowed to wash over him.

"Understood, Commander," Abuya responded, her voice steady despite the turmoil inside her. She watched as Scott and Henning continued their solemn work and then quickly turned away, unable to keep her gaze on the scene.

On all sides, the surface of Europa mirrored the chaos within her. The terrain was a jumbled mosaic of broken ice, where immense slabs had rafted into alien formations, starkly juxtaposed with smooth plains hinting at the hidden ocean beneath. Patches of reddish material, salts, and sulphur compounds, splotched the ice, lending a surreal, blood-splashed, quality to the landscape.

The rust-coloured patches reminded her of the apparent new life that lay beneath them. Her own research had focused on sampling such patches, hoping to find the tiniest of microbes and now the possibility of something much greater and more terrible flickered at the edges of her imagination. She shied away from the thought, tearing her eyes from the landscape to look upwards.

Above her hung the colossal presence of Jupiter, dominating the sky. The immense planet seemed to watch over them, a silent guardian, its turbulent, centuries old storms, rolling and twisting about each other. The swirling bands were a reminder of the immense forces at play in the universe. For a moment, she was transfixed by the sheer size and beauty, feeling both insignificant and awestruck under its gaze. The thought of Cole's final ravings echoed in her mind —*the great eye.*

Shaking herself from the trance, she turned back to the desolate surface and forced herself to look to where Scott and Henning were working. After just a few moments more, the two men finally freed Wei-Yun's body. Carefully lifting the man from the icy grave, they handled him with the respect due to the life that once animated the now-still form.

They moved in a slow procession back towards the rover. Abuya following in the rear, her steps mechanical. The icy terrain crunched underfoot.

Henning, with his usual quiet strength, took the lead in carefully placing Wei-Yun's body in the rover's storage compartment, which had been hastily cleared to serve as an impromptu transport for their deceased comrade. Scott assisted, his face an unreadable mask, his actions betraying none of the turmoil that must have been churning within.

Once Wei-Yun was securely placed, the trio climbed into the rover's cabin. Henning took the driver's seat, his large frame fitting awkwardly into the space. Scott sat beside him, staring blankly ahead, while Abuya found herself drawn to the window. She gazed out once more at the vast expanse of the landscape rolling away from them, trying to lose herself in the endless enormity.

The rover hummed to life, its lights piercing the encroaching darkness of twilight. Henning manoeuvred the vehicle with a steady hand, resuming their journey back to the base. The cabin held a clinging silence that none of them dared to break. The trip back to Cadmus felt longer than usual. Each minute stretched out, laden with loss and their unspoken fears.

Absently, Abuya began to unpick one of her braids, methodically parting and retwisting the small section of hair between her fingertips. The familiar, repetitive sensation of rolling the strands between her fingers helping to ground her a little.

As they approached the domes of Cadmus, the soft glow of warm light spilling from the viewports was a welcome counterpoint to the cold, unforgiving landscape surrounding them. The rover came to a gentle stop near the entrance, the inhabitants sitting at their controls for a long moment, unwilling to enter and inflict their nightmarish find on the warmth within.

CHAPTER FIFTEEN

Abyssal Confrontation

Jacob had been waiting for their arrival in the hangar, striding to and fro across the room like a caged animal, breaking off to gaze impatiently through the viewing port. He had contemplated Wei-Yun's form with a cold fierceness as he studied the stark symbol carved brutally into the man's flesh. The grim spectacle had held him spellbound, but rather than the further unravelling as Abuya had feared, the macabre sight seemed to have refocused him with an intensity that was almost frightening.

Now Henning had disappeared toward the medical bay with Wei-Yun's body cradled in his arms and Jacob was toe to toe with Scott, voices raised. Standing barely inches apart, their shouts reverberated through the hangar, both tight with strain and anger.

"We need to confront the miners about this, now!" Jacob declared, his voice flushed with sharp anger and an edge of inebriation. "Wei-Yun's death cannot be tolerated, I will not tolerate it. A line must be drawn!"

Scott, still grappling with the shock and exhaustion of the ordeal, removed his gloves distractedly, tossing them to the floor. "Jacob, you're not thinking straight. Going down there now, in this state—it's not safe."

He was trying to keep his tone level and reasonable although Abuya could hear that it was a strain.

Jacob's jaw tightened, his eyes narrowing. "I'm perfectly capable of handling this, Scott. While I was...absent, you may have stepped up, but I am still in command here."

"You were more than just absent, Jacob," Scott shot back, his voice raising in anger despite himself. "You left me to pick up the pieces while you wallowed in self-pity and liquor!"

The argument crescendoed, their shouts echoing off the metal walls of the hangar. Abuya watched, feeling a knot of anxiety twist in her stomach. She understood Scott's frustration, his feeling of being abandoned by their leader when they needed him most. Yet she couldn't help agreeing with Jacob. She couldn't stand waiting patiently for orders, not knowing what new horrors were to emerge from beneath them.

Finally, Scott, overwhelmed with emotion and fatigue, stormed off in the direction of the researchers' dormitory, leaving Abuya standing awkwardly with Jacob. She hesitated for a moment, unsure of what to do.

He stood, his shoulders rising and falling as he tried to master his anger and then he spun on his heel, heading out of the hangar, still muttering about justice for Wei-Yun and confronting the miners. Abuya followed at his heels concerned for him.

Scurrying along in Jacob's wake, she realised he was heading to the medical bay and she hurried to come level with him, determined not to let him take his frustrations out on Annika.

Jacob paused at the entrance, taking a deep breath as if bracing himself for the scene that awaited him. Abuya placed a gentle hand on his arm and he glanced down with a jerk, as if he had not been aware of her presence. Recovering his composure quickly, he nodded to her and clapped his own hand briefly over hers, before the two of them stepped through the hatchway together.

Henning was there, still in the orange surface suit which added significantly to his bulk. He seemed to take up half the room. Wei-Yun lay on the table which, until recently, had been occupied by Cole. His rigid form was covered with a sheet and draped in a collection of heating packs as the Doctor attempted to thaw his frozen flesh.

Annika looked to Jacob as they entered, noticing the new, fiercer expression. Her arms were filled with freshly warmed heat packs and she set about distributing them, addressing the Commander over her shoulder as she worked.

"You're going down then?"

Jacob nodded. "I have to."

Henning looked up at him sharply, clearly torn between rational safety and the desire to confront the terrors head-on.

"I'm coming down with you. I can't do any examination for some hours yet in any case, not until he warms up."

"It won't be safe Doctor."

"I don't feel particularly safe in any case. Besides, if this has happened, who knows what other injuries may have taken place below, people down there might need me."

Jacob didn't argue further, simply turning to lead the way to the elevator terminus.

Henning followed close behind the commander, peeling off layers of his surface suit as he went. The discarded pieces formed a trail behind him, marking their passage through the corridors and obliging Annika and Abuya to dodge the obstacles as they kept pace.

Arriving at the terminus, Jacob approached the control panel. There was a large red knob set with a keyhole, currently turned to 'maintenance', preventing the elevator from moving. Reaching into his pocket for the key he quickly returned the elevator to normal service. Stepping to the opposite wall, he thumbed the all-broadcast button of the intercom panel, his voice resonating through the base.

"Mark, I'm coming down. Be there to meet me."

His tone brooked no argument and he did not wait for a response as he stepped forward through the grating.

As the elevator descended, the atmosphere among the four was tense. Flashes of her last journey down flickered through Abuya's mind. That journey had been marked by fear, trepidation. This time, there was no fear, only fury. Jacob's anger was white-hot, a blazing inferno that had burned his complacency from him and which he barely seemed to keep in check. His fists repeatedly jerked open as if he were trying to control himself before curling tightly once again, knuckles white. In contrast, Abuya could feel her own vehement fury smouldering quietly—a deep-seated rage at the injustice and violence that had befallen Wei-Yun. It was like a hot ember in the pit of her stomach, burning and warming her.

After the usual long, rattling journey and groaning of gears, the elevator reached the mining platform. Jacob wrenched aside the grating before they had even come to a final stop.

Stepping out, they were at once face to face with Mark, Evans and perhaps a dozen miners. Their expressions ranged from wary to outright hostile, an unwelcoming welcome committee for the unexpected visitors.

Mark seemed taken aback at the ferocity in Jacob's eyes. Swallowing nervously, he tried to speak. "Jacob, I have the situation in hand, you're not needed down here. I…"

But Jacob was in no mood to listen or to be placated. Ignoring the miners arrayed hostilely before him, he stepped in close to his brother, uncomfortably close. With his voice laden with barely controlled fury, he growled into the man's face. "Come with me."

Ignoring Mark's protests, Jacob pushed past him, making him stumble. His gait purposeful and unwavering as he strode towards one of the nearby corridors. The miners and Evans, taken aback by the commander's assertiveness, exchanged uncertain glances but made no move to stop him.

Mark, visibly shaken by Jacob's uncharacteristic aggression, hesitated briefly before following. His steps seemed reluctant, fear and defiance clear on his features, but neither strong enough to deny Jacob's force of will. The rest of the group – Evans, the miners, Abuya, Henning and Annika – trailed in their wake, forming a tense procession down the corridor. The austere lighting of the mining platform cast long, ominous shadows as they moved. Along with the heavy metal hatchways and their clanging, echoing footsteps, the procession held a decidedly inquisitorial air.

Jacob led them with a single-minded focus, his anger and determination setting a brisk, unyielding pace, a relentless march towards confrontation. Abuya couldn't help but feel a surge of both admiration and concern for Jacob. His transformation from despondent inaction to fiery resolve had been as sudden as it was startling. She wondered what his new temper might mean for them all.

Jacob led them directly to the level one pressure lock. The heavy slab of the hatchway filled the small space, still daubed with the gory symbol they had discovered on their last visit only a day before.

As they reached the lock, Jacob spun round to face the group, his eyes scanning the faces before him, his own face a thundercloud. Mark, his expression defiant but uneasy, met Jacob's gaze.

"What," spat Jacob, his rage barely contained, "is that?"

He gestured at the symbol on the door. Mark's eyes flashed defiantly but he did not answer.

"Where is Wei-Yun, Mark?" Jacob continued despite his unanswered question.

"He's below," Mark muttered, breaking eye contact with Jacob and looking away.

Jacob leaned in close to him and grasped the front of his jumpsuit, repeating the question in a low, vengeful hiss. "Where is Wei-Yun?"

"I told you, he's below. He's running routine maintenance

on th..."

"No, he's fucking not!" Jacob screamed the words into Mark's face before shoving him backwards.

"He's lying dead in the fucking medical bay with that damned symbol carved into his damned chest." Jacob's own chest heaved as he towered over his cowering brother.

"What have you done Mark?!" his voice was hoarse and cracked. "What have you done?"

Mark remained silent, his eyes averted, unwilling or unable to answer Jacob's accusatory questions. Tension hung thickly in the air as neither man spoke, each glaring at the other. It was Evans who finally broke the silence, stepping forward with an unsettling calmness in his demeanour.

"He was chosen."

Evans's voice sounded eerily composed and calm. His words hung in the air, heavy with their implications. Jacob turned slowly to face him, his mouth agape at the words.

"Wei-Yun was chosen to appease her, to keep us safe. The symbol, it's an honour, a tribute to her grace. She protects us, keeps the dangers of Europa at bay."

Annika's hand found Abuya's and she clenched it tight at this shocking proclamation. Evans spoke with conviction, his face serene, almost reverent, as he talked of the creature. His tone was kindly and matter of fact, as if explaining something simple and obvious to a child.

Evans continued, undeterred by the horrified expressions of his audience. "You don't understand. She demands tribute. We must appease her, or we all are in danger. Wei-Yun's contribution was... necessary. It was the only way to ensure the safety of all."

Jacob's face contorted with a mix of anger and disbelief. "You're talking about murder, Evans. This is insanity!"

But Evans merely smiled, a chilling, disconnected smile that made Abuya's blood run cold. "No, Commander. It is survival. You've angered her by coming here, by questioning her ways. She will need to be appeased again."

"And what does that mean, *she will need to be appeased*?" Jacob's voice was a barely controlled growl, his hands clenched into fists at his sides.

Evans's smile broadened into a rictus grin, his eyes alight as if he was relaying a blessing. "She shall feed."

"And we shall witness."

Abuya nearly leapt out of her skin as the miners at Evans's back chorused together. The chant reverberated through the corridors of the mining platform, a menacing echo that filled the space with a sense of inevitable doom. Jacob, Henning, Abuya and Annika stood frozen, trying to comprehend the absurd and terrifying situation.

Jacob, recovering from his initial shock, stepped forward, his voice as stern and commanding as he could muster. "This ends now. We are taking control of this situation and we are going to get to the bottom of this madness."

Henning nodded, his expression grim and moved towards Evans, who made no attempt to resist. The miners, however, began to murmur among themselves, their expressions varying from defiant to fearful.

Turning to address them, Jacob's voice rose above the murmurs. "Listen to me. This...creature, this delusion, it's not real. It's a figment of fear and isolation. We are going to get to the bottom of this, but we need your cooperation. We are all in this together."

"No!" Mark stepped forward, standing between Evans and the advancing Henning. "Get out of here Jacob, you aren't part of this. Get out!"

He snapped then. Whether it was fear, or anger or alcohol or even just his little brother's effrontery in standing up to him, Jacob snapped. His fist shot out, rocking Mark back with a blow to his jaw that sent him sprawling into the arms of his fellow miners. There was stunned silence for a long second before the chamber erupted. With a bestial scream from Evans, the miners surged forward like a tidal wave of fury. They lunged at Jacob and the others, their faces twisted with anger and fear.

Jacob, caught off guard by the sudden onslaught, tried to fend off the attackers but was quickly overwhelmed. With a below like an ox, Henning, his huge fists swinging like hammers, battered his way through the throng and bodily pulled the commander back to his feet. The man's face was already bloodied and bruised. The air was filled with grunts and shouts and the sickening thud of flesh on flesh. If it were not for the tight confines of the space, the small group would have been overwhelmed immediately.

Abuya found herself grappling with a tall red-headed woman, struggling to break free. The assailant's grip was iron, her eyes wild with a mad intensity. With a desperate effort, she managed to push the woman away, only to be struck from behind. The world spun as her head hit the hard metal floor, stars bursting behind her eyes.

In the chaotic heart of the melee, Evans's screams tore through the air, an unholy sound that drove the miners into a frenzied assault. His face, once the picture of calm rationale, was now a grotesque mask of unbridled fury, twisted and distorted beyond recognition. Henning, a towering presence amidst the fray, advanced towards Evans. He moved with a singular purpose, the miners, falling back before the imposing figure.

With a single fluid motion, Henning's arm lashed out and his fist connected with the bridge of Evans's nose. The sound of breaking bone was almost lost in the chaos, but its impact was undeniable. Evans's eyes rolled back as he collapsed in a heap, his maniacal screams abruptly silenced. The miners, their frenzy momentarily halted, looked on in shock. Henning, seizing the moment of stunned silence, bellowed for a retreat.

Scooping the disoriented Abuya from the ground, Henning half-carried, half-dragged her towards the elevator. Abuya, her vision blurred and her head throbbing, could barely comprehend their escape. Jacob, his face a canvas of bruises and cuts, covered their retreat, swinging wildly at any miner who dared approach.

The elevator loomed ahead, their refuge from the madness. Henning, with a force born of desperation, threw Abuya through the open grating. She landed with a thud, her body aching from the impact. Jacob and Henning turned to hold off the remaining miners—Henning, brandishing an emergency oxygen tank he had snatched up in the mayhem, swinging it like a medieval mace. Step by step, the miners were forced back with each heavy, threatening arc.

Jacob took advantage of the resulting lull in the onslaught, slamming the grating closed. His fingers fumbled at the control panel, punching the buttons to initiate the elevator's ascent. The grating rattled as the miners threw themselves against it, their faces twisted in mindless rage.

As the elevator jolted into motion, Jacob and Henning leaned against the walls, their chests heaving with exertion and adrenaline. A small, disoriented voice cut through the din of their laboured breathing.

"Annika? Anni!"

It was Abuya, panicked and confused. She clutched the back of her head, her eyes darting around the confined space in a frantic search.

"Annika!"

She cried out again, her voice breaking with fear.

Jacob and Henning exchanged a look of dawning horror. In the pandemonium of their escape, amidst the struggle and desperation, they had left the doctor behind.

The dim, flickering light of the elevator illuminated Abuya's anguished face, her eyes brimming with tears. The cold, metallic walls of the elevator car seemed to close in around her. Abuya's wails echoed through the elevator shaft as they made their inexorable way to the surface, leaving behind the woman she loved.

Abuya's vision was blurry and her head throbbed with pain. She tried to focus, but the world tilted and swayed around her nauseatingly. Henning gently pressed her back against the wall, parting her braids to examine the wound on her scalp, his voice a distant echo in her ears. "Be still, Abuya. Let me see how bad it is."

Jacob stood nearby, his chest still heaving with exertion as he nursed his swollen jaw.

The confined space of the elevator closed in on her, the metallic walls pulsating with the rhythm of her heartbeat and the throbbing of her skull. Flickering lights cast disjointed shadows, adding to the sense of unreality.

Her thoughts were a tangled mess; tugging on any one thread only made it worse. She struggled to hold onto a single coherent idea. Flashbacks of the recent chaos flooded her mind, mingling with snippets of fragmented memories.

Abuya blinked hard, trying to clear her vision and her mind. She focused on Henning's face, his familiar features helping to anchor her. Her breathing steadied as she forced herself to take slow, deliberate breaths and gradually, slowly, the fog began to clear.

"We have to… Annika…" she murmured, her voice barely a moan.

"Sei still. Don't move too much," Henning cautioned, his eyes scanning her face for signs of concussion.

Abuya's thoughts started to crystallise around a single, burning need—to rescue Annika. She pushed past the pain and disorientation, her mind honing in on the urgency of the situation. Her voice, still shaky but gaining strength, broke the silence. "We have to go back for her," she insisted, but no one answered.

The elevator ground to a halt at the surface as they reached the relative safety of the upper levels of Cadmus. Abuya, Jacob and Henning staggered out in a daze, their bodies and spirits battered from the harrowing ordeal below. The familiar, utilitarian corridor of the surface base seemed almost alien to Abuya now, such a vivid contrast to the chaos they had just fled. Her mind was clearer now, filled with a tumultuous storm of emotions—fear, anger, and an all-consuming sense of desperation for Annika, left behind in the madness.

Jacob turned to her, forestalling her further protestations. "We can't go back down, not now," he stated firmly.

His expression was unyielding, the lines on his face deepening with the gravity of his words.

Abuya's response was visceral, her voice echoing through the corridors with its shrill intensity. "We can't just leave her there!" she screamed at him, her eyes blazing with fear, anger, and an indomitable urge to act. "She's stuck down there, alone. What if it were you, Jacob? what if it were someone you cared about?" Her voice broke and she angrily dashed tears from her eyes with the cuff of her jumpsuit.

Jacob's jaw tightened as he continued, trying to reason with her, his hands clenching and unclenching in a visible struggle to maintain his composure.

"I care about Annika, truly I do, but rushing back down there could do more harm than good. Think about it, Abuya. If she has managed to stay hidden, our return could compromise her safety. We can't risk her life on a gamble. If she hasn't stayed hidden then… then I don't see what good we can do by rushing in blindly. We need to be smart about this, for her sake."

His words were logical, but Abuya was driven by raw emotion, her voice cracking under the strain of the turmoil. "We have to do something!" she insisted, tears welling in her eyes, panic and helplessness threatening to engulf her.

Jacob's voice softened slightly, trying to reach her through the storm of her emotions. "I understand your need to act, but rushing back down without a plan is too dangerous. We need to be strategic."

Abuya was inconsolable, her gaze imploring Jacob to understand the urgency she felt. Each second wasted felt like a betrayal. "She's down there alone, possibly hurt. We can't just...give up," she pleaded, her voice incredulous and desperate.

"We're not giving up on her, but we have to approach this carefully. Annika is resourceful. We have to trust in her ability to stay safe until we can reach her."

Her breath came in short, ragged gasps. "We can't abandon her, Jacob. We can't," Abuya pleaded, her love and fear so desperate that they overrode all else.

Henning, his usually stoic face lined with concern and sadness, stepped forward and gently, but firmly, grasped Abuya's shoulders. "Abuya, we must think first. We can not help her if we get ourselves killed."

Abuya's heart raced, her thoughts a whirlwind. Every fibre of her being screamed to go back, to plunge into the depths and rescue Annika, but the rational part of her mind, however small and distant, knew Jacob and Henning were right. Torn between her heart and her head, she struggled against

Henning's grip, but his strength was unyielding.

With a deep, resigned sigh, Jacob turned back to the elevator terminal. His fingers found the still present key and with finality, he turned the knob back to maintenance. The control panel blinked a confirmation and once more the elevator was locked in its position. It was a necessary precaution, one that put a physical barrier between them and the madmen below, yet it felt to Abuya like a prison door slamming shut.

Henning led her away from the elevator, half dragging and half carrying her. Her mind was a cacophony of images—Annika's smile, her laugh, the way her nose crinkled when she was deep in thought. The idea of her down there, alone and in danger, was unbearable. Tears blurred her vision and a throbbing ache built at the base of her skull.

They moved slowly through the base, the usual hum of activity a distant, incomprehensible backdrop. The walls felt like the boundaries of a cage and they pressed tightly about her, closing in further with each hatchway and turn. Each step took her further away from Annika, each second that passed a torment, her mind filled with the worst of possibilities.

Henning's grip was gentle yet firm, his presence supportive but forceful. They reached the researcher's common area and Henning guided her to a seat, his expression a mix of sympathy and resolve. "We will find a way," he said softly, but his words were no comfort against the raging storm in Abuya's heart.

She slumped into the chair, her body trembling with pent-up emotion. The room felt cold and sterile, a stark contrast to the warmth and life Annika brought into her world. The walls continued to close in on her, the weight of the situation a crushing burden on her chest.

Henning stood by her, a silent sentinel, his presence something of a comfort but more a reminder of her inability to act. Abuya's mind raced with scenarios, plans and desperate ideas to bring Annika back. But with each passing moment, the reality of their situation sank in deeper, the cold, unyielding truth that she was trapped on the surface, powerless to act.

CHAPTER SIXTEEN

Lost In The Depths

Annika's perspective of the fight had been a mad whirlwind of disarray. The initial shock of the miners' sudden aggression, their faces twisted in manic rage, had initially jolted her into a state of heightened alertness. But as the brawl erupted on all sides, her surroundings had transformed into a senseless blur. Fists flew, bodies collided and the metallic walls of the mining platform rang with the sounds of the conflict.

Caught in the tumult, Annika tried to maintain her balance, dodging the flailing limbs and frantic movements of the miners. She was focused on reaching Jacob, on trying to exert some calming influence on the volatile situation. However, her intentions were abruptly derailed when a miner, sent sprawling by Henning's formidable strength, crashed into her. The impact was sudden and forceful, knocking the wind out of her and sending her tumbling to the ground.

The world spun as she hit the hard metal floor, her head striking with a sharp pain that radiated through her skull. For a moment, everything was a haze. Sounds were muffled, the shouts and cries of the brawl around her seeming distant. As she tried to regain her senses, she realised that she was pinned beneath the unconscious miner, his body a dead weight across her legs.

Struggling beneath him, Annika pushed and heaved with all her strength. Her ears rang and her vision swam, but the instinct to escape the madness that had enveloped the platform drove her. She felt a sudden onrush of bodies clambering and leaping over her as if she was sheltering from a stampede of buffalo. She tucked her head into her hands, relying on the unconscious miner for shelter from the trampling feet. At last, the noises diminished, the shouts, scuffles and yelps of pain receding into echoes. Finally, with a grunt of effort, she managed to free herself from beneath the miner's inert form, scrambling to her feet with a gasp. She took shuddering, unsteady breaths and looked around at the aftermath. She found herself to be quite alone—at least discounting the prostrated figures scattered about the floor, unconscious or perhaps worse.

In addition to the man she had lain under, there were three limp forms sprawled about the cramped chamber. She hurried towards the nearest, stooping to peel back the woman's eyelid. The eye beneath flickered at the sudden light and she let the lid fall. The man she'd laid under was likewise stunned; poleaxed by a blow to the temple from the look of a rapidly developing bruise. Moving on she let out a small groan at the sight of the body of the next woman. She had not fared well and Annika's stomach lurched queasily at the site of her crushed chest. She could imagine the sickening crunch as one or more of the running miners had come down with their full weight across the woman's ribs.

Finally, she came to Evans, lying in a pool of the blood that had gushed from his nose. It was already drying stickily on the floor about him. She checked for a pulse, relieved to find it strong and steady despite his unconscious state. The nose was definitely broken, nastily so, but she was confident he would recover.

Having done her duty to the fallen as best as she could in the situation, Annika made to rise. It was as she did so that she heard it – a faint noise, a hesitant shuffle of feet. Looking up, she saw one of the miners, Tara she thought her name was, standing in the entrance to the corridor. Their eyes met, a moment of silent something like understanding passing between them. Tara's face was filled with fear and confusion, a marked contrast to the fervour that had consumed her and her compatriots just moments ago. Then, with a last fearful glance at Annika, Tara turned and hurried away down the corridor towards the elevator terminus.

Annika's heart pounded in her chest, spoiling her attempt at calm reasoning as she tried to determine her next move. The platform felt like a trap, a cage of metal and madness. She needed to leave, to find safety. With Evans stirring, groaning faintly as consciousness began to return to him, Annika made her decision. She couldn't risk encountering Tara or any of the other miners who might still be in the grips of their delusion. For now at least she had been overlooked.

Moving as quietly as she could, Annika slipped away, choosing the outer ring of the platform to take her away from the pressure lock as quickly as possible. Her steps were cautious, her mind racing with thoughts of the confrontation and the chaos it had left behind. She felt a pang of guilt for leaving the injured behind her, but her survival instincts urged her onward.

The corridor was dimly lit, the usual hum of machinery eerily absent. As she moved, her footfalls seemed too loud, each echoing step a reminder of her vulnerable position. She glanced back frequently, trying to ensure she wasn't being followed as she quickened her pace.

Annika's mind was a whirlwind of fear, concern, and anger, all smothered by an overwhelming sense of urgency. She needed to find a way back up to the surface, to reunite with her team, to understand the full extent of the madness that had taken hold of the mining platform. But first, she had to survive the labyrinthine corridors of the platform, each turn and twist filled with potential unknown dangers.

Suddenly, behind her, she heard a roar of pain and fury. She knew instinctively it was Evans, roused from his insensibility. Suppressing a squeak of fear, she continued on as fast as she dared. There were other footsteps now—running, echoing all around and from all directions. She had no idea if they were chasing her from behind or up ahead or somewhere else entirely, the metallic walkways transmitting the running beat throughout the entire platform.

Breaking into a sprint, now heedless her own clanging footfalls, she hared around the gentle curve of the outer ring and found herself at the head of the ladderway down to the lower levels. She did not want to go that way and leave herself further from safety, but as she looked down the perpendicular corridor that would lead her back towards the terminus the forms of two of miners loomed out of a connecting corridor. The men spotted her and yelled and she did not wait. She hurled herself down the ladderway, scrabbling at the rungs and dropping the last dozen feet with a clang which would in earth gravity have knocked the wind from her.

She didn't wait to see if she was pursued and set off at a mad dash, further into the twisting maze. Annika's heart pounded furiously against her chest as she ran through the second level, her breath coming in short, ragged gasps.

The corridors seemed to stretch on endlessly, each turn and twist a potential trap. She could hear the echo of footsteps and shouts reverberating through the metal structure; she was certain now that she was being pursued.

In a desperate bid for respite, she ducked into a laboratory, pressing her back against the cold metal wall. She held her breath, listening as a group of miners charged past the doorway, their heavy boots pounding on the metal grating. Once the sound of their footsteps had faded, she peeked out, her heart sinking as she heard more miners coming up behind her. Glimpsing round the corner she could make out the ladderway at the far end of the corridor—bodies were tumbling down it from above.

Her plan to double back towards safety was quickly foiled by the increasing number of miners. Panic rising in her throat, she glimpsed Evans among them as he descended the ladder, his voice ringing out above the din in a manic cry.

"Find her!"

His words reignited her primal panic and she spun around, fleeing in the opposite direction.

She had seldom ventured beyond the first level of the mining platform and Annika navigated now with a mix of instinct and sheer luck. She rounded a corner and collided with a broad-shouldered miner at an intersection. The impact sent them both tumbling to the ground. Rolling with the momentum, she scrambled back to her feet and continued her desperate sprint. Her mind was singularly focused on escape, each stride fuelled by an overwhelming need to survive.

Passing the next ladderway down to the third level, she had a sudden burst of inspiration and flung herself down it, hoping the pursuers would assume she wouldn't want to go further below. Her lungs burned with exertion but she pushed her body onwards, needing to get as far away from the miners and Evans as possible.

Descending to the third level, she sprinted around the mercifully deserted outer ring, counting the corridors as she went. Finally, having traversed half of the entire circumference, she reached that level's pressure lock. It looked identical to the one on the first level, save for the absence of bodies and bloodstained symbols. She did however see the same symbol scratched into the perspex of the hatchway, hardly as grotesque or disturbing as its gory counterpart above.

Annika yanked open the door of a locker and pulled out a heavy sub-suit. The thick fabric and rigid joints made it unwieldy and she had to wrestle it free from the narrow confines. Dragging the cumbersome gear into the pressure lock, she stumbled, her foot catching on the coaming, almost sending her sprawling. With a grunt, she recovered and slammed the hatch shut with a sullen thunk, the sound reverberating through the confined space like a gong.

Panting heavily, she leaned against the hatch, trying to control her breathing and calm the frantic pounding of her heart. She fumbled with the sub-suit, her fingers trembling as she struggled to remember her basic training. The thought of needing to use a sub-suit had always seemed so remote, so unlikely. Yet here she was, her life potentially depending on her ability to don it quickly and correctly.

After several agonising minutes, she managed to secure the suit about her, ensuring every seal was tight, every connection secure. Her hands trembled as she forced herself to meticulously check each fastening, her breath coming in short, panicked bursts. She double-checked the oxygen supply, watching the needle hover reassuringly in the green zone and scanned the dials, percentages, and gauges on the suit's readouts to confirm everything was in working order. Finally, she reached out for the helmet, cursing her mane of white-blond hair. She tried to focus as she clumsily tucked every last tress inside with the suit's stiff gloves. The helmet's inner padding snagged on a few strands, but eventually it clicked into place with a satisfying hiss. She felt the gentle pressure increase as the suit began to inflate, signalling it was secure and airtight.

Annika closed her eyes, forcing herself to take slow, deep breaths. She needed to stay calm, to think clearly. Finally, with a beep and a gentle popping of her ears, the suit was fully inflated. She approached the control panel and initiated the pressurisation cycle, the clanging of valves and rumbling of water filling the small space around her.

The pressurisation cycle was always unnerving at the best of times, but now it was all Annika could do to choke down a panic attack as the gushing water threatened to knock her over. Her fingers flickered over the neck seals, double and triple-checking them as the water gurgled up over the face plate. The rushing noise was loud and unbearable, filling her ears until suddenly… Silence. The pressure lock was full. Annika listened to the sound of her own panting, magnified by the sub-suit's rebreather. She tried to ignore how terrified she sounded, swallowing down her anxiety to focus on the task at hand.

She turned back towards the control panel and screamed, filling the suit with the sound. Glaring at her, his ruined face twisted into a rictus of anger, was Evans. His eyes were wild, bloodshot, and full of the madness that had consumed him. His hand clawed at the toughened glass, fingers splayed wide, nails scraping and tearing against the surrounding bolts. Each desperate scratch left faint smears of blood on the surface. His breath fogged the glass, his mouth opening and closing in silent, furious roars. He was like an animal trapped in a cage, driven by a primal urge to escape and hunt. The sight was terrifying, his once familiar face now almost unrecognisable, contorted by rage and a desperate malice.

Annika didn't wait to see what he would do, she struck out with her foot, pushing herself towards the outer hatch. Transmitted dully through the water she heard a staccato rumble of metallic clanks. She knew Evans couldn't open the door—the safety measures used the huge water pressure to force the door closed—but she was not going to be sticking around in any case.

The pressure light turned on and glowed a dull green, Annika yanked the handle down and the outer hatch swung open. Activating the sub-suit's mobility unit, she moved out of the pressure lock as quickly as she could.

She looked up to the surface ice almost a kilometre above her. The ice was too thick to allow any light through and yet there was a pinprick, a thin line of radiance shafting feebly through the water before petering out. It was the plume vent hole and it was what she was looking for.

Using her wrist-mounted interface she programmed her target depth and initiated a controlled ascent. The sub-suit hissed as its ballast was released, pushed out by compressed nitrogen from the suit's main tank. She felt herself accelerate towards the surface.

There was nothing else now to distract her and the darkness and misery of what had happened rushed in to consume her. She drifted in the dark cold of the water and the dark cold of her mind. Images of Okoreye and of Wei-Yun and of Cole flashed before her eyes and she squeezed them tightly shut. A few tears spilt out and fogged her visor. She was alone in the void, utterly alone. Or was she? Thoughts of the alleged creature intruded on her isolation and her heart began to race once more, her anxiety and fear reaching fever pitch.

In this infinite void of cold and darkness, it was easy to believe in almost anything. Patches seemed to break off from the blackness, flitting towards her and then dissolving into nothingness. Her own mind manifested tentacles clutching at her limbs, teeth flashing in the dark, a low rumbling growl.

Striving to rid herself of these thoughts, she let an image of Abuya fill her mind. Abuya's kindness, Abuya's strength, Abuya's smile. She could see it before her, a bright white flash in a dark face. It drove away the imagined beasts of the water, giving her warmth and hope. She let herself go then, sinking into the smile, allowing herself to be fully immersed in her memories of Abuya. She felt her warmth, felt her hand on hers.

"Keep swimming little one."

The words drifted unbidden into Annika's mind with Abuya's voice and made her smile.

The depth gauge chimed, startling her out of the comfortable reverie as her eyes shot open. She had reached the target depth, just a few metres below the ice. She turned to find the shaft of light only a few hundred or so metres behind her. She engaged the mobility unit, letting it push her towards the light. It looked like a solid column and she half expected to slam into the side as the sub-suit pushed her into the brightness.

She looked up at the surface, the orange light shining ruddily through the water. She manipulated the interface again, setting it for maximum buoyancy. The bright disc of the surface surged down towards her and burst across the faceplate of her helmet. She gasped as she breached the thin crust of ice across the vent's surface as if she had been holding her breath under the water.

She lay on her back panting, the suit's buoyancy supporting her weight as she bobbed gently on the waves she had caused with her ascent. She had felt convinced she was going to die down on the mining platform and she was inexpressibly glad to see the sun again, even what feeble, warmthless sun that reached this far.

The struggle to the edge of the vent was ungainly and splashy in the bulky suit but it was nothing compared to the scramble up the steep sides onto the ice. She eventually managed it after several unfruitful attempts, dragging her body forward inch by inch and pulling herself into a standing position. She stood with rivulets of water dripping down the suit, destined to freeze or to sublimate before they could hit the ice at her feet.

The eye of Jupiter gazed grimly down at her, its great maelstrom churning. She ignored the unsettling sight as best she could and cast about for the tether cable. It was easy enough to find, less than a kilometre away and there at the bottom, the far-off domes of Cadmus. The distance would have made for a long and miserable slog in a surface suit but in the sub suit, she wasn't even sure if she could make it. The suit had very little range of motion, she would have to half shuffle, half bounce.

Setting her mouth into a grim slash of resignation she began, trying to pretend she looked a little more dignified as she awkwardly skipped across the frozen landscape.

CHAPTER SEVENTEEN
Cold Embrace

In the sombre quiet of the corridor, Jacob walked alone towards his office, his mind clouded with the weight of recent events. The darkness of his familiar black depression pulled at him, making each step feel like a monumental effort, while the manic urge to act without thinking buzzed incessantly at the edges of his consciousness. One moment he felt the crushing inertia of hopelessness, the next an almost uncontrollable need to fix everything at once, regardless of the risks. His hands fluttered restlessly at his sides, fingers twitching as if searching for something to hold onto. As he approached his office, Jacob forced himself to take deep breaths, each inhale and exhale an attempt to calm the conflicting forces within him and bring himself back to his usual fragile balance.

He entered the room to find Scott waiting there, his posture tense, a look of contrition on his face, quickly replaced by shock as he took in Jacob's battered state. "What the fuck happened to you?!"

Jacob merely shook his head tiredly.

The two men looked at each other for a long moment before Scott broke the silence again. "Jacob, I was out of line earlier. I apologise."

He paused, looking expectantly at Jacob, hoping for an explanation of the man's faceful of bruises and cuts.

Jacob, letting out a deep sigh, sank into his chair. The fatigue of the day's events was written clearly on his face. "You weren't out of line Scott; you made a lot of sense and I ran in with my eyes wide shut like an idiot."

His voice was slow and heavy, words falling leadenly from his mouth."The situation below...It's worse than we feared. The miners...They're completely lost, Evans too. They attacked us and we barely escaped."

Scott's eyes widened."Evans as well? He's barely been down there more than a day. This thing, whatever it is, is spreading fast."

He looked at Jacob's face, worried by the clear distress he could see there. "Anyone hurt worse than you?"

Jacob sighed, pinching the bridge of his nose and pausing a long moment before answering. "The Doctor… Annika. She's still down there."

Jacob couldn't meet Scott's eyes as he shared this news. "She got left behind in the chaos."

He stared down at his desk, gazing dully at the backs of his twitching hands. Without thinking, he picked up a pen and began methodically to pull it to pieces.

Scott sat in stunned silence, the awfulness of the situation pressing upon him as he absorbed this information. After a long moment, Jacob sat up, his tone resolute. "We need to evacuate. If this thing below is contagious then it's the only safe thing to do."

Scott nodded slowly as he considered, his expression grave. "You may be right. Not all the way back to Earth, not till we hear from ground control, but we could get everyone up to the ship at least."

"I don't see what else we can do."

Scott mumbled an agreement as Jacob opened his laptop, initiating a call to the Fulgur in orbit above them.

After a few moments of cheerful dialling tones, Captain Lukas appeared on the screen, hovering before the camera. Her hair floated out in a halo around her head and her face showed the puffiness of someone living in micro-gravity.

In slow, emotionless sentences, Jacob relayed their new information to the Captain, updating her on the latest developments. "We think it would be safest to remove ourselves to the Fulgur, at least for the next thirty hours or so until we hear back from Earth. You're well supplied?"

"We are, enough for my crew and four passengers all the way to Earth, so we can definitely manage the eight of you for a few days."

"I hope it will be nine of us," replied Jacob, "but that's good to hear. Send down the climber right away."

"Will do, it should reach you in just under seventeen hours. Be careful down there while you're waiting."

Jacob nodded his response and cut off the call, half closing the laptop's lid.

"So," said Scott, as Captain Lukas' face disappeared from the screen, "we've got seventeen hours to get her out of there."

Jacob leaned back in his chair, his eyes fixed on a distant point as if he could find the answer in the cold metallic walls of his office. "But how, Scott? We've seen what they're capable of. They're not predictable anymore; they're zealots, blinded by this...this delusion."

Scott stood and paced the small room, his steps echoing in the confined space. "I think you're right about going down again, it's a suicide mission with them in that state. There's no way they wouldn't have someone watching the elevator..."

Jacob rubbed his temples, feeling keenly every second ticking by. "Even if we get down there, finding Annika while she's hiding in that maze...It'll be like looking for a needle in a haystack. And that's assuming she's still..."

His voice trailed off, unable to finish the thought.

The room fell into a brooding silence, the two men lost in their thoughts, grappling with the grim reality of their situation. The possibility of successfully rescuing Annika seemed to diminish with each passing moment, hopelessness settling over them like a shroud.

Jacob finally spoke, his voice low. "We also have to think of the rest of the crew. We can't risk more lives on a rescue that seems...impossible."

He hated the words even as he said them, each one a betrayal of the promise he had made to Abuya and his duty of care to Annika.

Scott sighed, throwing up his hands in frustration and helplessness. "If only we could communicate with her, find out where she is, or what's happening down there, but the intercom isn't private. She'd have to get to a computer in one of the main offices."

Even as he said those words, the laptop on the desk between them chimed once more, this time with an incoming call. Jacob nearly fell out of his chair at the sudden sound and Scott whipped about to face the desk. The screen flashed with Evans's name. Jacob and Scott exchanged a look of apprehension, the tension in the room spiking.

"Could she have reached his office?"

Neither of them made a move as they gazed at the laptop.

"Only one way to find out I guess."

Jacob nodded, hesitating only a moment longer before accepting the call.

The face that appeared on the screen was not Annika. It was Evans and the pair tensed in disappointment and nervous anticipation. Evans glared out at them, his cheek and chin still smeared with dried blood, his nose awry from Henning's felling blow.

Evans's face on the screen was contorted with anger, his voice a harsh growl. "Your little raid, your intrusion… She is enraged."

The man's eyes burned with a fervent light and flecks of spittle flew with every plosive. "You have disturbed the peace we had; the understanding, the safety."

Jacob leaned forward, anger and desperation fighting for dominance against his attempt at rational thought. "Evans, listen to me. This is madness. There is no creature–"

But Evans cut him off, raising his voice. "She was appeased! We held her beneficence!"

Evans spat, oblivious to their reactions, his voice rising in a maniacal crescendo. "But now, another must be chosen. Another sacrifice to calm Her wrath. And you, Jacob, you have brought this upon us. You should be humbled, brought before Her, to witness Her glory and atone for what you've done."

Jacob tried to interject, to reason with Evans, but his words fell on deaf ears. Evans's speech was relentless, his tone becoming almost sermon-like, filled with a twisted reverence for the entity he believed lurked in the depths of Europa.

We should have given Her that sneaky bitch, before she slipped away."

His words sent a jolt through the two men, their eyes widening at the implication. "But now it will be another. One of our own. A willing supplicant."

Scott cried out in horror and disbelief. "Evans, you need to stop this. Think about what you're saying. You're talking about a human life here."

But Evans seemed lost in his own world, his eyes not even registering their presence on the screen. "She will be appeased," he intoned, his voice carrying an eerie finality. "Her will be done. She will feed and we shall witness. YOU shall witness!"

Jacob clenched his fists, his frustration boiling over. "Evans, there is no creature! This is a delusion, a madness that's taken hold of you all!"

But Evans's face remained unyielding, his gaze distant and unfocused, as if he were looking past them, seeing something they couldn't. His voice was a monotonous drone, repeating his chilling mantra.

"She will feed and we shall witness."

Jacob and Scott shared a glance, a silent communication passing between them. Evans was beyond reason, lost in the grip of his delusion. The man's voice echoed strangely, as if more voices had joined his own in the chant. And then the screen flickered and changed. Jacob cried out and grasped the monitor, holding it with white knuckles as if he could climb through to the other side.

Evans's face was gone, replaced with the grainy feed from one of the pressure locks. There, framed by the heavy hatchway behind him, stood Mark. He stood in the centre of the small room, stripped to the waist. His chest was slick with blood—the same symbol that had been carved into Wei-Yun now etched deeply into his flesh. The sight was a visceral blow to Jacob, who let out an anguished cry at the sight of his brother in such a state. "Mark!" Jacob yelled, his voice raw with terror and disbelief. "Mark, what are you doing? Get out of there!"

But the only response was Evans's voice, eerily calm and detached, repeating over the intercom. "You shall witness!"

Jacob's face crumpled, tears streaming down as he sobbed in terror. Scott sat beside him, his body rigid with shock, unable to move or speak, his eyes glued to the monitor.

On the screen, Mark's gaze was fixed on the camera. There was an unsettling serenity in his eyes, a beatific smile on his lips. He was not a victim; he was a willing participant, a believer in the delusion that had gripped the miners. He seemed almost joyous, ready to embrace his fate as a sacrifice to the non-existent creature.

As they watched, paralysed by horror, the pressure lock activated. Water began to rush in, icy and unrelenting. It swirled around Mark's feet, slowly rising up his legs, but he remained unmoved by the frigid cold, his arms outstretched as if in welcome. The water climbed higher, engulfing his waist, his chest, but still, he did not flinch. His smile never wavered.

The chanting continued, more voices joined Evans's, overlaying discordantly. "She will feed and we shall witness."

It created a haunting background to the tragedy, echoing through the tinny speakers and filling the room with its morbid sound.

Scott, finally tearing himself from his stunned stupor, let out a guttural cry of revulsion. He couldn't bear to watch any longer. He stumbled to his feet and fled the room, leaving Jacob alone with the screen.

Jacob was curled around the monitor, gripping its edge with white knuckles as if he could climb through the screen, his body wracked with sobs. He watched helplessly as the water continued to rise, now covering Mark's shoulders, his neck, his chin. Mark's eyes remained fixed on the camera, his rapturous smile unwavering, even as the water closed over his head.

In the final moments, as Mark's figure disappeared beneath the swirling, dark waters, his arms remained outstretched, a final, chilling embrace. The water continued to churn for a moment as the pressure equalised before stilling. And then with slow finality, the outer hatch swung open and a dark shape drifted out to be swallowed by the inky blackness.

Jacob was left alone in the room, the screen now showing nothing but the still, dark waters of the pressure lock, eerily illuminated by the chamber's lighting. The chant had ceased, leaving behind a deafening silence. Jacob's sobs filled the room, a solitary sound of grief and despair echoing off the walls. He remained there, a broken man, mourning the horrific demise of his brother, unable to tear himself away from the screen that had borne witness to such an unspeakable act.

. .• . .

Abuya lay sprawled dejectedly on her cot, her mind a morass of conflicting emotions. The cot's thin mattress did little to cushion her from the webbing underneath, but discomfort didn't matter anymore. She gazed blankly up at the sloping ceiling, her eyes unfocused, listening to every distant hum of machinery and creak of the base's fabric. Half-baked rescue plans and gruesome imaginings of what might be happening to Annika tumbled through her thoughts.

Henning had been watching over her since their return from the mining platform, sitting silently, his eyes never leaving her. While his usual stoicism did a lot to hide it, he too had been shaken by the day's events.

Neither of them was fully conscious of the time passing, both zoning out into their own thoughts. The minutes and the silence stretched on with neither of them having the heart to say anything.

Eventually, Alistair arrived and was shocked to see the state of Henning. The man's face and arms bore a welter of bruises, scratches and cuts and Alistair insisted on tending to him.

He fussed over Henning like a mother hen with her chick, clucking and murmuring as he applied antiseptic and bandages to the wounds. Henning, for his part, was a reluctant patient, grimacing and grunting as Alistair worked. Abuya watched this interaction from the corner of her eye, biding her time and waiting for the right moment.

As soon as Alistair had fully immersed himself in his task, Abuya seized her chance. Slipping away quietly and passing out of the dormitory. She moved with a singular focus—getting back down to the mining platform to find Annika. Guilt and desperation had won out over all Jacob's arguments; the thought of Annika alone and in danger was unbearable.

Abuya moved with purpose, her heart racing in her chest as she he crept along the corridor towards the elevator terminus. She passed out of the researchers dome and into one of the main corridors, taking the longer route to avoid going past the Commander's office.

As she reached the next junction, she heard footsteps approaching. Her breath caught in her throat and she quickly ducked into the nearby head to avoid whoever it was. The scent of antiseptic and the hum of the ventilation system filled the small, sterile space. Abuya pressed herself against the cool metal of the door and heard the person walk by, muttering to themselves in what sounded like Polish. Tomas then, on his way to some unknown duty.

As his footsteps receded, Abuya slowly exhaled and slipped

back into the corridor, resuming her cautious journey. Her steps quickened as she neared the elevator terminus, her breath coming in short, sharp pants.

Reaching the control panel beside the elevator, she glanced over her shoulder to ensure she was alone. Jacob had neglected to remove the control key, only concerned with security against those below. Her fingers trembling, she turned the key, twisting the knob away from maintenance. The corresponding light on the panel blinked off and the elevator was unlocked once again.

Just then, a cacophony of sound erupted behind her—a series of clanging crashes and a bellowing roar. It sounded like a maddened wildebeest charging down the corridor in her direction. Her heart leapt into her throat and she spun around, her eyes wide.

"HALT!!"

She stumbled back into the elevator, her hand frantically scrabbling for the grating. In the next instant, Henning burst into the terminus, his face red and contorted with exertion, his eyes wild with urgency. He skidded to a halt in front of her, panting heavily, thrusting his arm across the grating to prevent it from closing. They stood for a moment, chests heaving, staring each other down.

The clattering behind Henning continued and, after a few moments, Alistair and Delun appeared, their faces flushed from the pursuit. Alistair's usually tidy hair was dishevelled, and Delun was clearly confused, not knowing what was going on or why he had been pulled into a chase.

Henning, without a word, reached for Abuya, his large

hands gripping her firmly to pull her from the elevator car with a force that left no room for resistance. She struggled against his grasp, her desperation telling her to fight back, but to no avail. Henning, regretful yet determined, hoisted her over his shoulder as if she weighed nothing. Abuya pounded on his back, her fists making muffled thuds against his broad shoulders, her nails scraping at his neck.

"Put me down! I need to go to her!" she cried out, her voice muffled against the fabric of his uniform. Henning, his brow furrowed against the pain of her blows, continued down the corridor, his steps heavy and resolute.

Delun and Alistair, positioned themselves between the pair and the elevator, effectively blocking any attempt Abuya might make to return. They exchanged concerned glances, uncertain of what the right thing to do might be. They were not unmoved by the Doctor's predicament and their inability to act chafed at them all.

Unable to tolerate any more of her stinging blows to his already beaten and bruised frame, Henning set Abuya down. The two of them collapsed onto the floor of the corridor, panting heavily. Abuya's face was streaked with tears, her body shaking with her exhaustion and emotional turmoil.

"I have to go back for her," Abuya sobbed desperately. "You don't understand...I can't leave her there, alone."

Her eyes pleaded with them all, begging for their understanding as the three men shared uneasy glances, unable to meet her imploring gaze.

Alistair was the first to speak, his voice hesitant. "Abuya, you know how dangerous it is down there just now. We can't go rushing in blindly."

"We would need a plan," Delun added, "or we could just make things worse for her."

Abuya nodded vigorously, her tears flowing freely. "We can make a plan, whatever it takes, just help me bring her back."

Delun and Alistair looked at each other, They already felt the guilt of leaving Annika below strongly and Abuya's impassioned pleas moved them. They both knew the risks, the sheer danger of what Abuya was proposing, but the need to help a friend in peril was too strong to ignore.

"We...We can't just let you go alone," Alistair finally said, his voice tentative. "If you're determined to go back down there, then...then we'll come with you. But we need a strategy and we need to be careful."

Delun nodded in agreement, his face set in a grim line. "We have to be smart about this. We can't just barge in there."

Abuya's eyes shone with gratitude and renewed determination. She dashed the tears from her cheeks, nodding her agreement. "Thank you," she whispered, her voice hoarse. "We'll be careful, I promise. We just need to find her, to bring her back."

"Just how do you propose getting down there without alerting the miners?" Alistair asked, his voice low and thoughtful. "A direct approach will get us nowhere."

"We would need a distraction. Some way to divert their attention. Maybe an emergency alarm?" Delun suggested.

Henning snorted, still unconvinced. "I have been thinking about this for the last hour. In the case of an alarm, they would gather in the terminus ready to evacuate. If we try and send a message to trick them, we can not be confident that they will be fooled with the cameras still down. I have thought of no way to be certain of getting down unobserved."

Abuya's frustration boiled over. "So, what then? We do nothing? We leave her down there alone, hoping she survives? We need to try, Henning! We can't just abandon her because we can't come up with a fool proof plan. We have to take the chance, to at least learn what's happened, to show Annika that we haven't given up on her. We—" CLANG!

They all froze as the unexpected sound echoed around them. The clang was followed by another and another.

"Someone is knocking maybe?" Henning looked baffled.

The sound came again, three blows, almost as if someone was hammering on the outside of the bulkhead.

Alistair, his curiosity piqued, cautiously approached a nearby viewing port. Tentatively, he reached for the shutter. "Let's see what all the fuss is about, shall we?"

As he lifted the shutter, Alistair recoiled sharply, stumbling backwards with a yelp. "Bloody Hell!" he exclaimed, his eyes wide with shock as he pointed a trembling hand.

On the other side of the port, pressed against the glass, was a helmeted head, its visor inscrutable, blooming with scarlet reflections from the planet above.

Henning and Abuya scrambled to their feet, the sudden adrenaline rush in the corridor was palpable. Could one of the miners possibly be outside? Were they under attack? The figure outside began pounding on the viewing port with their gloved fist, their movements desperate and urgent, trying to get in.

Abuya, driven both by fear and curiosity, edged closer to the window. Her heart hammered in her chest as she peered through the perspex. The figure outside leaned in closer, their breath fogging their visor. For a moment, the reflection of Jupiter's light on the curved glass obscured their face, casting them in an eerie, celestial glow. Then, as the figure shifted closer into the shadow cast by the base itself, the glare on the visor lessened and the face within became visible. Abuya's breath caught in her throat, her knees buckling with a wave of relief so powerful it nearly sent her to the floor.

"It's Anni!" She gasped, her disbelieving voice filled with an all-consuming joy. Her hands flew to her mouth, tears of relief welling up in her eyes. The face on the other side of the glass was unmistakably Annika's, her eyes wide and glassy with utter exhaustion.

Alistair, recovering from his initial shock, stepped forward to wave through the port, his demeanour shifting from startled fear to delight."Annika! Nice of you to join us, we missed you something awful."

"She cannot hear you Knallkopf!"

Henning barged him out of the way. Peering through the viewing port, he too waved to Annika, gesturing for her to follow the corridor along to her right.

Delun was still nonplussed. "How on earth did she..."

"Never mind, let's just get her in!" Abuya's faculties were returning to her as the warmth and joy of Annika's reprieve flowed through every nerve in her body. She dashed away down the corridor in the direction Henning had indicated, towards the hangar and its airlock, the others following eagerly along in her wake.

CHAPTER EIGHTEEN

In The Wake Of Tragedy

Annika, having finally made it through the airlock after a last desperate scramble along the outside of Cadmus, was a picture of utter exhaustion. Her breaths came in short gasps, almost sobs, and her usually pale face was scarlet with exertion. She had wrenched off her helmet as soon as she could, gasping for air and revealing the sweat matted clump of hair underneath. She stood before the airlock, swaying slightly, too tired to even sit.

A whirlwind of weeping, profanities and joyous exclamations surrounded her in the form of Abuya who was alternating between enveloping her in tight, desperate hugs and assisting her with the removal of the heavy sub-suit. Each piece that came off revealed more of Annika's slight, weary form, shivering as the dry air evaporated her sweat.

Alistair, unable to contain his relief and joy at Annika's safe return, chattered happily, his words a stream of barely coherent well-wishes and exclamations.

"Absolutely brilliant to have you back Annika! We were

worried sick, I can tell you! Poor old Abs here was all ready to storm the breach down below and bring you out single handed."

Annika, her voice barely above a whisper, tried to respond, but the sheer exhaustion made each word feel like lifting a heavy weight. She leaned heavily on Abuya, her eyes conveying the gratitude her lips struggled to articulate.

As Abuya began gently to ask Annika about her escape, the moment was interrupted by Scott's abrupt entrance. He staggered into the room, his complexion pale and his eyes wild with dread. His breathing was laboured and he kept glancing over his shoulder as if afraid he was being chased.

"Scott, what's happened?" Abuya asked, her concern immediately shifting to him.

Scott took a moment, trying to steady his breathing, to collect himself enough to speak. He leaned against the door frame, his hand gripping it as if it were the only thing keeping him upright.

"Mark's gone." He eventually managed to get the words out, the statement echoing leadenly in the room. His voice was hollow, the trauma of what he had witnessed clear in each syllable.

The room fell into a stunned silence, the chilling implication of his words settling over them like a cold, heavy blanket. Annika, despite her exhaustion, looked up at Scott, her eyes wide with shock. "How?"

Scott, still reeling from the horrific spectacle he had witnessed and struggling to keep nausea at bay, was nonetheless startled as he took in Annika's presence for the first time. He swallowed hard, trying to push back the bile that threatened to rise in his throat. "He... He was a sacrifice for the creature, Doctor."

Annika bowed her head at the news, too tired even to shed a tear. The last of the suit removed, Abuya gently raised her to her feet and led her from the room, leaving Alistair and the others to their frantic quizzing of Scott. Her arm wrapped supportively around Annika's waist, she guided her slowly through the dimly lit corridors towards her quarters.

Despite their situation, the silence between them was a comfortable one, filled with the unsaid understanding and shared relief of Annika's safe return. Abuya's concern and care were palpable, her eyes frequently flitting to Annika's face for any sign of the trauma she must have felt.

Upon reaching Annika's quarters, Abuya steered her into a sitting position on the cot and began gently to help her undress, removing the last vestiges of her sweat stained uniform. She moved with a tenderness that belied the frantic thoughts still racing through her mind, her hands careful and attentive as she aided the woman she loved.

Eventually, with Annika dressed once more in fresh clothes, Abuya began to work on detangling her hair, which had become a knotted mess during her ordeal. Annika, exhausted beyond words, simply let her head rest in Abuya's lap, her eyes closing in fatigue.

The quiet of the room was only broken by the soft sound of Abuya's fingers working through the tangles, separating and smoothing the strands with a rhythmic, almost meditative motion. In this serene moment, with Annika's head in her lap,

Abuya finally allowed herself to process recent events. Her thoughts laboured through the harrowing experiences, the relief of Annika's return taking some of the sting out of the dark memories. Each one surfaced with a sharpness that made her wince. The chaotic fight on the mining platform, the raw fury and fear in the eyes of the miners, people she had known and worked alongside. She could still feel the shock of Henning's massive hand gripping her, the desperation as she struggled against him, her resolve to return for Annika clashing with the awful reality of their situation.

This was replaced by the image of Wei-Yun, frozen and twisted, his clawing hand reaching up from the ice which held him fast. She pushed that particular traumatic vision aside hurriedly.

Then there was Jacob's breakdown—that had shaken her more than she'd even realised at the time. Now, with Mark gone, she could hardly imagine what state he must be in. The loss would undoubtedly push him further into despair, compounding the toll on his mental well-being. She found herself dreading any impulsive decisions he might make. The last thing they needed was some risky cowboy mission back down below.

Abuya's hand paused in Annika's hair, her eyes unfocused, staring at a point somewhere beyond the walls of the room. Her mind continued to race, imagining the desperate ventures and grizzly consequences that might befall them if Jacob's despair was allowed rein. The sense of helplessness was overwhelming, a gnawing void that seemed to consume all hope. They were trapped in a nightmare, and with each passing moment, the darkness about them seemed to deepen.

Closing her eyes, she drew in a deep breath through her nose, seeking to find her calm. The relief of having Annika back, safe and alive, was a balm, but it couldn't erase the horrors she had witnessed, the traumas they had both endured. The fragility of their situation on this distant moon, a speck of humanity in the vast, indifferent expanse of space, had never been more apparent. Gently, but firmly, she pushed those thoughts away, calling her rational self to the fore. She would talk to Scott about the Commander, and by the end of the day, she and Annika would be safely aboard the Fulgur, out of reach of monsters, fictional and human alike.

Abuya's fingers resumed their work, untangling a particularly stubborn knot. Each pull of the comb, each freed strand, allowed her to bring herself more into the present, to put aside the misery and focus on the now. In this quiet moment, with Annika's soft breaths as the only sound in the room, she could clutch at a tiny fragment of peace.

Annika's breathing deepened, slipping into the steady rhythm of sleep, her body finally giving in to the exhaustion. Abuya continued her gentle ministrations, the repetitive motion of her hands through Annika's hair soothed her mind, allowing it to wander, to reflect, to hope.

In the stillness of the room, with the soft warmth of Annika's body against her, Abuya gazed down at the woman's pale form. Despite the uncertainty that lay ahead, this moment of quiet connection grounded her, reminding her of the strength they found in each other. They would survive this, Abuya suddenly felt sure. Nothing could overcome her, could stop her from protecting her love.

After a long time, as Abuya's head had begun to droop over her work, Annika's eyes flickered open and a gentle smile shone up at Abuya.

"Hi kosepus." She reached up to lay a hand on Abuya's cheek.

And at that moment, there was a loud crackling, a bang that reverberated through the superstructure about them, and darkness fell as every single light snuffed out.

Abuya jolted in alarm in the sudden dark. Annika's eyes snapped fully open, mirroring the anxiety that gripped Abuya.

Annika bolted upright and grasped at Abuya's arm in the sudden darkness. The ruddy jovelight falling through the window was barely enough for Abuya to pick out Annika's glinting eyes in the gloom. They sat in silence for a long moment, listening to the eerie quiet of the base, suddenly without the usual background hum of ventilation.

Finally, after just long enough for them to fear it never would, the emergency power kicked in. The dim glow of the overhead lights flickered back to life, illuminating their worried faces. The vents above them sighed as air was once again circulated, maintaining their atmosphere.

Power cuts were not that uncommon on Cadmus, but now, with tensions running high, it felt like yet another calamity reaching out for them. With a shared sense of urgency, Abuya and Annika sprang off the cot. They heard footsteps coming towards them and stepping out through the hatchway they encountered Alistair hurrying down the corridor. He was clearly trying to hide his concern as he grinned at them.

"Thought I'd find you two here."

Before he could go on, Scott's voice crackled through the intercom panel at the end of the corridor. "Power outage. Don't know what caused it, but I want everyone together now. Meet in the research dome."

Nodding to each other, they hurried along the corridor and through the various intersections to the research dome. As they neared the entrance hatch, Lena and Tomas, the two maintenance engineers, approached from the command section. "Any idea what's going on?" Tomas asked them as they met.

"Not a clue, I suppose we'll have to see what our dauntless leaders have to say."

Alistair gestured them through the hatchway ahead of himself as they all entered the dome's common area. They found Henning and Delun already there, engaged in conversation with Scott but they broke off as the new arrivals entered. "Just the Commander left," commented Scott as they all found seats.

Abuya sat cross-legged on the floor and leaned back against Annika's knees.

Scott, assuming a position of leadership in Jacob's absence, addressed the crew. "Obviously, there was a power outage, which under normal circumstances wouldn't be a cause for alarm. However, given the recent events and the threat from below, we're taking no chances. I want everyone to stay here, in the research dome, where we can keep an eye on each other."

The group exchanged anxious glances, but Scott's decision

to keep everyone together was met with nods of agreement.

"The climber is on its way down from the Fulgur. Before… Before the call from Evans, the commander requested that Captain Lukas send it down to allow us to evacuate."

There were murmurs at this, but no one argued, it was clearly the sensible thing to do.

"We've got about fourteen hours now till it reaches the surface. I suggest we spend the time together in here. It may be a little cramped, but I think we'll all feel safer."

"The emergency batteries should have enough juice to run the essentials for twenty-four hours," Lena piped up.

Scott nodded at her.

"Good."

Turning to the intercom panel, he spoke into it again. "Jacob, are you joining us? Please respond if you're at a panel."

Silence.

"Shit," muttered Scott under his breath.

"Do you wish me to look for him?" Henning volunteered.

Scott considered for a moment.

"Not alone Henning. We'll go together. Lena, you come too, we'll take a swing by the power centre if we can. Sleep Doctor, that's an order."

Annika had begun to clamber to her feet to join them and Abuya was grateful to Scott for stopping her. Annika was too exhausted to contest the point as she sank back to her seat.

"I'll come too," volunteered Abuya clambering to her feet. "Like you said, safety in numbers," she said in response to Scott's disapproving expression.

He grunted his assent.

Together the group set off back into the rest of the base, closing the dome's hatchway behind them.

The team, led by Scott, began a cautious sweep of the station. The corridors echoed to the soft clank of their boots on the metal floors as they moved through the base methodically, checking each room and compartment. The possibility that the miners might have found a way up, much as Annika had, loomed large in their minds. Every creak and groan of the station's superstructure set them on edge, their senses heightened to every potential threat.

The metal walls of the corridors, usually a reassuring barrier against the harshness of Europa, now felt like the cold, unyielding sides of a trap. Pipes and conduits ran along the ceiling and walls, part of the intricate life-support system that kept them alive. Some still thrummed with life, others were gently ticking and creaking as they cooled—dormant now under the emergency power measures.

Scott, still visibly shaken from the traumatic experience of witnessing Mark's death, led them with a grim determination. He had seen now first-hand the depths of madness the miners had descended into and seemed prepared for anything they might encounter.

Arriving at Jacob's office, they found the door slightly ajar. Inside, the room was in disarray, a concerning contrast to its usual meticulous order. The laptop lay on the ground, its screen shattered, a physical manifestation of Jacob's despair at witnessing his brother's sacrifice. Papers were strewn about and a chair lay on its side as if pushed away in haste or anger.

With no sign of Jacob in any part of the command section, they continued on to the maintenance dome, their footsteps echoing through the empty hallways. The atmosphere grew increasingly tense as they neared the heart of the station's operations.

"Let us check the power centre," Henning suggested, his voice low. "Perhaps Jacob went there when the power outage happened, and if not, perhaps we can effect repairs."

Scott nodded, his expression set in a hard line.

"Do you smell that?" asked Lena, sniffing the air. Smells like something burnt, I'd guess one of the big circuit breakers overloaded and burnt out."

As they walked through the maintenance dome, they all began to scent the unpleasant odour of burnt plastic, and as they rounded the corner and saw the entrance to the power centre, they knew she was right. The warning light flashed above the hatch, indicating that the room had been voided. Given the chance of fire at such an electrical junction, the section was rigged to slam its hatchway shut before venting its atmosphere, starving any fire of oxygen before it could spread.

Lena hurried over to the control panel and began the sequence to pressurise the room once more. It only took a few minutes before the light stopped its flashing and Lena announced the room was safe to enter.

The power centre was a compact space, filled with monitoring equipment surrounding thick cables that snaked their way through conduits to the outside world. Those cables then made their way across the surface over kilometre before connecting with the small nuclear reactor in the offsite facility.

The room was dimly lit by flashing emergency lights, the various screens and displays casting a soft glow in the gloom—all illuminating the charred and huddled object which had stopped them in their tracks.

The figure lay motionless and distorted, barely recognisable. They knew it could only be Jacob. His proximity to the high-voltage equipment and the evident signs of electrical damage around him left little doubt about the cause of death. The air was thick with the acrid scent of burnt hair, burnt clothing, burnt flesh. Abuya had to work hard to keep herself from retching.

They all stood frozen, each grappling with the shock and disbelief that gripped them. They all could picture the sad scene that must have unfolded. The horrific shock of watching his brother's own suicide. The mad rage which had cast his office into disarray. The desperate staggering through corridors, fleeing with nowhere to escape. And finally, the realisation of an ending within his grasp.

Henning stepped forward first, his face lined with sorrow. He approached Jacob slowly, respect and reluctance in his movements. The others followed, their steps hesitant, as if moving through a nightmare they hoped to wake from.

"No!"

Lena called out making them jump back from the grizzly remains. "Things may still be live," she explained.

They all froze again, not wanting to repeat the gruesome tableau before them.

Scott's gaze lingered on Jacob, his eyes reflecting a tumult of emotions—regret, sorrow, and an underlying sense of responsibility. He had seen the signs of Jacob's unravelling and then, when faced with Mark's death, he had run and left Jacob alone to his despair. Now, confronted with the finality of Jacob's decision, he felt the burden of command settle with finality on his shoulders.

"We…We can't…There's nothing we can do for him now. We can mourn him and the others we have lost when we're safely in orbit."

The others didn't reply. They had nothing to say. There were six to grieve now, even if no other atrocities had occurred without their knowledge deep below their feet.

"Lena," Scott continued, "any chance of getting the power back online and quickly?"

Lena's voice quavered with emotion as she replied.

"Not quickly I don't think. Maybe a few hours to replace the burnt-out components."

"We'll leave it then. We've got enough emergency power to see us through till the climber arrives."

Abuya was glad, not wanting to stay another second in that room. They turned to leave and processed in single file back into the comparatively fresh air of the dome outside.

The group made their slow way back through the base, their steps less cautious now, their minds occupied by the tragic discovery of Jacob. The corridors, with only essential systems active, were eerily quiet, adding to the depressed mood that enveloped them.

As they traversed the main intersecting corridors, a distant noise caught Abuya's attention. It was faint, almost imperceptible at first, but gradually growing clearer. She halted, her hand instinctively reaching out to signal the others to stop. The group fell silent, listening intently.

And then, with a bitter curse, Scott identified the sound. It was the metallic clanging of the elevator arriving at the terminus. A chill ran down Abuya's spine as the subsequent rattling of the grating being pulled aside reached their ears. A collective sense of horror gripped them, the realisation that the miners had found their way to the surface after all.

Without a word, they turned on their heels and began a desperate dash towards the safety of the research dome and the remainder of the surface crew. Their pace was frantic, reckless given the loudness of their passage, but fear drove them on heedlessly.

Every shadow cast by the overhead light strips contained an assailant. Every distant echo was a hinted at their mortal danger. The madness had made its way into their safe haven and the once benign, familiar corridors twisted before them into a malevolent maze.

Finally, they rounded the corner of the final stretch, the corridor off which the research dome was accessed. But before they could take more than a few steps, the tall figure of Evans, backed by a group of miners, appeared at the opposite end of the corridor. Evans's face was set with a grim determination, made ghastly by the misshapen nose and remnants of dried gore. Both groups froze in surprise, each gazing at the other. Slowly, Evans face split into a dreadful grin that chilled them where they stood.

The hatchway to the research dome lay in the middle of the corridor, the entrance to their sanctuary now turned into the prize in a deadly race. They were slightly closer than the miners, but not by much. At a bellow from Scott, the group sprinted towards it, matched only a moment later by the miners leaping forward and dashing towards them down the corridor.

They reached the hatchway barely ahead, tumbling through just as hands scrabbled on the coaming behind them. Henning turned and slammed the hatch home, shattering the fingers of one miner as she tried to grasp the rim and pull it open. The miner let out a cry of pain as the hatch clamped down on her hand and the questing fingers withdrew. Henning spun the locking wheel and Delun ran up to thrust a chair through its spokes, blocking the mechanism from being turned.

The miners' frustrated pounding and yelling echoed through the metal as the group stepped slowly back.

The adrenaline that had fuelled her escape ebbed away and Abuya felt a wave of exhaustion crash over her. She sat heavily on the floor and hugged her knees when suddenly a dreadful realisation hit her like a freight train and without warning she burst into tears. In her desperate, aborted attempt to rescue Annika, she had unlocked the elevator. It had never been locked again, and now the miners were here. Her well-intentioned actions had inadvertently endangered them all. The guilt was crushing and she could not bear its weight as she allowed it to press her down into the aluminium floor below.

CHAPTER NINETEEN

Up & Over

For ten agonising hours the relentless pounding and screaming from the miners outside the hatchway had echoed incessantly. Inside the research dome, the tension was thick, hanging in the air like a fog. The crew members of Cadmus Outpost, those who had managed to survive thus far, huddled together—a small bastion of sanity amidst the chaos. They were besieged, trapped within their own sanctuary.

They had set a watch on the door, taking turns to monitor the only access point to their temporary refuge. In theory this meant the others could rest. In practice, few eyes left the hatchway, whether on watch or not.

Despite their exhaustion, not one of them could find the peace needed to sleep. The fear of an attack, the anxiety of being trapped and the relentless clamouring kept them all on a razor's edge.

Alistair, always the one to think ahead, had pointed out a chilling possibility. "If any of those miners is particularly resourceful, they might think to bring a sub-suit up from below. They could come at us through the back door, so to speak."

This possibility had added another layer of anxiety to their wait. Thankfully though, there was as yet no sign of such tactics from the miners. The only surface suits were stored in the rover hangar, which branched off the research dome. As long as they controlled the main hatchway, they should be safe from any external breach.

However, the prolonged stress was taking its toll on the crew. Tempers flared over trivial matters and harsh words were exchanged in the heightened tension. They were all struggling to hold themselves together, their nerves frayed and raw.

Finally, with the climber now only an hour or so away, Scott called them together for a discussion. They gathered around, their fatigue and worry clearly in evidence on every face.

"Listen up," Scott started, his voice carrying authority in spite of his weariness. "The climber will be here soon. We need to be ready to move quickly."

He scanned the faces around him, seeing nothing but despondency and fear. "We'll have to make a break for it. It's going to be dangerous, but it's our only chance to get out of here."

His words were met with dull silence. It was likely suicide and they could all see it. The miners were still out there, delirious, and dangerous and they would have to somehow make it through as many as thirty of them to reach the climber station on the other side of the base.

"We'll stick together, no heroics." Scott pressed on, trying to instil a sense of solidarity. "We move as one, quickly and quietly. Once we're in the climber station, we seal it and wait for the climber to arrive."

The others shifted restlessly at his words, but no one leapt into action.

"Sounds awfully dangerous, don't you think, Scott?"

Murmurs of assent greeted Alistair's statement and Scott scowled at the man.

"If you have something better to suggest then please enlighten us," he replied through gritted teeth.

"With pleasure." Alistair's unending chirpiness and instinct to be extremely irritating could not it seemed be cowed even by a life-or-death struggle on a frozen wasteland six hundred million miles from home.

Scott sighed exasperatedly and gestured for him to continue.

"Well, the climber has two hatches, doesn't it. One for those of us on the ground to enter it and another on the far side for those on the ship to enter it. Why don't we go around the outside and climb in through the top hatch? Avoid those nasty buggers out there all together."

Scott nodded thoughtfully. It actually made sense; indeed, he cursed inwardly for not thinking of the idea himself.

"There are only the five researchers' surface suits," Delun pointed out, "and a single spare in case of damage. There's eight of us."

"No one wants to squeeze in with me then?" Alistair asked with forced joviality; he had clearly considered this objection and did not have a good answer.

"You and me Al, we can cuddle up." Henning's deadpan offer raised a few smiles around the table, even despite the dread of their circumstances.

The group pondered Alistair's suggestion, their trepidation quelling the atmosphere of hope that had briefly been engendered. The idea of avoiding a direct confrontation with the miners was appealing, but with the limited number of suits it would be a challenge.

"We could make multiple trips," Annika proposed, breaking the silence. "Six of us go first, leave two in the climber, then return with the suits for the others."

The idea still wasn't without its challenges. This was especially true for those among the group who weren't accustomed to the physical demands of surface activity on Europa. As the base's doctor, Annika had limited experience in a surface suit beyond her recent return from the plume hole. Tomas had rarely needed to venture outside beyond trips in and out of the rover en route to the offsite facility and Lena had never even donned a surface suit outside of training scenarios on Earth.

"I'm not sure about this," Abuya voiced her concern, her expression reflecting the anxiety she felt. "Hauling ourselves up the side of the dome, scrambling over to the climber station, it really won't be easy."

Tomas nodded in agreement. "And I've only been out a couple of times for minor repairs. Nothing this...intense."

Lena was clearly worried, but she spoke up with determination. "I'll try, of course I will. But I'm worried I might slow everyone down, or worse, cause an accident."

Scott looked at them both sympathetically.

"I don't think we have many options. We'll take it slow, help each other out. It's about surviving, not setting any speed records."

It was a daunting prospect, but with no other viable options, it was all they had.

"What if the miners notice the climber is arriving?" Delun pointed out. "If they realise we're making for it, they might try to enter it themselves from the inside."

They all considered the problem for a long moment.

It was Henning who suggested a solution. "We will be needing a distraction. I could go around the far side of the base and let myself be seen—make some loud noises against the bulkheads maybe."

Scott nodded in agreement. "It's worth a try. It's a pretty obvious ploy, but I don't think there are many clear heads out beyond that door."

He gestured to the hatchway which still resonated with fist blows and the maddened yells beyond.

"Surely the devils need a nap at some point!" Alistair exclaimed, giving a little shudder as his attention refocused on their attackers.

"I don't think so," Annika answered sadly. "Cole died of massive dopamine toxicity. If they are on the same track, then I don't think they could sleep if they tried. Not without heavy sedation at least. I could barely get Cole to stay under."

A pensive silence greeted her words. Already it was all too easy to think of those slavering without as a faceless horde of monsters, when in fact they were colleagues. Friends. People.

Abuya slapped her hand down on the table to break the spell.

"Right then. We don't have long, we should get to it.

Hope overcoming their inertia, the group sprang into action, voices overlapping as they worked the problem. Abuya, still grappling with her guilt over inadvertently leaving the elevator unlocked, forced herself to focus on the task at hand. She and Annika helped the others to prepare, making sure every strap and seal of each one of the suits was secure. The thought of leaving soon steadied her frayed nerves, giving her a sense of purpose after hours of helpless waiting.

Scott coordinated their efforts, his leadership providing stability amidst the chaos as the six of them suited up, leaving only Annika and Abuya. The pair looked almost child-sized surrounded by the bulky figures.

The atmosphere in the dome shifted from one of despair to a cautious optimism as they worked. The idea of escape, of leaving behind the madness that had consumed the base, was a powerful motivator.

As the six suited crew members made their clumsy way to the airlock, Annika's arm snaked about Abuya's waist, pulling her close. The two of them would be alone until Delun and Scott returned with the suits for them and each was working hard to put on a brave face for the other.

With the usual whooshing of atmosphere and clattering of valves, the airlock cycled. The two women held each other and watched as their compatriots opened the far hatch. As they stepped out into the orange light of Jupiter the pair turned back to the room and settled down for a long and anxious wait.

Alone now in the hangar, Annika and Abuya sat huddled together, their feeling of isolation magnified by the lack of visibility to the outside world. After a short while, the clamour at the hatchway reduced and then ceased, leaving behind an eerie calm. The sudden silence was a relief, if a little unnerving. Presumably, though it meant that Henning's diversion had been successful.

To keep their spirits up, and to distract themselves from their situation, they talked, their voices low as if speaking in a library, or in a tomb. Annika shared her experiences from her harrowing journey through the mining platform across the ice —her voice trembling as she recounted how close to death she had felt. Abuya listened, her grip tightening around Annika whenever the story grew particularly distressing.

"And then, seeing the base in the distance...it was like a beacon," Annika concluded, a small smile flickering across her tired features. "I knew I just had to keep going."

Abuya pulled her closer, her heart swelling with pride and love.

"You're incredible, I hope you know that. I don't know if I could have done what you did."

Their conversation meandered, touching on memories of better times, shared laughter and dreams for a future that now seemed so fragile. It was a way to hold onto their sanity, to keep the looming fear at bay.

As the minutes stretched into what felt like hours, the eerie silence persisted. They flinched at every creak and groan of the station, each sound a jarring reminder of their precarious situation.

Suddenly, the airlock hatchway clattered loudly, causing both women to jump. The inner hatch swung open and Scott and Delun stumbled in, their bulky suits making their movements awkward and laboured. Relief washed over Annika and Abuya at the sight of them, safe and sound.

"We made it," Scott panted, as he removed his helmet. "The others are safely inside the climber and they've barred the lower hatchway."

His words were greeted by cries, even sobs as some of their tension was alleviated.

Abuya rushed forward to help with the suits that Delun was manhandling out of the airlock, her hands shaking with adrenaline now that it was time to act.

"Any sign of Henning?" she asked.

"He's still there doing his thing. We'll pick him up as we go." Scott began helping Annika on with one of the spare suits while Abuya clambered into her own. "He was telling us on the suit radio—the miners are really raving."

Delun looked disturbed. "He said they were clawing at the viewing port, fighting each other to get closer to him."

Annika sighed and nodded as if she had feared as much. "I don't think they have long then. I'm afraid they'll be beyond saving long before any help can reach them."

Delun bowed his head at the words solemnly, before pulling his helmet back on.

Abuya ran one last check over Annika's suit, more to calm her own nerves than any real expectation that Scott had missed something. Content that all was in order, they made their way into the airlock and decompressed, leaving the safety of Cadmus base for what was hopefully the last time.

Outside the airlock, Abuya found herself once again in Europa's unforgiving landscape of ice and rock, bathed in the pale, ghostly light of Jupiter. The four figures, clad in their bulky surface suits, made their way cautiously along the edge of the research dome, their movements slow and deliberate. The silence of the outside was a welcome relief from the chaos they had left behind, the only sound the crunch of their boots against the icy surface, transmitted to their ears through the suits themselves.

Above them, the climber's tether stretched skyward, a thin line disappearing into the void above. Its presence was reassuring, their only lifeline to the world beyond this frozen moon.

The climber itself, an ungainly, unlovely structure, sat perched in its cradle, nestled awkwardly between the three principal domes of the base. Its angular form loomed over them; safety only a few hundred metres away.

To reach it, they began the arduous climb up the side of the research dome. The dome's surface was a series of sheets of high-tech canvas, ribbed with aluminium struts. The canvas was slick, offering no handhold, but the ribs themselves were flanged and could be gripped, even with the clumsy gloves of their surface suits. They used the ribs to pull themselves up the slope, inch by inch. The task would have been beyond any of them on Earth, but the low gravity made the impossible task merely a gruelling, laborious ordeal.

As they climbed, the curvature of the dome became more pronounced, the rib bending away from them as more of the landscape became visible. They focused on the task, each movement careful and deliberate, aware that a single misstep could be disastrous.

From the top of the dome, they had to traverse across and then descend down the next strut, the only way to navigate over the connecting corridor that linked the domes. They paused to catch their breath at the summit, and from that vantage point, Abuya spotted Henning below them, pointing him out to the others.

He was doggedly trotting up and down along the far corridor on the opposite side of the base. His figure disappeared behind either the maintenance or command domes at either end of his route. With every few steps, he would reach out and pound with his fist on the bulkhead of the corridor.

Abuya called out to him on the suit's radio. "We're about halfway, what's your status there Henning?"

Henning replied his tone distressed and gloomy. "The miners are still focused on me. They are like animals—tearing at the viewing ports, trying to reach through. It is...It is horrible."

He paused, his next words faltering in his sorrow. "Mayumi is here. She is brandishing something, a chair leg, I think. It is twisted and sharp and it is already blood-stained. There has been some fighting I think."

Abuya felt sickened by his words, her mind drawn back to Cole's animalistic behaviour. "Get to the climber, Henning.

We're almost there, you can't do much more good," she urged him.

"Understood," Henning replied. His voice was resolute despite the spectacle he was witnessing.

He started moving towards the command dome, his figure soon disappearing from their sight behind it as he prepared to climb.

Moments later, a loud curse erupted over the comms, Henning's voice filled with shock and despair. "Nein, nein, nein, oh Gott, nein!" His words were a horrified shout, almost pleading.

As he cried out, the canvas beneath Abuya and the others began to ripple and judder violently and a billowing cloud of ice crystals shot upward from near where Henning had been. They all clung to the dome's rib, desperate to weather the storm that seemed suddenly to be whipping about beneath them.

As quickly as it began, the juddering stopped, replaced by utter stillness.

"Henning, what happened? Report!" Scott called out over the radio, his voice panicked.

There was a moment of anxious silence before Henning's voice came through again in response, sounding winded but alive. "The base...it is breached. The air blew outwards, threw me back. Some of the miners were blown out through the rent."

They all absorbed this in silence, realising the gruesome implications. Eventually Scott broke through the spell, grimly trying to be matter of fact. "One of them must have tried to cut their way through the dome to get to you, Henning."

"Ja, I think that must be so."

Abuya looked around in shock, noticing that the domes, previously taut and firm as a basketball, were now sagging against the metal ribs, deflated and lifeless. From the direction of the command dome, Henning appeared, clambering up the rib of the deflated structure.

Slithering down their own dome, they met him in the centre of the triangle of corridors and together, they began the final climb up the side of the cradle to reach the top hatch of the climber.

The climb was treacherous, it never having crossed the designers' minds that such a thing would need to be done. They moved with cautious haste, aware that time was against them.

Finally, they reached the top of the cradle, their hands grasping the metal of the climber's outer hull. Alistair's grinning face appeared, waving at them through a viewing port, clearly unaware of the mass deaths that had just occurred. With a collective effort, they opened the top hatch and clambered inside, sealing themselves into the too-small airlock as it pressurised.

As they removed their bulky suits in the cramped confines of the climber's airlock, Alistair's chatter filled the space, his voice a stark contrast to the melancholic mood that lay on them. He was blissfully unaware of the events that had just transpired.

Annika, her face expressionless, turned to him, her voice low but firm."Alistair, the miners are all dead. The base is breached. It's over."

The words hung in the air and Alistair's demeanour shifted instantly. His usual garrulousness replaced by shock.

Delun, focused and methodical, worked the controls of the climber. With a soft whirr and a gentle vibration, the vehicle began its slow, steady ascent towards the Fulgur in orbit. The long journey ahead finally taking them away from the misery that had come to claim the surface.

Annika and Abuya moved to one of the viewing ports, looking out together at the moon below. The landscape of Europa, faintly lit by distant Jupiter, was a scene of silent, frozen desolation, already far below them.

Abuya's thoughts wandered as she gazed at the barren moon. Now that they were climbing away from it, the chaos and madness they had faced down there already seemed like a distant nightmare. The moon was once again a bare, uninhabited speck in the solar system. There were no miners left, no surface crew and certainly no creature—just a cold, indifferent lump of rock and ice, drifting through the void of space.

She reached out to take Annika's hand and squeezed it. She could hardly believe that the two of them were finally safe, that they had made it through together. In silence, they turned away from the port and away from Europa, moving towards the cots that lined the wall of the climber. Without a word, they settled into one, finally freed of immediate peril and able to give in to their exhaustion. It was the sleep of the saved—of those who had faced unimaginable horrors and had emerged, battered and scarred, but alive. They held each other as the moon receded away beneath them and they drifted away from consciousness.

CHAPTER TWENTY

The Red Marble

Abuya awoke gradually to the soft, rhythmic snoring filling the climber. The sound was oddly comforting in its normality. The familiar, strange sensation of lightness and unease churned in her stomach, a tell-tale sign that they had reached a sufficient orbit and velocity to experience microgravity. Her body felt oddly detached, her movements slow and ungainly as she adjusted to the apparent absence of gravity. The sensation told her they must be well into the ascent with perhaps only a few hours left until they reached the Fulgur.

As her eyes fluttered open, still heavy with sleep, she found herself entranced by a peculiar sight. Hovering before her in the dim light of the climber's cabin was a small orb. It was a delicate globe of deep red, suspended in the weightless environment. It seemed to dance in the air, a solitary jewel cast adrift in an endless sea of tranquillity.

The orb shimmered like a ruby as it caught the light. It quivered with the push of her breath, each subtle movement sending gentle ripples across it, distorting and reforming in a mesmerising display. The droplet reflected the sparse light of the cabin, bending it into iridescent arcs that played across the curved surface.

In this quiet, otherworldly moment, it was as if a tiny planet had been born anew in the confines of their spacecraft. She reached out tentatively towards it and the droplet adhered to her finger, distorting into an elongated shape in a fluid motion that was both fascinating and unsettling.

As the droplet clung to her, trailing a shimmering line down the length of her finger, the dreamlike quality of the moment shattered. With a jolt of realisation, Abuya came fully awake and understood what she was seeing—it was a globule of blood.

Jolting upright in the cot, she scanned the cabin. The rest of the crew seemed to be asleep, their shapes discernible drifting within the sleeping bags of their cots. One figure, however, was drifting near the floor of the cabin, face down and motionless. It was surrounded by more of the orbs, like a planet with its moons. She thought it might be Tomas but, in the gloom, she couldn't be sure.

Her gaze then drifted upward to where another figure floated in the air above her, silhouetted against a viewport. The shadow was facing away, gazing out into the vastness of space, their arm outstretched towards the port as if reaching for something just beyond their grasp. As she carefully manoeuvred herself free of the cot, she could make out the unmistakable profile of Evans's ruined nose. His body was oriented towards the star-strewn void, his posture one of reverence and longing.

A cold shiver ran down Abuya's spine. The sight of Evans, alive and seemingly entranced by the void, was deeply unsettling. It raised a myriad of questions, the foremost being how he had managed to board the climber unnoticed.

Drifting as gently and quietly as she could, she made her way to the sleeping form of Henning, her eyes not once leaving the back of Evans's head. She kept her movements slow and deliberate in the zero-gravity environment. Feeling about behind her, she gently clamped her hand across her friend's mouth, feeling him stiffen beneath the touch but thankfully not cry out.

Still not daring to drop her gaze, she waved her hand before his eyes and gestured urgently to the floating figure. Feeling a tap on her shoulder she knew he understood and she allowed herself to drift away slightly, giving him room to disentangle himself from his cot.

Risking a quick glance, she saw him inching his way carefully away from her and she understood his intention from his gestures. The two of them would rush the floating man from different angles, hopefully catching him unawares.

Abuya returned her gaze to the drifting form of Evans. She could hear him speaking softly under his breath."Beautiful, so beautiful."

The copper light of Jupiter bathed his face and he spoke reverentially. "She calls. She calls to me. So beautiful. Can you not hear it Abs?"

With a shock like a bucket of ice water being tossed over her, Evans turned to look her straight in the eye. He smiled and beckoned.

"It is so beautiful."

She did not, could not reply. She was rooted to the spot by fear. Evans did not seem deterred.

"Can you not hear the call, the cry of the universe, the music of the spheres? It is all about us. Come Abuya, hear it with me, we can—"

Henning struck him in the small of the back like an avalanche. He had bunched his legs against the far wall and torpedoed himself across the cabin. The breath left Evans with an audible whumpf and he and Henning went tumbling away across the cabin. The small, bladed multi-tool the man had been wielding turned lazy somersaults as it drifted away to be lost somewhere in the ceiling.

At the moment of Henning's strike, Abuya had cried out at the top of her lungs, looking to rouse her companions while she herself leapt forward to help Henning. They scrambled and jerked, tangling themselves in their sleeping bags, but the danger had passed. Evans could barely breathe, let alone resist. He hung limply in Henning's bear hug, wheezing against the blow he had received and the two broken ribs they would later find that it had caused him.

The rest of the crew awoke in confusion; Abuya and Henning grappling with a limp and wheezing Evans, his face contorted in pain and poor Tomas drifting through the cabin, quite dead. Scott was the first to fully comprehend the situation, his eyes widening in disbelief at the sight of Evans.

"How the hell did he get here?" Scott exclaimed, his shocked voice despairing as he pushed himself across the cabin to assist them.

A search of the climber revealed an open locker in the cargo hold, its contents askew, where Evans had presumably hidden himself during the departure from Europa. The discovery sent a ripple of unease through the crew and they thoroughly inspected every inch of the craft to ensure they were truly alone. Apparently though, only Evans, perhaps due to his relatively short exposure to the madness, had retained the guile necessary to board the climber and conceal himself.

Henning, with Scott's assistance, bound Evans securely using strips torn from sleeping bags. The makeshift restraints were tight, ensuring he couldn't pose any further threat. Annika, despite her own exhaustion and shock, tended to Evans, examining him for injuries. She confirmed Henning's suspicion of broken ribs and did her best to minister to him as far as possible.

By the time the climber finally docked with the Fulgur, Evans's mental state had deteriorated further. He sobbed incoherently, his tears forming a bulbous blob of water around his face, unable to fall in the microgravity of the climber. The sight was both pitiful and unnerving and it was all the crew could do to look at the broken and forlorn figure.

The hatchway to the Fulgur opened, revealing Captain Lukas and her two crewmen floating in the threshold. Her expression shifted from relief to shock as she took in the sight of Evans, bound and broken, amidst the weary crew.

"My God, what happened?" she asked, her eyes flicking between the crew and Evans.

"Later," Scott replied wearily and he drifted past her, the fatigue and stress evident in his voice. "Let's just get underway from this cursed place."

One by one, they made their way into the Fulgur, Captain Lukas welcoming them aboard. She guided them to the living quarters, where they could finally settle in for the long journey.

As the Fulgur set its course for Earth, the crew settled into the rhythm of space travel, each person lost in their thoughts, their hearts weighed down with the memories of those left behind. They were safe now, but the journey back to Earth could never be a journey back to themselves, to who they were before. Europa had changed them forever.

Epilogue

In the spacious hall, an air of grandeur and modernity was evident in every detail. The architecture of the room was a testament to both the wealth and technological focus of TAURS, with sleek lines and a design that spoke of efficiency and elegance. Expansive glass panels allowed natural light to flood the space, complementing the theatrical lighting system that bathed the room in a soft, ambient glow.

At the front, a large dais stood, equipped with state-of-the-art audio-visual technology, including a vast screen that spanned the width of the room. The seating was arranged in a semi-circular fashion, ensuring that every attendee had an unobstructed view of the woman on the dais.

The overall ambience was one of subdued sophistication. The colour scheme was a tasteful blend of neutral tones, accented by the occasional splash of TAURS's corporate colours. Above, a high ceiling added to the sense of openness and space, with acoustically engineered panels ensuring that sound was crisp and clear throughout the room. The air was fresh and clean, a silent and efficient ventilation system working unnoticed.

Abuya stood upon the dais, looking out at the audience before her. More than three years had elapsed since their escape from Europa and now here she stood, alive and on Earth. The room was filled with an eclectic mix of TAURS officials, scientists, journalists and interested members of the public as well as the panel officiating over the enquiry. The investigation into the Cadmus base disaster was not a trial, but standing there it almost felt that way.

Abuya swallowed nervously as she prepared to begin. She was just one of several speakers today, but being the only one with direct experience of the tragedy held a unique gravity. She could feel the audience leaning forward expectantly in a way they had not for the previous presentations. The weight of her own story pressed down on her. She found the encouraging face of her wife in the crowd. Holding her gaze for a moment, she found her calm and brought up the first slide.

Beneath the title *'Thalassoarchaea Okoreyensis'* the large screen behind her displayed annotated microscope images, showing the minute organisms that were about to be the focus of her presentation.

"These," she began, pointing to the images, "are samples of the chemolithoautotrophic Archaea found in the basal ganglia of James Evans. They are an extremophile organism, now known to exist in the oceans of Europa."

She marvelled at the steadiness of her own voice, ill-reflecting the fluttering of her heart as memories were dredged unbidden back to the surface.

She continued, explaining the nature of the organisms. "They metabolise ammonia, which is naturally present in Europa's oceans. Due to a malfunction in the water filtration system on the mining platform, these organisms contaminated the miners' drinking water."

She paused for a moment, letting the implications sink in.

"The majority were likely killed by the temperature change," she continued. "But, being extremophiles, a significant number survived and were subsequently ingested by the miners."

The room was utterly silent as she delved into the more technical aspects of her findings. "Ammonia is a key element in the metabolism of several neurotransmitters. The archaea, once consumed, managed to survive and reproduce in the miners' brains, predominantly the striatum. This led to an enormous increase in dopamine production, severe physical brain damage and ultimately, the delusions and paranoia witnessed."

Abuya's tone grew solemn as she described the tragic end result. "This imbalance would eventually lead to death through dopamine toxicity. Doctor Pedersen will be discussing this in more detail in this afternoon's session as she walks us through her case study of James Evans."

Her eyes met Annika's and she once again received her silent support. Returning her focus to the audience, Abuya's address shifted away from the desolate past to a more hopeful future.

"A recovery mission is currently en route to Europa, led by Commander Scott Taylor. Its primary objectives are to recover the bodies of our lost colleagues and to collect samples for further investigation."

"As you all know, part of this enquiry committee's responsibility is to determine the feasibility of further research missions, to rebuild the Cadmus Outpost and study this new life form. The tragedy on Cadmus"—here she bowed her head briefly as the memories threatened to overwhelm her—"has opened a new chapter in our understanding of life beyond Earth. The first extra-terrestrial life to be discovered by humanity. The remainder of my lecture today will be the discussion of this micro-organism, of the potential for future research and in general the arguments in support of funding for future expeditions."

. . . •

Abuya stepped down from the lectern some forty minutes later to a mixture of subdued applause and murmuring conversations. The revelations she had shared were ground-breaking, offering the promise of new scientific frontiers. And yet to her and to Annika and to the other survivors of Cadmus base, they were sad reminders of the friends they had lost.

Annika was standing waiting for her, a rock about which the river of lunch-bound audience members flowed. They left the hall together, politely acknowledging the respectful nods and greetings of those they passed.

The pair, their arms entwined, walked in companionable silence through the corridors of the Jemison Library in which the lecture hall was housed.

As they stepped outside, the crisp winter air greeted them. The TAURS campus lay under a thin blanket of snow, its pristine white contrasting with the dark, angular forms of the buildings. The snow crunched softly beneath their feet, a peaceful sound in the otherwise quiet campus. Despite the cold, neither of the two women felt the chill; their time on Europa had left them quite immune to all but the worst that Earth could throw at them.

Without a word, as if guided by a shared instinct, they made their way through the campus grounds to the memorial. It stood at the intersection of two avenues, a sleek, black stone slab, solemn against the snow-covered landscape.

It was simple, yet elegant, its surface engraved and silvered with the names of those friends whom they had lost. Beneath these, the epitaph read:

'Dedicated to the pioneers whose dreams transcended Earth's bounds.
Their bravery lights our way through the darkness.'

The pair stood before the slab, their eyes tracing the names etched into the stone. Each one was a reminder of a life lost, of a story left unfinished. They remembered their friends. Remembered their laughter, their quirks, the shared moments of joy and the harrowing experiences they had endured together. The stillness between them was filled with memories, both happy and heart-breaking.

Eventually, Annika broke the silence, her voice soft. "I suppose they were right in the end. There really was a creature." She lifted her face to look up past the memorial, into the sky above. "It consumed them as thoroughly as any monster could have."

Abuya nodded absently, her gaze still fixed on the names, her mind six hundred million miles away.

They lingered a moment longer in silent tribute. Then, as if on cue, they turned to leave. Arm in arm, they walked away from the monument, their steps leaving a trail in the fresh snow.

The world was hushed and serene as they walked, leaving the memorial and their memories behind them in the snow.

Afterword

If you hadn't worked it out yet, I'm a bit of a space nerd. Perhaps you are too, in which case I hope you weren't too annoyed at the moments I took some artistic license. If, however, you're just starting to explore the wonders of our universe, you might appreciate a bit of context for the story you've just read.

We humans exist on an insignificant fleck of dirt in the vast expanse of the universe, like ants debating the mysteries of a colossal garden they can barely comprehend. If Earth were the size of an ant, our 'garden'—the solar system—would be slightly larger than the city of Chicago. Far off in the distance, too small for our ant to see, would be Jupiter, about the size of a softball and nearly five football pitches away. It's a long journey for an ant, and it's a long journey for us, but nevertheless, we are on our way.

This book is set on Europa, the third largest moon of the planet Jupiter. Although we have never landed on Europa, several missions, including Galileo and Voyager, have flown past and seen some amazing things. Its icy surface is thought to hide a vast, global ocean, kept warm by the immense tidal forces exerted by Jupiter's gravity. These forces create a dynamic and geologically active environment, with the surface cracking and shifting like a living entity. Enormous plumes of water shoot out from the surface, some as much as 200 kilometres high, about 25 Mt. Everests! Because of this ocean, Europa is considered the most likely place in the solar system to find life beyond Earth.

Europa orbits Jupiter, the colossal giant of our solar system, which looms as an awe-inspiring presence in the sky above. Jupiter is a swirling, stormy world, famous for its eye, the Great Red Spot, a massive storm larger than Earth that has raged for centuries. The planet's thick atmosphere is composed primarily of hydrogen and helium, with bands of clouds creating stunning, colourful patterns.

In the next few years, NASA's Europa Clipper and ESA's JUICE missions will launch to study Jupiter and its moons. These missions will explore Europa's icy shell and subsurface ocean, and may get us a little closer to answering the big question: are we alone?

Closer to home, NASA's Artemis missions are gearing up to bring humanity back to the Moon. Artemis III aims to return humanity to the Moon as early as 2026, including landing the first woman and the first person of colour on its surface. These missions mark a new chapter in space exploration, focusing on a sustainable lunar presence and paving the way for future journeys deeper into the solar system.

As we prepare to moonwalk once more, the idea of venturing further out, to places like Europa, starts to feel more achievable. The technological advances and international collaborations from Artemis could set the stage for ambitious missions. Perhaps even manned expeditions to Europa to mine its rare earth metals, as imagined in this novel, might be possible one day. While it may seem like science fiction today, each step forward with Artemis brings us closer to making these extraordinary visions a reality.

Thank you for reading, I hope you've enjoyed "In Jupiter's Shadow." Your support means the world to me. If you have a moment, I would love to hear your thoughts.

Leave a review: Your honest reviews on Amazon or Good Reads help other readers discover the book.

Spread the Word: Share your thoughts on social media using the hashtag #InJupitersShadow

Stay Connected: Scan the QR code to join my mailing list for updates on upcoming books, special offers, and more.

Printed in Great Britain
by Amazon

49610205R00158